Foreward

This story has technically been on the internet since 2000 as an ebook with ebooksonthe.net. It was being run from Ellsworth, Maine and one basically bought the right to print off one copy to read - or you read it on the internet. There was a limited edition print I did myself.

Then Write Words Inc. bought ebooksonthe.net in 2002, re-edited this book, and it became a Kindle and Nook offering when those reading devices came out. They began offering it as a paperback in 2008.

All versions had a few goofs, some perpetrated by yours truly and some done in the re-editing, as was pointed out by observant readers. When Northern Bard Publications offered to let me have one more try at correcting the gaffs so that this could be sold as a three pack with the sequels they've published, I jumped at the chance.

Yes, there are two other books in this series and another waiting in the wings, but I'll discuss that in an afterward so that, for those reading this the first time, there will be no spoilers in this foreward.

But for those who HAVE read this before…

"The Author's Cut" indicates that some of the gaffs people have pointed out have been corrected, especially the one that changed the feel of the pivotal scene in Chapter Eighteen. I left the ending the same, however, as it was what the characters insisted happened.

Thank you for your feedback, and I hope the corrections meet with your approval.

Debi Emmons

September 14, 2015

P.S. I almost forgot to include the "warning label" several readers insisted it needs: "Don't start reading in the evening, as it has been known to keep people up all night."

Dedicated to my mother,

Monique Dow,

who always knew I was different -

and always encouraged me to be so

With special thanks to the crew at

Northern Bard Publications, especially
Dee Jae Dow, who took photographs and
created the cover.

Northern Bard Publications

53 Cambell Shore Road

Gray, ME 04039

ISBN: 978-0-578-17269-9

Night of the Tiger: The Author's Cut

Book One of the Tiger Series

By

Debi Emmons

PROLOGUE: TERESANNA

One week before Prom Night, 1988

Sixteen-year-old Teresanna Montesallo smiled as she walked toward the door of the apartment she shared with her mother, her dark eyes glowing with happiness. After three years of pain, her life was finally turning around, and it had all started with the restraining order that her mother had finally placed on her stepfather!

For three wonderful months, Teresanna had been able to go to school every day instead of spending her days healing from "Big Daddy Long's" so-called "loving" attention. Many of the kids at her school had come forward when the story made its way through the grapevine to offer their sympathies, and she had found herself suddenly popular, never having realized before that it was her own attempts at hiding the truth that had erected barriers between herself and her classmates.

The best thing of all, however, had come to pass that very afternoon. Tom Gormley, whom she had always thought of as one of the nicest guys in school, had asked her to the Junior/Senior Prom. She hurried up to the door with her key in hand, eager to tell her mother, thinking only that her mother had anticipated her return when the door pushed open before the key was fully in the lock. As she pushed the door the rest of the way open, she called out "Hey Mom, guess what?"— and stopped with a gasp, unable to believe what she was seeing.

Linda Montesallo-Long lay on the living room carpet, bleeding profusely from her ears and nose as her face swelled and darkened, the bruises combining into one huge, reddish-blue mask. As Teresanna took another step forward, a wheezing laugh that sent shivers down her spine at its familiarity came from her right. She turned to look in that direction just as a fist came her way.

Seeing it just a split second too late to avoid it completely, she dodged to one side and caught the blow on her cheek and shoulder instead of on the nose. Spun off-balance, she stumbled back, wondering distantly how long it would take to recover this time, and found herself suddenly bursting with renewed hope as the sound of sirens reached her. She turned to look at her abuser with narrowed eyes and a fierce demeanor that hid the fear she was feeling.

"They're on their way, Big Daddy. Our new neighbors were once abused women, and they know what to do when a little weasel like you invades the hen house. You call the cops when someone starts beating on one of your own."

Teresanna didn't know if this was fact or not, but she was willing to lie if it meant sending Big Daddy running for cover, despite her mother's insistence on always telling the truth. The sirens got louder, and Big Daddy's lips curled back to reveal his large front teeth, whose irregular spacing beneath his long, thin nose gave him a rat-like appearance. His small, black eyes peered at her with sheer hatred from beneath his disheveled shock of black hair, and then he was moving toward the door, his hand snaking out as he went past to tangle in her thick, chocolate-brown locks and snap her head around so that her eyes were forced to meet his.

"Wherever you go, I'll find you, because no matter what you and that bitch you call Momma may think, you're MINE!"

His liquor-tainted breath touched her face, making her want to retch, and his mouth covered hers in a sloppy semblance of a lusting kiss, producing nothing but hatred in his stepdaughter's heart.

Then he was suddenly gone, leaving his unwashed odor in the air and his rancid taste on Teresanna's lips.

With utter revulsion, she wiped at her mouth as she hurried over to the phone in the kitchen to make sure an ambulance really DID come for her mother. With the calm assurance that came from three years of practice, she gave the address to the operator, then quietly hung up the phone and slipped back to her mother's side.

After seeing her mother in bad shape uncountable times before, Teresanna could never remember seeing Linda's ears bleed, and she worried that Big Daddy had finally gone too far. Rocking back and forth, unable to do anything for her mother but pray, her eyes suddenly focused on the small metal box under the edge of the couch where all their important papers were kept.

As if drawn by a force outside of herself, Teresanna got her mother's keys off the kitchen table and unlocked the box, pulling out the envelope that held both her Birth Certificate and her Social Security card. She thought long and hard about going into

Linda's purse for a driver's license, but decided that would never do, even if there was the vaguest chance of getting a car. Her mother was very obviously Caucasian, with big blue eyes and pale ivory skin. Teresanna showed the influence of her Asian father in her brown, almond-shaped eyes and olive skin tone. The only things the two women had in common were their small size and soft, chocolate-brown hair. Trained well by the fists that had pummeled her for leaving even a pen in the wrong place when she was done with it, Teresanna re-locked the box and returned the keys to the table where she'd found them.

Running into the apartment's one bedroom, she dumped her school books out of her backpack and quickly threw in some clean clothes, slipping the envelope inside as well so it wouldn't get lost. She nearly jumped out of her skin when the doorbell sounded, then forced herself to take a deep, calming breath as she realized that the red flashes that lit the room meant that the ambulance had arrived.

Tossing her backpack over her shoulder, she hurried out to open the door, hovering anxiously close as her mother was lightly and quickly bandaged, then loaded carefully onto the gurney. Grabbing her mother's purse and keys last-minute, she followed the paramedics out to the ambulance, where a police officer gently herded her into his car. He wanted to hear what had happened on the way to the hospital while allowing the paramedics the extra room necessary to work on Linda.

By the time they arrived at the hospital, the officer had a fair idea of what happened and had called it in over the car's radio, putting out an APB on one Mark "Big Daddy" Long. In return, he had been assigned to protect the one witness to the deed until re-enforcements could be dispatched, and didn't seem to be too upset at the idea of protecting the very young, but already exotically pretty brunette from her abusive stepfather.

Teresanna was smoothly polite to her assigned guard, but spent most of her time in the waiting room trying to decide what to do if, as she feared, this beating was too severe for her mother to recover from. Plan after plan was thought of and rejected as she tried to come up with a place where Big Daddy wouldn't be able to find her, but where she wouldn't need money to go. She was having no luck at all until she looked over at her so-called "protector" and saw an advertisement on the back page of the newspaper he was reading.

It was for "Amateur Night" at a local strip club, and announced the grand prize in big, bold letters. It wasn't a huge amount, but it was enough to see her to the next city, where there just might be another "Amateur Night" and another grand prize. Part of her argued that Big Daddy just might go into a strip club and see her, but then another part of her, a deeper instinct that had preserved her more than once, insisted that he would be far too busy following police cars around and looking in all the places she had already rejected to ever think of looking for his errant stepdaughter in a strip club. This was especially true since that same stepdaughter refused to even wear a one-piece bathing suit in front of him without having extra clothes over it, fearful of the leeringly hungry gazes he tossed her way more and more as she developed from a bone-thin, flat-chested girl to a small, trim, yet well-rounded young woman.

By the time the doctor came out to tell Teresanna that her mother was in a coma and showing no normal brain wave activity, Teresanna's path was clear. She would go to the home of a computer-geek friend she had never mentioned to Big Daddy, a boy who had bragged about forging himself an ID with the help of his computer and his mom's home office equipment so he could go into bars at 17. He had once looked at the black eye she was trying to pass off as an accident on the way to the bathroom in the middle of the night and offered to make minor changes to her Birth Certificate and Social Security card so she could "escape". At that time, she had angrily turned him down, her pride stung by the fact that he had so easily seen through her lie, but now, when she needed him, she hoped he might still be willing to help her if she apologized and asked for his help.

She would start by making herself old enough to work in a strip club as well as changing her name to make it harder for Big Daddy to find her, especially since her given name wasn't a common one. Disowned by her well-to-do parents for having a child out of wedlock, Linda Montesallo had named her half-Asian daughter for her maternal and paternal grandmothers, Teresa Wadsworth and Anna Montesallo. It was the first time that Teresanna found fault with that touch of sentimentality, and she would now have to get used to being called something entirely different in order to stay hidden.

With any luck, she would win that contest and get out of town before Big Daddy finished making the rounds of her known friends and started checking on anyone who had ever been to school with her. If she wasn't lucky, she'd probably end up sharing her mother's fate for daring to slip away from the dubious "protection" of the ones who were supposed to make sure that Big Daddy obeyed the restraining order.

Escorted to a safe house by the police officer, Teresanna pretended to make herself comfortable and even managed to doze briefly. Her eyes popped open just as everything got quiet, and she listened for a long time to the policeman who had been left to watch her snoring in his chair, almost deciding that her plan was suicide. With a deep sigh, she collected her bag and slipped silently out the window and into the darkness, disappearing into the shadows with only one regret.

She didn't tell her mother good-bye.

Book One

Tanya

Chapter One

The Friday before Labor Day, 1995

"Oh, come on, Jack! You can't be serious!"

Kyle Benton closed his eyes to shut out the curious looks thrown his way by the men working to unload his trailer at a warehouse in the New York City garment district. In a patient tone, his partner and dispatcher, safely out of reach in an office in northern Maine, carefully repeated that there would be no outgoing loads until at least two days after Labor Day, leaving Kyle to cool his heels in the city for the long weekend.

"Enjoy some time off for a change!" Jack cheerfully advised, hanging up the phone on Kyle's muttered curse.

Pushing his too-long hair off his forehead with one hand in frustration, Kyle returned the telephone handset to its cradle and spun around with his emerald-green eyes shooting sparks. Taking note of the fear in some of the eyes that watched him as they took note of the strength in his tall, muscular form, he controlled his anger through the concentration techniques he'd learned through martial arts training without even breaking stride. Yanking a pair of heavy work gloves out of his back pocket, he pulled them on and strode passively into the trailer, throwing off the last of his anger with a heavy outward puff of air as he began to help the others unload his truck. Deep within his constantly active mind, he tried to come up with something he could do for five days in the city he privately thought of as "The Armpit of the Universe".

"Wha's up, buddy?" A scruffy fellow in smeared coveralls asked, his accent quickly marking him as a New York native. Kyle sighed dramatically and lifted a box that would have sent the smaller man to the hospital with strained back muscles.

"Nothing serious. I'm just stuck here for the long weekend with no plans because my boss decided I needed a vacation," he grunted.

"Well, you's can come wit' us to BoxCars tonight!" the worker offered.

Working hard to control his annoyance as the accent grated on his nerves, Kyle forced himself to relax as they moved together across the floor to where the shipment was being stacked. When he was sure he could speak calmly, he asked "What's so special about BoxCars?"

The worker grinned, and Kyle couldn't help but grin in return at the man's animated delivery of the facts.

"It's one a' the strip joints just a few blocks from here, an' 'bout three weeks back, this new gal starts dancin' there. Like most of the dancers these days, she's a sexy little babe with curves in all the right places, if you know what I mean."—his leering smile said more than enough — "But what REALLY draws the crowd is that she comes out all in cat makeup, head to toe, and ain't nobody seen her, 'cept on stage. She comes out, does a couple sets, then disappears just like that." He snapped his fingers to demonstrate, then smiled again as Kyle frowned thoughtfully.

"Nobody knows who she is?" Kyle just couldn't quite believe NO one knew!

"Tha's why her act is so special." Kyle fought a frown at the man's tone which was reminiscent of a teacher instructing an extremely slow student on something they'd been over repeatedly. As if he felt Kyle's disapproval at his tone, the worker thought for a moment, then continued in a softer tone.

"All the other dancers are a lot more— 'friendly', if you know what I mean, which is why BoxCars is such a dive. It's the kind a' place that gets you divorced if your wife finds out where you been," The worker chuckled softly while Kyle thought about the women he and his trucking friends called "leather lizards", a term used to describe the prostitutes who mostly dressed in leather and hung out at truck stops to pick up truckers.

"O'course, the fun part for us guys is takin' bets on who she might be. Made myself a fair bundle just by bettin' against whoever was so sure he had it right he was willin' to stake money on it."

He eyed Kyle as if assessing his ability to make such a bet, taking in the slightly ratty, wrinkled T-shirt, worn jeans and battered work boots that Kyle wore, then turned away without offering to make a bet. Kyle almost called the man back, well aware that he could afford to lose any bet he might make, but decided to see the girl for himself before making any bets—OR any statement about his ability to unmask her. At the very least, it would provide him entertainment for the coming evening. He'd worry about what he was doing tomorrow when tomorrow became today.

Another worker, a tall, thin fellow whom Kyle had been seeing at the warehouse for several years and who went by the name of Vinnie, bumped Kyle playfully with his elbow as he slipped past to collect another box.

"So, Superman, you comin' with us to BoxCars tonight? You just might see something you like!"

Vinnie's cheeky use of Kyle's CB handle and infectious smile, as well as the soothing lack of any hint of the local accent in Vinnie's voice, brought back Kyle's good humor full force. His left eyebrow lifted, an unconscious habit that preceded any wisecrack, and his green eyes sparkled like jewels. He put on his best imitation of the hated accent and came off sounding like Rocky Balboa.

"What else am I supposed to do, knit doilies?"

Vinnie's burst of laughter lightened the mood of the whole crew, and the rest of the unloading was spent in happy camaraderie, complete with a boisterous exchange of jokes too colorful to be told in mixed company. Kyle was still chuckling over the last of these as he parked his semi among others being left in the locked, fenced-in yard at the warehouse for the long weekend and gathered what he would need for the extended hotel stay. As he locked his truck and started for the gate, intending to call a cab, he heard the blast of a car horn and turned to find a beat-up Ford sliding up beside him. As the car came to a stop, he saw Vinnie grinning at him from the driver's seat.

"Even Superman sometimes needs a hand—or a ride." Vinnie teased, and Kyle fought a grin as he slipped into the passenger seat, a battle well hidden beneath his heavy beard and mustache even as his high-flying eyebrow fouled his best efforts at appearing serious.

"Just drive, Vinnie, or I'll have to fry you with my x-ray vision. And you'd better know where the best hotel is at the best price!" He growled in mock anger. Vinnie simply grinned in response, well aware of what the arched eyebrow meant, and soon deposited him outside a fairly well kept motel that Vinnie insisted combined cleanliness, safety and a reasonable price.

After settling into his room, Kyle enjoyed a nice, hot shower to ease the aches from long hours on the road, then changed into fresh clothes and enjoyed a hearty meal in the motel restaurant. As he was preparing to step outside for a cigarette, he discovered that Vinnie was back—and had a few friends in tow.

Kyle stepped onto the sidewalk amid cheers and whistles, pulling a leather jacket on over his T-shirt. Insuring that his cigarettes and lighter were still in the pocket with one hand, he reacted to their playfulness with his own good cheer. By the time they reached the bar, which had its own small parking lot, Kyle felt as if he had known them all his life, and he was more than ready for an evening of playing Sherlock Holmes in "The Mystery of the Disappearing Dancer."

He began his investigation while they waited in line on the sidewalk for the bouncer to collect their money, looking over all the vehicles in sight and placing a personality type with each one, trying to place one with a young lady who would be trying to keep a low profile. A Kawasaki Ninja motorcycle, a flashy red-and-black crotch rocket that promised speed and maneuverability, was passed over entirely as being highly unlikely simply by the fact that it would command attention. As he waited, however, his eyes seemed inexplicably drawn to the machine, imagining the result of someone drinking before driving such a powerful piece of equipment. As he stepped through the door and paid the cover charge, he couldn't help but wonder if there would even be enough pieces left after a high-speed crash to identify the body.

He pushed his thoughts to the back of his mind as he and his companions settled at a table close to the edge of the stage. As he pulled off his jacket and put it over the back of his chair, he seemed oblivious to the many feminine eyes that turned his way, but Vinnie noticed, and was quick to comment on it.

"Looks like we brought in the right guy to get good service!" He teased loudly as a waitress hurried their way, almost licking her lips as she eyed the well-built trucker. Kyle's brow lifted, but he withheld his wisecrack as the woman came within earshot, choosing instead to order a Bloody Mary and offer to pay for the first round with amusement in his tone. While his companions ordered, he looked around at the waitresses and dancers who watched him, smiling at them as if admiring all the scantily clad bodies that paraded in front of him. Systematically, he counted noses and took note of such things as height, weight and basic measurements. As the waitress moved away, he turned back to his companions and sighed softly, one thought coming to the front of his mind and stopping just short of falling from his lips:

Blasted leather lizards are everywhere!

Chapter Two

In a former broom closet backstage at BoxCars, Tanya LaMonte looked at herself with the aid of several mirrors, examining the cap that covered her thick chocolate-brown curls to make sure that not a single hair escaped. Very carefully, she smoothed on tiger-striped pantyhose that seemed almost to become a part of her skin, then used greasepaint to paint stripes over her arms and torso, leaving unpainted circles around her eyes, nose, and lips while also leaving her palms paint-free.

She filled in around each eye with white eye shadow, then elongated the slight Oriental slant of her eyes with black eyeliner to enhance the tiger image. Fake eyelashes brought back a little bit of the woman under the makeup, and Tanya couldn't resist batting her eyes, smiling at the image she created. Her next step was to darken her nose with black paint, carefully using a paintbrush and insuring that her own skin tone didn't show through, then coated her lips with black lipstick. Like with her eyes, she enhanced the cat image by using the brush to extend the edges a little before painting a thin line from the center of her nose to the center of her mouth. Small dots gave the impression of whiskers, and false teeth insured that, when she smiled, she had cat-like fangs peeping out between her slightly distorted lips.

With her makeup done, she added the wig—a short, black-and-gold striped punk 'do that fit snugly over the elastic cap. She carefully secured it with a plethora of hairpins, making sure that the hairpins were as invisible as possible against her scalp. What she couldn't hide would be masked by the glittery hair grease she'd used on the wig to make the hair stand on end.

Looking from mirror to mirror, Tanya made sure that no inch of her natural olive-toned skin or dark hair showed through to allow anyone to place her as the woman beneath the makeup when she left the building. Satisfied with her appearance, she slipped into the character she had created for this gig. She had based Tigré on the characters she had seen in the Broadway show, "Cats", which she'd gone to see her first time in New York. Her soft brown eyes grew cold and fierce, her lips curled back, her back arched, and she hissed at her reflection, seeing for just a moment the sexy tiger-woman that the men outside would soon see.

Hoping that even her own mother wouldn't be able to recognize her, she turned away from the mirrors and stepped over to the rack of silky lingerie that awaited, choosing a black silky bikini top and matching g-string with a lacy black jacket and black lace gloves as her outfit for the first set. The gloves had half-fingers, cut so that the ragged edge made it appear the tips were bitten off rather than cut, making one imagine that the gloves were on someone else when the biting happened.

Each item was slowly and carefully pulled on so as not to smudge the still drying paint job, and Tanya again checked in the mirror to make sure none of the makeup was smudged and everything was placed just right. Sitting gingerly on the edge of a slightly rickety wooden chair, she finished off the look with 4-inch spike heeled black sandals, bringing her up to a more statuesque 5 foot 6 inches from her normal diminutive 5 foot 2. For added color, she fastened a gold dog's collar, studded with rhinestones, around her neck and slid a heavy gold ring, a roaring tiger's face with tiger-eye stones set in its eye sockets, on her right middle finger, repairing her smudged paint immediately. With all her other preparations done, she carefully put on long, fake fingernails that were painted a dark black and clipped to resemble sharp claws. She was just placing the last of these when there was a knock at the door and a hushed voice whispered through the crack.

"It's me!"

Careful not to disturb her newly-applied nails or her body paint, Tanya unlocked the door and let a petite blonde dancer slip inside, checking the corridor to make sure no one saw Christi before she closed the door and locked it again. As she turned, she accepted a glass of orange juice from her friend, sitting down again on the edge of the chair and sipping through the straw to avoid damage to her makeup. Just like always, Christi launched into what they had come to refer to as 'The Buns Rush' before she was even able to settle on her customary stool.

"You won't believe what I saw in the audience tonight!" Christi began in a breathless tone, making Tanya smile.

Christi always began with that same line, but it was only when a man was particularly cute that she used her special breathless tone. Before Tanya could wonder about the man who had caught the blonde's eye this time, Christi was launching into a description.

"He's tall and dark-haired, and he's obviously a body builder. He's got a body that just won't quit and biceps as big as our waists." She flexed her arms and puffed herself up as she talked to give the impression of the man's size.

"And his eyes!" She fanned herself dramatically with one carefully manicured hand. "Oh, man! Those things could melt a hole in a vault!"

Tanya tried to hide her amusement, but Christi saw it anyway and pushed a full lower lip out in an exaggerated pout.

"Here I am telling you about the hunkiest piece of man ever to grace this dump and you think I'm pulling your leg. You just wait until he sets those eyes on you!"

"But he won't be setting his eyes on me. He'll be setting them on Tigré, and she'll eat him for lunch." Tanya hissed slightly and snapped her teeth together in imitation of a tiger snapping up a mouse to emphasize her point, but Christi only smiled.

"This guy's so big, he couldn't be less than a ten-course meal, even for a man-eater like Tigré!"

"You're warped, Christi!" Tanya admonished, but couldn't help giggling at Christi's lust-loaded tone. Sobering after only a moment or two, she added the note of practical cynicism that Christi had come to expect. "But seriously, how rich does he look?"

The comment was delivered with a note of feigned boredom as she studied her nails, as if looking for flaws.

Tanya pretended she didn't like men, yet didn't go after girls either, which baffled most of her co-workers. They called her "the Ice Princess" and whispered among themselves, wondering if the references to money whenever they spoke about falling in lust with cute guys meant she only had sex if it was for cash. Tanya heard the whispering, but didn't care what they thought about her. She thought it better to pretend that money was all that mattered to her when it came to sex—and no one was ever rich enough for her to bestow her charms on—than to admit what she was really doing dancing in places like BoxCars.

Christi frowned slightly, her attention shifting from the new man who had caught her eye to the pending disappearance of the biggest draw BoxCars had ever seen. The arrival of Tigré, with her air of mystery that had all the men talking, had brought about an increase in patrons as well as the bouncers necessary to keep them under control. Before Tigré came, the tiny blonde dancer had gone home many nights covered with bruises from the pinches and playful slaps of the rough crowds drawn to the neglected bar to watch the women disrobe. With the added bouncers, BoxCars had become a safer and saner place to work, and Christi feared that, when the petite brunette moved on, the place would go back to being rough.

"I can't believe you could be worrying about how rich a truly sexy man looks when you're moving on and taking all the rich ones with you!" Christi snorted, too busy being grumpy about her foreseen future to note the slight smile that touched Tanya's face.

"Well, I do have this one little problem with that," Tanya began, looking down at her feet as if embarrassed so Christi wouldn't see the laughter in her eyes before she had it controlled. Christi's rapt attention when Tanya was able to sneak a peek from beneath her lashes told the brunette all she needed to know. Her fish was hooked, even before she had cast out the bait!

"You see," she continued, "I forgot that I already had a booking in Jacksonville when I booked a return gig here for the first three weeks of November." Finally daring to look up, she gave a shamefaced half-smile. "Now I'm supposed to be Asia in Jacksonville and Tigré in New York at the same time!"

Christi absorbed that information for a long moment, unable to believe that her normally meticulous friend could have made such a blunder. Booking two gigs for the same dates over 1,000 miles away from each other? It sounded like something Christi herself may have done, being a less than careful bookkeeper, but Tanya?

"I hope you can help me out." Tanya added, and Christi was struck with an inspired thought that drove all questions from her mind.

"You and I are pretty close to the same size, so if I keep up with the aerobics classes while I'm doing my next few gigs, I could double for you when I get back to the city from Niagara Falls. It'll save me having to beg for a return gig."

Tanya allowed her real grin to surface. Christi had grumbled often about having to book return gigs. Neither used agents, so return gigs had to be set up before leaving town to assure that they could continue to move around enough to always be the "fresh face" in the bar. It assured better tips, and for both, tips assured a better future. But Tanya would never let Christi know she had double-booked on purpose.

"I was hoping you'd be able to take it. I'll sell you the supplies as soon as I get done with them, at the end of this weekend, at the latest."

Christi squealed with joy. Without another word, they solemnly sealed the deal with a handshake, then Tanya carefully repaired her paint job, not letting on that it was a deal that would allow them both some peace of mind. For Tanya, it meant making sure that anyone trying to follow her would be thrown off track, especially if they saw advertisements for Tigré in New York when Tanya planned on being miles away, using a new character for her dance routines.

Christi's next words had nothing to do with their newly sealed bargain, however, as her mind had bounced back to the original subject of the hunk in the audience.

"Now about this guy I saw. Do you like beards?"

Chapter Three

Kyle was sitting back in his chair, sipping on his second Bloody Mary and listening to the spirited banter going on between his companions about the various dancers on the stage, trying hard to enjoy himself. After spending his youth in a small Maine town, his early adult years in a small, elite group in the Navy, and all the years since mostly alone in his truck, Kyle found the constant banter to be a bit unnerving. The girls on the stage looked even more like the leather lizards than the waitresses did, and they all seemed to be eyeing him rather well. Their type didn't appeal to Kyle at all, and the one currently on stage seemed to be on some kind of drug, laughing and talking to herself while she danced to a beat that wasn't included in her music selection.

The dancer came out of her private world long enough to notice the big, dark-haired man with sexy green eyes, and began to move toward their table. Kyle pretended to be deeply interested in digging a cigarette out of his pack, keeping his eyes down, refusing to even look her way. He lit the cigarette and took a long drag before turning cold eyes up to stare at her, and the dancer gave a half-smile and turned away, closing her eyes briefly to return to her private world. Vinnie looked at Kyle in some surprise, never having seen anyone who came to BoxCars ignore even the ugliest of the women, and Kyle also appeared to be getting annoyed. Vinnie leaned forward with a concerned frown, signaling until Kyle followed suit.

"What's wrong, Superman? Not happy with tonight's menu?"

Kyle sighed and gave an awkward shrug.

"Haven't seen much of particular interest yet."

Vinnie grinned.

"Patience, my man. They tend to save the best for last, have a long intermission, then start another set. Most of the guys here will leave after the first set, but I like to stay until they close—even if there are only two dancers of any interest."

Kyle distinctly remembered hearing about only one: Tigré. He was about to ask who the second dancer might be when the drugged-looking dancer made her exit and Vinnie started a chant that their tablemates quickly joined in on.

"We want Christi! We want Christi!"

It wasn't long before the whole place was chanting, and the DJ laughed and smiled his approval when Christi peeped out through the curtains and nodded her head. It took him a moment to regain the peace after she pulled her head back, but a quick darkening of the lights and the slow buildup of her opening music did the trick.

"Here, doing her set a little out of sequence by popular demand, is a little firecracker we were supposed to call Cheerleader Cherry, but you boys all know her as: (he paused and the whole crowd bellowed the name with him) Christi!"

The men at Kyle's table whistled and cheered as the petite blonde in a cheerleader's uniform came back-flipping and cart-wheeling onto the stage, stopping directly in front of their table to kick one nicely-shaped leg over her head and shake her pompons as if cheering on the team at the Homecoming game. Her small, well-rounded form and wide smile caught Kyle's eye and he set his drink down to fish a few bills out of his wallet in appreciation of the first dancer who was of any interest. His companions poked each other and grinned in amusement, but once again, it was Vinnie who leaned forward to make the comment Kyle knew was coming.

"Guess you ain't bored anymore, huh Superman?"

Kyle's grin was little more than a flash of straight, white teeth against the darkness of his beard, but Vinnie saw it and grinned back. Christi saw it, too, along with the wallet, and turned her back so that her short skirt bared her sexy bottom, clad only in a thong bikini, before starting a raunchy cheer that had the crowd roaring their approval.

Then she looked directly into Kyle's eyes and signaled him forward as the next selection of music began and the DJ's voice enticed the men to come forward to try to coax Christi out of her clothes.

Kyle stepped up to the edge of the stage, his brilliant emerald eyes dancing with appreciation, and Christi pretended she was going to take off her sneaker for his first offer of a single bill. Kyle shook his head and mimed pulling off his shirt, holding up two bills for Christi to see. She pouted until he added three more, then she smiled brilliantly as she slowly and tantalizingly lifted her sweater off over her head, prolonging the moment of actual removal as long as possible.

Kyle gave her a grin and a wink as she leaned forward to allow him to tuck his offering into her bikini strap, then turned and slipped back to his seat while others pushed forward to get their turn at giving Christi a tip to try to entice her to take off more.

Kyle sat back and enjoyed the rest of Christi's entertaining set, flirting outrageously with the dancer. At thirty-two years old, he was all too aware of the effect his firm, heavily muscled form, dark hair and bright emerald-green eyes had on women, and found himself actually enjoying it for the first time in years. Christi didn't seem to mind the flirtation at all, encouraging him with every flip of her blonde head and every smile that touched her full lips, putting on a better show because of her efforts to attract the man she'd described to Tanya as "the sexiest thing this side of Heaven".

Almost as soon as she finished her set, Christi was at Kyle's side, tugging a knot in the belt of her silk dressing gown as she slid through the crowd. He graciously stood and offered her his seat, waving at a waitress before sliding smoothly into a comfortable, balanced crouch at the blonde's side. Impressed by his manners as well as his generosity, Christi gave him her best high-voltage smile and started the conversation with the first really obvious come on line she could think of, her blue eyes sparkling with mischief.

"So, do you come here often?"

Kyle's return grin made hers pale in comparison and his left brow lifted slightly just before he answered in kind.

"No, but can I buy you a drink?"

Christi seemed to think a moment.

"Can you make it two? I promised the bookkeeper I'd bring her an orange juice."

Kyle sighed and dug into his wallet, acting for all the world like he was the sore loser in a fierce competition, but his soaring eyebrow made the other men at the table laugh.

Another tall, thin lady in a police uniform began her set right in front of them, having heard about the muscle man with the sexy green eyes, but was unnoticed by the trucker. Kyle was too busy watching Christi and wondering why the dancer would be getting drinks for the bookkeeper.

Could Christi be the reason that Tigré didn't come out for drinks between sets?

Unaware of Kyle's thoughts, Christi bummed a cigarette off one of Vinnie's friends and a light off another, drank the sombrero, and checked the time on Vinnie's watch by gently grabbing his arm as if she'd done so a thousand times before, disappearing backstage just as the police woman finished her set. The stage door was barely closed behind Christi when the lights went out, and a hush fell over the crowd as they sat in the darkness. A soft drum beat started, a strange African rhythm that set a man's heart pounding, followed by the DJ's voice, hushed and reverent.

"And now, gentlemen, the moment you've all been waiting for. BoxCars is proud to present the cream of the crop, the best of the rest, the one, the only Tigré!"

The roar that followed the announcement made Kyle think he was going to go deaf, but he soon lost all interest in such dire thoughts as a single spotlight lit the center of the stage, where a large cage with heavy brass bars had been rolled on silent wheels. In the center of the cage, a small, striped form was curled into a ball, and the ball didn't move until the cacophony began to dim beneath the onslaught of the African drums, which grew slowly louder.

Kyle's chin dropped as one small, well-formed limb emerged from the ball at an odd angle to stretch like a waking cat, followed by another and another until, at last, the black-and-gold striped head lifted and Kyle got his first glimpse of the tiger-woman's face.

She had eyes that appeared to be as black as coal within the shadows of the cage, blazing with an animalistic hatred, and she let her gaze travel from man to man as if searching for an extra tasty morsel she might use to fill her belly. With the grace of the jungle cat she portrayed, the girl moved around within the cage, tricking the eye into believing she really was part tiger, her firm muscles even taking up the game, imitating the beast with every strong, smooth movement.

Never in his life had Kyle found himself so intrigued by an on-stage persona! Whoever the girl was under the makeup, she certainly knew how to make an entrance, and Kyle was as dazed as the regulars had been the first night the elusive Tigré had made an appearance. Once again, his tablemates poked each other and grinned, but Kyle was too busy trying to see Tigré's face to give them much attention. If he was to figure out who this heavily made-up creature was, he would have to use all his skills. The only dancer who this wondrous creature even vaguely resembled was the only one Kyle could immediately cross off his list.

Christi wouldn't have had time to put on the makeup between the time she stepped backstage and the time that Tigré emerged!

Meanwhile, his attention was entirely centered on the dancer as she mimed a growl at the exact moment that the music included a growl, rising the hackles on the back of Kyle's neck at her exquisite sense of timing. The imitation of the beast was so well done that even some of the regulars couldn't resist gasping as the cage door came open at her touch, and she slithered out onto the floor, pulling along a length of lightweight gold chain that ran from the rhinestone collar to a ring on the side of the cage, keeping the tiger-woman from leaping into the audience.

Two waitresses made their way to the edges of the stage and cat-walk, each setting two top hats where they could be easily reached by the men, yet still be picked up by the dancer at the end of the set. The DJ's voice was dark and mysterious as he explained that, due to the fact that their lovely kitty wasn't domesticated, tips for this particular dancer should be placed in the hats 'for your own safety'.

Kyle laughed at all the fuss being made about an exotic dancer, especially since it was his understanding that they earned their tips by allowing the men to put the bills between their breasts or under whatever they wore that passed for clothing. He changed his mind quickly when one very drunk soul stood up and walked to the edge of the stage nearest the dancer, insisting he would put his dollar wherever he wanted—and Tigré lunged at him like a wild beast, hissing loudly. The man dropped his dollar on the edge of the stage and jumped back, shaking. The DJ sighed dramatically and his amplified voice was belittling.

"That's why I warned you to put your money into the hats! She's sweet as a kitten if you keep your distance, but she hasn't met the man yet who can tame her!"

Kyle smiled just as Tigré started to pace down the catwalk toward him, thinking that perhaps he was just the man for the task, and she stopped for just a moment as the woman beneath the makeup found herself eye-to-eye with the man Christi had been describing while straight, white teeth flashed against the darkness of his beard. Kyle's eyes, a most startling shade of green even in the semi-darkness of the bar, sparkled with so much vital energy, he almost seemed to pulse with it, and Tanya understood Christi's comment that they could melt a hole through a vault. If she looked too deep, they just might melt a hole to her heart!

Growling like a tiger, she drew back her lips and narrowed her eyes to keep him from getting a good look at her face, and it was Kyle's turn to be startled when he saw the fangs for the first time. Although his mind insisted they were fakes, they were of such fine quality that they looked real, and for just a moment, he found himself almost believing that the stage persona was real, and that he was actually seeing something that should have been in a circus sideshow.

It suddenly dawned on him that it wasn't so much the thought of seeing an exotic dancer that brought the men to see Tigré, but rather to admire the impressive talent she had for becoming a beast—and for keeping her true identity a secret. As she moved back to the cage with the sinuous grace of a big cat, Kyle admired her shapely curves, but was unaware that he was about to be introduced to yet another talent that drew the men to see this particular exotic dancer.

As she neared the cage door, Tigré removed the lace jacket inch by tantalizing inch, but was very careful not to smear her makeup as she did so. More eyes than Kyle's were watching carefully, waiting for the chance to see her true skin tone, and she felt them all! She dropped the jacket, then the music changed and she began to sway to a different beat, performing gyrations that reminded Kyle of a belly dancer he'd seen once.

Turning to face the back of the stage, she smiled slightly, then bent until her chest touched her legs with such ease that several of the newcomers groaned, wanting to be standing behind her while she did the same movement in private—while naked! Making it look effortless, she swung one leg up, then the other until she was doing an upside down split with her entire weight supported by her hands on the stage, and groans turned to gasps of appreciation and a sprinkling of applause for the show of strength. After holding her position for several beats, she bent both legs back until her feet touched the floor, then completed the maneuver by flipping herself back upright.

Kyle drank in the grace and beauty of the woman on stage, finding that his libido was going into overdrive even as a wide grin of purest pleasure turned up the corners of his lips and crinkled his eyes. His drink sat, forgotten, by his hand, and he was totally unaware of the way some of his tablemates were smiling and taking money from others who wore big frowns. The exchange, however, caught Tigré's eye, and she glared at them fiercely. Kyle, lost in his thoughts, saw only the darkness of her eyes in the narrowed slits and wondered at their true color, trying to get as much information about her features as he could in the few short times that she was allowing her face to relax completely during her set.

For Tanya, trying to hide behind the makeup and persona of the tiger woman, the watchful eyes of the tall, dark haired muscleman in the audience were most unnerving. Usually, Christi's "hunks" were just regular looking men with one particularly fetching feature, but there was indeed something about this one that really drew attention. Beneath the stunning emerald eyes was a well-muscled body that women ached to touch, and yet the way he watched her had Tanya worried that he might figure out what she really looked like—and bring the man of her nightmares to her door.

Trying to ignore Kyle's table, she reminded herself that the only thing that mattered was the money, so that she could pay off the travel trailer she called home and keep moving so she could feel safe. Safe from the fans, safe from pushy roomies, but most importantly, safe from the man who had made three years of her childhood into a living nightmare and who still haunted her tortured dreams. Then she looked down as a tall, lean form with biceps almost as big around as her waist stood to move toward the stage with his bright emerald eyes gleaming.

Kyle held up a bill, making sure that he had the tiger woman's attention before carefully folding it into an airplane, smiling while she snarled at his approach. When he reached the edge of the stage, staying carefully out of her reach, he took careful aim and sent the airplane flying toward her with a flip of his wrist. The shot was a study in perfection, landing directly at her feet. She glared at him, but snapped up the bill and unfolded it.

Kyle watched as her eyes snapped open in shock at finding he had given her a ten-dollar bill instead of the one dollar bill she expected. For the space of a breath, maybe two, he was able to see the woman under the makeup, then she snapped back into character as easily as if she'd put back on a mask. Hatred flared out of the dark eyes and she snarled menacingly, then carried the bill over to a hat and dropped it in, discouraging any others from following his example.

But for Kyle, he had already won the prize he sought. As he made his way back to his seat, he tried to look disappointed even as his heart was soaring in triumph. He had seen the shape and color of her eyes by the stage lights and could now go home secure in the knowledge that the girl behind the tiger woman's makeup had big, beautiful brown eyes with a most intriguing Oriental tilt!

Throughout the second set, Kyle mostly ignored the other dancers, trying to think of a way that he could find out more about Tigré. It wasn't until Christi came out that he once again noticed the similarities between the two—and the differences. Although very close to the same height and about the same size around the bust and hips,

Tigré was firmly muscled under the layer of makeup in areas where Christi was softer and somewhat flabbier. As Christi turned and looked at him, he took a good look at her eyes, and became even more positive about the Oriental tilt to Tigré's eyes. The latter's brown orbs were definitely almond shaped while Christi's blue ones were a pretty, but very average American oval.

Tigré appeared a second time, and this time the routine involved a series of tumbling moves that were meant to keep a man's head in the bedroom, but Kyle's thoughts were firmly on the identity of the exotic creature. His eyes scanned her again and again while she covertly took note of the T-shirt he wore, which was tight across the shoulders and upper arms where his bulging muscles stretched it to the limits, but loose across the abdomen, where she suspected a washboard stomach was hidden. Kyle smiled and Tigré gave him a sharp glare in return, but he continued to smile even when she turned and moved away.

Once again, Kyle reached into his pocket and drew out a bill, knowing full well that his buddies would think he'd flipped if they knew that it was another ten. Always before, he had spent his money frugally and had often been teased about his well-worn clothing, so his sudden generosity would have raised a few eyebrows. In truth, he only wanted to make sure he got the dancer's attention, assuming (and quite correctly) that she was mostly in it for the money.

Working quickly but carefully, he folded the bill into an origami figure in the shape of a cat's face. Quietly, his eyes on the face of the woman before him, he made a second trip toward the stage, holding up the folded bill and seeing her frown as he approached.

Kyle's left brow lifted just before he smiled, and Tanya's heartbeat quickened as she was treated to smile so sexy it set fires in places she never knew existed. Frightened by the feelings, she retreated into the fierceness of the tiger and hissed at him, but it only made his smile change slightly: from mildly sexy to knee-melting.

When he saw the look in her eyes change from fierce hatred to mild confusion, Kyle knew she was watching him. He made a show of kissing the cat face before dropping it into the nearest hat, then turned and moved away, smiling at her over his shoulder. With a glare, she continued her routine, but couldn't help wondering why her body seemed determined to react to the stranger with the beautiful bedroom eyes. As the lights went out, she grabbed the hats (with the one that contained Kyle's offering on top) and ran backstage before the lights could go on again.

She hurried to her dressing room and barely got the door closed and locked before digging for the folded greenback.

When she found it, she didn't bother to unfold it. The word TEN was clearly visible on the cat's forehead, sending her mind spinning off in a thousand different directions, many involving making contact with a certain green-eyed trucker. She sat for a long time, trying to gather her thoughts, but in the end, there was only one thing she was able to do. Like she always did, she carefully wiped off all the makeup and put on the baggy clothes that hid her figure before working her sweat-slick curls into a greasy-looking mop. Looking rather dirty, tired and pale, she wasn't anything like the energetic, exotic beast that had appeared on the stage.

Kyle was outside having a breath of air and a hand steadying cigarette when the small brunette with greasy hair slipped out of the bar. Looking like a ragamuffin from a back street, she wasn't the type he would normally have noted, but tonight was different. Tonight, he was searching for a small woman with Oriental eyes. His eyes roamed over every inch of her, watching from the shadows as she pulled on a helmet, climbed onto the Kawasaki he'd noted on the way in, and rode away. He found it odd that he didn't recall seeing a small waitress with greasy dark hair in the bar, and he finished his cigarette deep in thought, going over the faces he'd seen earlier. No matter how many times he went through the faces, he couldn't recall seeing a small waitress with greasy dark hair.

Tanya, lost in her thoughts about the first man who had ever started a fire in her blood, never saw the tiny glow from Kyle's cigarette—and the man himself was lost in shadow. She rode away from the very man who was currently on her mind without knowing that he was watching her and trying to figure out who she was!

Chapter Four

Tanya met Christi outside their favorite gym at 10:15 the next morning, allowing them plenty of time to change and warm up before the 11:00 aerobics class started. As usual, Christi was going into vivid detail about the man who had taken her home for a "private dance" the night before and Tanya was only half listening, barely registering the fact that the man Christi took home had been sitting with the green-eyed trucker that all the girls had found to be so sexy. When Christi came to a sudden stop and frowned at a group of women who had gathered at the door of the aerobics room, Tanya walked on four steps before realizing Christi was gone.

"What's going on?" Christi wondered aloud, and made her way toward the door to see. Stifling a yawn, Tanya followed, more worried about the dreams she'd had about the tall, dark stranger with the sexy green eyes turning into the man of her nightmares than curious about whatever was drawing the attention of a bunch of giggling women.

She woke up suddenly when she found herself peeking through the crowd to see the man who had haunted her dreams doing a morning stretch consisting of a series of martial arts moves done with a slow, studied grace. His eyes were closed as he turned to face the women, but even when they opened, it was obvious from the far-away look in the green orbs that he didn't see any of them, concentrating on his breathing and movements in a world of his own. Tanya found herself entranced by the suppleness in the tall, firmly muscled form.

As he sped up the movements to enhance the cardiovascular workout, she was impressed by the fluid grace of his body as he displayed both speed and accuracy, pushing his body to its limits and giving the rapt audience quite a show. It was only when he finished his final bow and became aware of his surroundings that he realized he was the center of attention for some twenty women. A wide grin produced straight, white teeth in the middle of his dark auburn beard and a twinkle lit his eyes.

"Good morning, ladies. Hope I haven't monopolized your warm-up time with my morning mantra." He rumbled, and Tanya tried to shrink out of sight as his eyes traveled over the group.

"Monopolize my time whenever you want, sweetheart!" A voice called from the depths of the crowd, and Kyle laughed along with the ladies, his deep, bass voice seeming to harmonize with the higher female outburst. His eyes calmly scanned the grouped women, and his attention was drawn to Christi, waving from the front of the crowd, and then slid to a petite brunette close to Christi's elbow who appeared to be trying to disappear into the crowd like a salmon trying to swim upstream. For some reason that Kyle couldn't fathom, the brunette seemed alarmed when their eyes briefly met, and turned swiftly away before he was able to get a really good look at her.

Tanya slid desperately toward the back of the gathered females, feeling her body warm at even the slightest glance from the strange man—and not appreciating the thought that she might be feeling the first twinges of a crush, her first since high school. Christi, still waving and smiling from ear to ear, was too busy trying to get Kyle's attention to notice when her friend left her side.

Tanya hurried into the locker room and to her usual locker, trying to slow the trip-hammer beat of her heart. She pulled clothing out of her bag with hands that shook and muttered to herself, trying to find some flaw in the muscleman that would allow her to stop herself from reacting to him.

"With a body like that, he must have an ego as big as Texas!" she muttered, and that seemed to make her feel better, so she elaborated on that theme. "He's so full of himself that no woman could ever be good enough for him."

She continued telling herself such things as she changed, and was feeling much better by the time Christi hurried in, her face flushed with excitement. As she tied her sneakers, she listened as Christi gushed on and on about the wonderful man with the stunning green eyes and the lady-killer smile. Then Christi concluded with, "And you just sneak off like there's nothing to see that's of any interest!"

The accusation in her tone startled Tanya for a moment, and she looked up to find Christi looking at her with a frown of confusion darkening the normally glitteringly happy blue eyes. But why? Because she had slipped off rather than allow herself to be drawn in by a charismatic man? Leaning in close so no one else would hear her, Christi pressed on a bit further.

"What are you, gay or something?"

Tanya was stunned, then found herself giggling hysterically. Did avoiding a man who got you hot and bothered without even trying make you gay? Deciding that her friend deserved to hear the truth, she laughingly admitted that the man certainly had a nice body and his eyes intrigued her, then found herself having to firmly defend her decision to avoid getting interested in him, thereby avoiding any romantic entanglements.

"I'm leaving for Atlanta in a few days, then it's Jacksonville, Miami, New Orleans. How can I possibly keep a relationship going when I'd be going one direction and he'd be going another?"

"A relationship?!" Christi's squeal echoed through the locker room and Tanya quickly shushed her. She continued in a slightly more hushed tone. "Why worry about a relationship? What's wrong with a one night stand, a little fling with an interesting guy who cranks your motor?"

"I don't believe in sleeping around."

Christi started laughing, once again drawing attention to them and making Tanya frown heavily.

"Then you and this guy are made for each other!" Tanya looked confused, so Christi elaborated further. "Vinnie says this trucker, Carl or Ken or something like that, doesn't like loose women, and wouldn't normally have gone out to BoxCars with them, except he got a layover for the weekend and didn't have anything else to do. He came and saw the show to see Tigré and see if he could figure out her secret identity just for something to do."

Tanya felt hysterical laughter building somewhere deep inside her and managed to fight it down. The man who had turned her whole world upside-down with a mere look had just happened to be at BoxCars because he was trying to avoid getting bored? It was outrageous! Fate at her most fickle!

Managing to keep her thoughts hidden from her effervescent friend, she quietly finished tying her shoes and expressed her heartfelt opinion that Vinnie just might be lying in order to keep a certain cute blonde dancer to himself.

"Really?" Christi looked radiant as the thought took root, and she got even bubblier as she got excited about the possibility, despite the fact that her continued interest in the trucker might make Vinnie lose interest in her and stop sending her jobs. Vinnie and his companions had gotten Christi hired for several bachelor parties that had paid quite well, but the possibility of having such a well-built man in her bed got Christi all hot and bothered, making it well worth the possible loss in income, bringing forth a dreamy smile. Tanya smiled as well, secretly hoping to have the man's attention centered on anyone other than herself. His gaze was much too unnerving!

Walking back to the aerobics room with Christi preening at her side, Tanya looked up as she stepped through the door— and directly into the calm, yet unsettling gaze of the man she had decided should be avoided at all costs. Her heart leaped and she felt short of breath, but the spell was broken when Christi made good on her promise to go after him. Waving and giving him her best "come hither" smile, Christi cut off Tanya's view, allowing the petite brunette to slip off into a quiet corner to do her warm-ups while the equally petite blonde flirted outrageously.

Settling herself with her back to the big trucker, Tanya started her warm-up stretches, hiding the grace of several years of yoga and aerobics with a false clumsiness. She was painfully aware of the warm, green eyes that watched her every move, while Kyle continued to try to get a glimpse at the face that was seemingly innocently turned away from him, but which he was beginning to suspect was being hidden for some reason.

Across the room, Christi tried to draw Kyle into conversation, but although he was distantly polite, it was obvious that his attention was centered on the one female in the room who was pointedly ignoring him. With a sigh of resignation, she soon gave up to join Tanya in the corner.

Allowing herself a snort of anger that made Tanya jump, she flopped onto the floor beside her friend and began to try to warm up in stiff, angry jerks.

"Wouldn't you know it!" she finally snapped, "The first real man to walk into my life in this decade and he goes for the one lady in the room who doesn't want anything to do with him."

Tanya glanced over her shoulder, feeling foolish for believing the big trucker would be watching her, but curious about which of their number had garnered the man's attention—and again found herself looking directly into two warm, green pools. He smiled—a slow, sexy scorcher that made her soul catch fire—and she looked quickly away, unable to stand the heat of the flames he kindled with nothing more than a look. Her heart raced in her chest and she thought for a moment that she was going to embarrass herself further by fainting, then she managed to regain control of her emotions and chanced another glance.

Kyle was no longer standing next to the instructor, where he'd been only moments before, but he wasn't leaving the room in preparation for the beginning of class, either. Instead, he was walking toward her, his eyes leaving no doubt as to his intention, for they traveled over her quickly, and it seemed from the smile that again produced a flash of straight, white teeth against the dark beard and mustache that he liked what he saw. Tanya sat stunned, then suddenly got to her feet to attempt an escape. She was saved from further action by the instructor, who called for everyone to take their places.

True to form, the woman started giving explicit directions about the upcoming class while everyone complied with her first request, not giving anyone else a chance to speak. There was a brief moment of confusion as every woman in the room tried to find a place close to the well-built stranger, and in the confusion, Tanya slipped to the edge of the room, prepared to make a mad dash to the locker room if need be, overcome with the fear that the trucker had been hired to find her by the man she had run away from.

It didn't become necessary, for Kyle ended up several rows away from her, but she felt his eyes on her again and again throughout the class. As soon as the instructor released them, she bolted for the door, leaving Christi to make one more attempt at Kyle, who found himself the only man in a sea of admiring women, unable to pursue the prey that most interested him: a small, well-built brunette with almond-shaped brown eyes. Having watched her throughout the class, he had found himself more and more infatuated with her exotic beauty, and just wanted to see if her voice was as sexy as the rest of her small, well-built figure, but was puzzled by her obvious attempts at avoiding him. Her association with Christi also sparked his curiosity, but Christi's attentions were all too obvious.

She wanted nothing more than to have his attention for herself.

Safe in the locker room, Tanya did the one thing that always seemed to bring her worried mind some ease. She took a shower. In the comfortably small, steamy shower stall with the water drumming down on her head, she tried to justify her reasons for running away from any possible contact with the trucker. There was the tale she had told Christi, and then there was the truth. The truth was that, if she let her guard down, her stepfather, or possibly just a man like him, would find her, and her life would end in pain and misery just as her mother's had.

She stepped out of the shower to find Christi waiting for her, a frown of disapproval on her normally cheerful face. Feeling like a kid caught doing something dreadfully wrong by a favorite grown-up, she slunk over to a bench and sat down, preparing herself for the coming lecture. She didn't have to wait long.

"You really are going gay on me!" Christi snapped, and Tanya felt as if she'd been slapped.

"I'm not going gay on you," she responded sullenly, and Christi snorted.

"Then explain to me why you're running away from the most perfect man in the universe when it's obvious that he's interested in you!"

"If it's so obvious to everyone, why did he get mobbed as soon as class was over?"

Christi rolled her eyes, unable to believe how infantile the whole conversation was, but unwilling to let it slide. She would get the truth of her friend if it was the last thing she did!

"What was as obvious as his interest was the fact that you were ignoring him. Most of those ladies were trying to offer him a consolation prize! Me included!"

When Tanya only continued to frown, Christi sighed and tried another tactic.

"What would be so hard about giving the guy a minute or two? You don't have to sleep with him! Just give him the time of day!" she begged, but Tanya had made up her mind.

Kyle was much too stimulating for her to have a one-night fling with, and she wasn't interested in a formal relationship. The big man would just have to get over it, because she wanted nothing to do with him!

Trying to explain her position to Christi without explaining the events leading to her way of life made her feel guilty, somehow, especially when Christi continued to frown. But she couldn't reveal that part of her life to anyone, especially not someone who would be apt to ask all the questions she had asked herself again and again, questions that had no answers. She watched while Christi threw on her clothes and stormed out, not even taking a shower first, and knew that Christi was truly upset with her for the first time since they had become friends, but she couldn't go after her and give her the insight that would allow Christi to understand the 'why'. She couldn't bear the pain of letting someone else know how bad her life had been a long time ago in a town thousands of miles away—or that she was still running from a man who may well have given up the chase!

Sitting on the steps leading out of the gym, Kyle was having a cigarette and thinking about the little brunette who had fled before he had a chance to get anywhere near her. He was frowning distractedly at a familiar-looking black-and-red motorcycle when Christi joined him, bumming a cigarette with anger in her tone. Before he even opened his mouth, she went off on a tirade about the very person he was thinking about, the friend who had accompanied her to class. Christi didn't mention the young lady's name, but was apologizing profusely for her strange behavior.

"I don't know about her sometimes." Christi snorted. "I've even started to wonder if she might not be gay, because even though I always tell her about the cutest guys in the bar, she almost never seems interested."

Kyle looked away to hide his amusement while Christi went on about how seldom really cute guys actually came into places like BoxCars—then turned back when it seemed that she hit a stopping point right in the middle of a sentence. He realized the reason for her sudden silence as a small, brunette figure in baggy clothes slipped by them without a word. The silence between the two women spoke volumes.

Feeling guilty for causing strain between two friends, he sat in silence while Christi started talking again and the dark-clad figure made her way to the motorcycle, then he felt like he was having a serious attack of deja-vu. Just as when he was standing outside BoxCars the night before, he watched the small woman pull a helmet over her damp, slightly curly hair and climb aboard the big machine, then roar off into traffic. His heart started to pound with excitement as the truth hit him like a physical blow: The little brunette had been somewhere in the bar the night before and had slipped out virtually unnoticed to climb on that same motorcycle and ride away, totally ignored by most of the patrons of the bar!

Could it be that the petite brunette was the elusive Tigré?

When faced with Kyle's direct question, Christi found it hard to lie to the man who watched her so closely. There was just something in his eyes that made her tell him the truth. A plan started to form in his mind, and it brought a twinkle to his eyes and a smile to his face.

Christi barely knew what hit her when he turned his full-voltage lady killer smile her way. She was floating on cloud nine and knew deep in her heart that she would probably agree to anything he suggested, just on the off chance that his eyes would turn to his blonde co-conspirator should his plan to capture the elusive Tigré fail. And if that happened, Christi would do everything in her

power to make sure the trucker didn't leave
New York without first visiting HER bed!

Chapter Five

Kyle arrived at BoxCars that afternoon just as Jimmy, the bartender, was arriving to start his shift. Invited to have a seat at the bar for the beginning of Happy Hour, Kyle grinned and ordered a Bloody Mary. As Jimmy turned away to prepare the drink, Kyle started what appeared to be an innocent conversation.

"So, I hear you guys have some great acts here."

Jimmy's bright blue Irish eyes lit up as he grinned back at the trucker.

"You heard right, buddy. The best in the city."

"So what can you tell me about this Tigré character?"

Jimmy shrugged, having heard the question many times before, and gave his rehearsed speech about the mystery woman who appeared on stage and then disappeared without a trace. Kyle frowned as Jimmy placed his drink in front of him, then reached into his wallet and pulled out a twenty.

"Suppose I've heard all that and I want to hear more. Who would I have to talk to?"

Jimmy looked at the twenty, knowing what it meant, but he was making some good money off the little dancer to keep her identity a secret, so he didn't take the bait.

"I don't know of anyone who knows more than that."

Kyle sighed, then pulled out another twenty.

"How about if I wanted to get a little something delivered to her dressing room? Know anyone who could pull that off?" Although Kyle knew that Christi would do the deed for nothing, he wanted to make sure that the brunette dancer would not be able to pin the blame on just one person, and hopefully he could make sure that Christi and Tanya remained friends after all was said and done.

Jimmy tried not to show his weakening resolve, but Kyle pulled out another twenty and Jimmy licked his lips. The drink only cost $4.25, and Tanya was only forking over $50 a week! Could it really be that he could make almost as much for a single delivery as he usually made in a whole night in tips, yet still keep his promise to keep Tanya's identity a secret? It was the thought of what the extra 'found' money could do for his always-stretched budget that finally made up his mind.

"What did you have in mind?" he asked innocently enough, but Kyle's eyes sparkled merrily. Without a word, he reached in his pocket and pulled out a stuffed tiger with a pink ribbon around its neck that matched the color of the leotard she'd worn at the gym that morning, then handed it, along with the cash, to a mystified Jimmy. The bartender frowned for a moment, then smiled and shrugged before heading backstage. He had barely regained his accustomed place behind the bar when Tanya slipped through the door. She kept her head down and mumbled a greeting to Jimmy, slipping through the backstage door without realizing there was anyone else in the bar.

"She's the bookkeeper." Jimmy was quick to explain, but the way his eyes shifted as he spoke told Kyle he was lying. Kyle smiled at the suddenly nervous man and decided to let him off the hook.

"I saw your 'bookkeeper' with Christi at the gym this morning," Kyle murmured, "And I saw her leaving here last night. Christi's already confirmed that she's Tigré, but wouldn't tell me much more than that about her." Kyle grinned as he shrugged. "I just think she's really cute and would like to get to know her better, and figure a little nonthreatening present is a good start."

Although Kyle's voice was too soft to be overheard by anyone else in the bar, had there been anyone else to hear, Jimmy clearly heard and understood every word. As he brought his drink toward his lips, Kyle lifted it toward the bartender, then toward the stage door in a silent toast to the young woman who had just disappeared backstage, making Jimmy's Irish eyes smile. If there was one thing the bartender understood from experience, it was the infatuation that came with seeing a certain pretty face in the crowd and not knowing anything about the young woman the face belonged to.

Christi came in a short time later, and the trio sat quietly making plans while Tanya put on her makeup and looked repeatedly at the stuffed tiger that had been sitting outside the door of her dressing room with no indication of where it came from except for a single letter—K—that was written on the tag that held care instructions. At her regular time, Christi slipped backstage, but instead of the usual orange juice, she carried a glass of ice water and had her face set in stern, angry lines. She pounded fiercely on the door and snapped off her assigned line like a professional actor as soon as Tanya opened the door.

"Here! Since you're such an Ice Princess, you can drink ice water tonight!"

Shoving the glass into Tanya's hand, she spun on her heel and stalked off toward the dressing area she shared with the other dancers while Tanya's eyes swam with unshed tears. For the first time, Tanya had cause to wonder if she was really doing the right thing by keeping everyone at bay rather than risk getting hurt again by someone who swore he loved her. Shutting the door slowly, Tanya went back to her preparations with her mind whirling in confusion, wondering how so simple a thing as refusing to speak to a man could cause so much trouble—and how to prove to Christi that she really was straight, just terrified, without telling the blonde the full truth about her teen years.

By the time she stepped out on stage, she had managed to gain outward control her emotions, but she was still slightly in a daze, unaware of the dark-haired man who watched her from a dark corner of the bar. His vivid eyes took in every detail, and when she made a rare misstep, a smile touched the mouth that was hidden under his heavy beard. She was rattled! All was going according to "The Plan"!

Christi didn't deliver Tanya's next drink, sending it back with another dancer, and Tanya spent most of her time before her second set pacing the small room. She had started to feel like Christi was the sister she never had, and now Christi wouldn't even come and talk to her! More disturbing, though, was the feeling of being lost and alone that washed over her, reminding her yet again of her teenage years, when she had felt closed off from the whole world by the beast that ruled over her home with a fist of iron!

She was still lost in her thoughts when she stepped out on stage the second time, and went through the act on autopilot. She never even noticed when a tall, muscular man slipped through the crowd to put another origami figure into one of the top hats, nor did she note the calculating look he gave her. He was smiling as he returned to his seat, certain from the worry in the dark eyes that his little plan was working quite well, indeed!

Tanya, meanwhile, was truly shaken by Christi's odd behavior. She had very few people whom she counted as true friends, and Christi was one of the closest of them— until now. She was so shaken that she forgot about the ring she wore as part of the act and still had the big gold tiger ring on her right middle finger as she stepped up to the bar. In a daze, she ordered a glass of orange juice, unaware that she had stopped beside a tall, dark-haired man with sexy eyes who was watching her and plotting his next move.

She wasn't even aware that anyone was still in the bar until a deep, slightly husky voice sent shivers of pleasure racing down her spine.

"Do you know Tigré really well?" Kyle had noted the ring and knew she normally didn't wear it except on stage thanks to Christi!

Tanya's head snapped back so she was able to look up into the dancing emerald orbs, then she promptly looked away and swallowed hard as a vivid memory of the muscle man at her elbow in skin tight bicycle shorts set her heart to racing. Afraid to speak for a moment for fear her voice would betray the wayward path of her thoughts, she finally got up the courage to turn toward him as she shrugged and tried to sound nonchalant, putting on her best backstreet New York accent to hide the last traces of California culture that clung to her normal tones.

"I jus' do da books in a little room off in a cornah. I don' even know who you're talkin' about."

Kyle hid his irritation at her use of that specific accent behind a big smile.

"Then what are you doing with her ring?"

Before she could hide her reaction, Tanya looked down at her hand in shock, turning the ring so that it looked like a wedding band and silently cursing her luck. When she lifted her head, her eyes were as cold as ice and all attempts at acting were abandoned as she prepared to take this jerk down the same way she'd taken down many other greedy jerks before him.

"How much?" she growled, barely loud enough for Kyle to hear, suggesting that his was a less than savory character motivated by greed with her tone, but he only leaned in closer and dropped his voice, too.

"You really think you can buy me off?" He shook his head and leaned closer, as if about to press a kiss to her ear. "If so, I don't want cash. The price of my silence is a cup of coffee in a public place."

Tanya's eyes narrowed, hinting at her distrust. "One cup of coffee in public?"

Kyle nodded, his eyes glittering like gems. Trying to ignore the way his smile made her knees weak, she forced a note of sarcasm into her voice.

"And I'm supposed to believe that's all you want?"

Kyle's smile never faltered. If anything, it became even more dazzling as he nodded slowly in response. Tanya found herself fighting to maintain her train of thought as well as her anger beneath the onslaught of his too-obvious charms.

"The Donut Shoppe on Broadway. It's the closest. Be there in twenty minutes." Despite the fact that she had to appear to be giving in, Tanya's glare was so cutting that it should have made him fall into neat little slices. She started to turn away, too shaken by the conversation to worry about the juice Jimmy was supposed to be getting, intent on leaving without a second thought about setting him up for a fall, but Kyle's soft, deep voice in her ear as his warm breath touched her cheek made her heart flutter and stopped her in her tracks.

"You expect me to believe you'll actually go there and wait for me?" He gave her another quick grin as she turned back to face him. "I wasn't born yesterday."

Tanya frowned, unable to believe how fast he could think for someone who'd been sitting in a bar drinking all night. When she realized he was watching her quietly, his eyes steady and his soft smile almost hidden by his beard, she suddenly knew by the clarity in his gaze that he'd had very little liquor that evening. For some reason she couldn't quite fathom, she had the suspicion he could see right through her—and found what he saw amusing. The thought that he might be playing with her just to amuse himself brought her anger back full-force, although she chose not to wonder why it should make her angry to have him do anything less than behave like a total gentleman.

"Then call a cab and let's get this over with. I'm exhausted!" she hissed through clenched teeth, knowing she'd made a mistake in letting her anger show when the full-wattage lady-killer smile returned.

Kyle wanted to crow about his good fortune, unable to believe he had actually kept her off-balance enough to agree to a date of sorts, despite her reputation of being an Ice Queen. With the success of the earlier part of his plan, Kyle was determined to keep the lovely lady he'd won as his companion for a part of the evening as off-balance as he could. As if reading her earlier thoughts, he took Tanya's hand, brought it to his lips and kissed her knuckles like a gentleman of old, his breath warm on her skin. "Kyle Benton at your service, milady."

Surprised by the unexpected tingle in her fingers as his beard brushed her hand, Tanya was unaware of the shy smile that accompanied her blush. Her name came out of her mouth in a husky whisper. "Tanya LaMonte. Pleased to meet you."

Jimmy appeared with her juice and she used it as an excuse for pulling free of his touch, pausing to drink while Kyle paid for her drink and looked on, his eyes sparkling merrily. She allowed herself to look him over while hiding behind an angry glare, impressed by the firm bulges under his T-shirt and the massive biceps which, true to Christi's description, really did look as big around as her waist. When she could delay the moment no longer, she set her empty glass down and started away from the bar as Kyle stepped to her side, his hand sliding toward her waist.

"Keep your hands to yourself!" she hissed, and his hand promptly disappeared into the pocket of his tight-fitting jeans while he quietly apologized, his eyes gleaming in a spirited way that belied his somber voice. Frowning, she led the way to the door, offering not even the slightest hint of a smile as he opened the door for her. Outside, she stood in the area that was brightly lit by the street light like an actress taking center stage, glaring at him from under her lowered brows as he pulled out a cigarette and lit it before offering her one. The look of disgust she offered in response left no question as to what she thought about smoking.

Uncomfortably aware that she had no intention of being polite, Kyle sighed deeply, wondering if it would benefit him to let her just go home. Watching her carefully, he considerately blew his smoke away from her and watched for a cab, trying to pretend it didn't matter when she answered his silence-filling questions with fierce glares and no verbal responses whatsoever.

He was almost sure he had seen signs of an awkward shyness as he kissed her hand, but he could certainly understand her current mood. She had been set up, and that made her extremely angry. He even bit back a smile as he thought about how he would feel if one of the hookers the truckers referred to as "leather lizards" found a way to blackmail him into a date. He'd be one angry cuss, and would make sure she knew it by being rude!

Grinding the butt of his cigarette with the toe of his boot, Kyle tried to keep an eye on Tanya without seeming to stare as she either looked around, as if expecting a bogeyman to step out of the darkness, or glared at a point somewhere on the other side of the street, stubbornly refusing to look at him. He ran admiring eyes down her body, returning his gaze to her face just as she looked his way. He grinned at the blush on her cheeks, which she sought to cover with another glare, and finished snuffing out his cigarette just as a cab came along. Kyle gave a loud whistle to draw the driver's attention, and Tanya gave him a bitter smile to cover her envy of his ability to whistle that loudly without having to put his fingers into his mouth.

"The Broadway Donut Shoppe, lover boy. Make sure the cabby understands that you're to meet me there in fifteen minutes or I'm gone." She challenged, her eyes shooting sparks and her voice as cold as ice.

Tanya marched angrily over to her motorcycle and climbed aboard, unaware of the sparkle of amusement in Kyle's eyes as he took note of her anger in the rigidity of her spine as she moved away from him. He, on the other hand, noted all the things she did that indicated her feelings, right down to the shadow of doubt that crossed her mobile features in the form of a puzzled frown just before she pulled her helmet down to cover her visage. Seeing signs that she had never been treated like a lady and was a bit confused by his manners, Kyle found himself suddenly hoping that the pretty dancer would be thrown for a curve, allowing him to see past the Ice Princess façade that Christi had told him about and have a look at the real woman before the impromptu "date" was over. Passing a ten to the driver, Kyle told him his destination, adding "There's twenty more in it for you if you can get me to the

Broadway Donut Shoppe before the girl on the crotch rocket gets there."

The driver grinned and nodded, his eyes showing his greed. Minutes later, the driver pulled out of the Donut Shoppe's parking lot as Tanya pulled in. Looking fierce, she almost snarled as she put down her kick stand.

"After paying big bucks to get here first, what would you have done if I hadn't showed, big shot? Called the cops?"

Her ire at being outmaneuvered by the simple greed of a New York cabby was unmistakable, and Kyle laughed, his warm chuckle echoing off the nearby buildings.

"I would have just done the same as I did tonight. I figure you would have had to report to work sooner or later."

A look of surprise tinged with pleasure touched her features for only a moment, but allowed Kyle realize how hard she was fighting to maintain her angry façade in his presence. His spirits lifted again, prompting him to confuse her further by opening the door of the donut shop for her with a bright smile and a genteel bow.

"After you, milady."

Tanya passed him with a slight frown marring her face, sensing from his behavior that he wasn't bothered at all by her angry routine. Always before, her fierce demeanor had sent men away in a hurry, looking for a more gracious companion, yet this one, despite being treated to nothing but the very worst of her cutting remarks, seemed to be enjoying himself. When she turned to look up at him, she lost her concentration, for he was looking at her with the warmth of understanding in the deep green pools of his eyes despite the fact that she hadn't said a word about any of the things she wanted him to look at her like that for.

Kyle saw the confusion in her dark eyes fade to something softer, and his doubts about finding her warmer side took flight. The fact that Tanya's temper had always made men back off was apparent, but Kyle had never been the type to back away from a challenge, and he wasn't about to start by backing down from one tiny, seemingly angry young woman. Since extreme politeness seemed to confuse her the most, he stepped aside to let her order first, hiding his revulsion when she asked for her coffee with extra cream and extra sugar. He ordered his black, hiding a small grin beneath his beard as Tanya loudly announced what she thought of black coffee, just as he had expected she would. It fit the character she was trying so hard to portray.

"Black coffee rips holes in your stomach lining. Between black coffee and cigarettes, it's a wonder you stay healthy," she snapped and in return, Kyle gave her a wink and a grin, faking a heavy Irish brogue.

"Sure an' it's the black coffee an' cigarettes what keep me goin', lass. Have ye e'er heard o' a leprechaun wi'out his pipe?"

"You're too big to be a leprechaun!" Tanya growled, fighting the grin that wanted so badly to surface.

"Well, ye can't be blamin' me! Ma Gram wouldna let me smoke 'til I was in the military, an' by then, t'was too late to stunt ma growth."

Tanya tried to find something to say, some way to keep her anger as a wall between herself and Kyle, but found her eyes traveling over his firm frame instead, her mind's eye bringing forth a picture of him in the tight shorts and muscle shirt from the aerobics class, making her thoughts drift far afield. Her eyes slid up to his face, and she blushed furiously as she found him looking down, watching her with a smile. The gleam in his emerald eyes was too knowing, and Tanya felt shaky as she realized she was losing control of her lustful side for the first time in her life—and it seemed he knew it even before she did!

When Kyle's cup of coffee was delivered first, Tanya suggested sweetly that he find them a seat, planning to attempt an escape when he turned away. Kyle only lifted his left eyebrow as he leaned forward, smiling as he murmured in her ear, looking to anyone watching like he was sharing a lover's secret.

"Sorry, Angel Face, but I know that the minute I head for a seat, you'll head for the door, and that wasn't part of our deal." He drew away, and at her disgruntled frown, gave another grin. "Gram didn't raise no dummy."

"Why did your Gram raise you?" Tanya changed the subject rather than attempt to continue her angry farce in an attempt to lull Kyle into a false sense of security, but Kyle's killer smile came back at full voltage as he seemed to read the turnings of her mind. She was forced to look away from the deep pools of emerald green to avoid drowning in their depths, struggling to get back her anger at her stepfather to protect her from the virile man who stood before her.

"My folks died when I was seven, so my grandparents brought me up. Then Grampa passed on when I was sixteen, so it was just Gram and me from then on."

"Poor Gram!" Tanya's tone was meant to annoy, but Kyle continued to smile, and even laughed slightly as he remembered some of the antics of his younger days.

"She'd agree that I was quite a handful at times, but always says I turned out okay."

Tanya tried again to get angry, but her anger slipped further away each time she risked a glance into Kyle's glittering green eyes. She didn't usually find men with beards or long hair even vaguely interesting, but there was something about his eyes. What was it Christi had said? Something about his eyes melting a hole in a vault? Now she knew what Christi was talking about, because he had certainly melted a hole in the wall she'd built around herself, and didn't even seem to be trying all that hard!

Taking several deep breaths to gain some degree of control over herself, she accepted her coffee from the young female cashier, who stared at Kyle in much the same way as men stared at Tigré. Grudgingly, she admitted to herself that Christi was right on all counts. This Kyle was a lady killer in a very animalistic way, looking for all the world like a devil-may-care biker in his tight-fitting jeans and black leather jacket, open down the front to reveal rippling muscles under a tight black T-shirt. The heavy beard and long auburn hair added to the dangerous biker image, but his eyes drew the most attention. They revealed a certain intensity in his nature, proclaiming him vividly alive. Even now, they darted about the room, absorbing every minute detail about their surroundings so that he could analyze it at a later date. She couldn't explain why, but she tingled clear down to her toes every time they settled on her.

She turned to lead the way to the seat, feeling a pleasant warmth where she imagined his gaze touching her back. She shivered from the sensual sensation as she sat down, but looked at him steadily when he took the seat across from her, hoping he wouldn't notice her body's traitorous reaction. The knowing look in his eyes dashed her hopes immediately. It seemed he didn't miss a trick!

"Are you cold?" His deep bass voice added to the strange quaking that was possessing her, making her duck her head to keep him from seeing her confusion at the strange feelings overtaking her.

"I didn't sleep well last night, and I always get cold when I'm overtired," she grumbled, as if that explained everything he needed to know.

Kyle just sat staring at her for a long moment, then opened his mouth and came straight to the point, surprising her with his candid manner.

"I asked you here to find out why you don't make a little extra money on the side like the other ladies, but I think I already figured it out." He paused, and his brow furrowed slightly as he tried to find a polite way to say what he was thinking and grimaced after speaking when he said the lamest thing he'd ever heard. "You don't seem to like men much."

Tanya frowned, wondering why this conversation sounded so familiar, then remembered Christi's comments about Kyle after the incident at the gym and her accusations about a certain brunette's sexual preferences.

"I'm not gay!" she growled, and Kyle smiled and pretended to wipe sweat off his brow with a mischievous gleam in his eye. When he leaned forward and lowered his voice to a confidential level, Tanya found herself leaning in like a co-conspirator.

"But you don't like the company of men. Why?"

His soft, warm tone urged Tanya to answer before she was aware she was going to open her mouth, blushing at how lame it sounded.

"I like men just fine, and find them sexy and all that, but I just don't trust them."

Kyle looked incredulous, and Tanya tried to explain further while not giving away her the full embarrassment of her secret, choosing her words carefully.

"I had a really bad experience with a man once." She said quietly, and blushed even more, unable to continue.

Kyle tried to act angry, but his left brow lifted and his eyes glittered with suppressed amusement, spoiling the believability of his ruse. "Boy, that's really low. One bad experience and you take it out on millions of innocent men! Shame on you!"

Tanya caught his playfulness and pushed out her lip in a very exaggerated pout, dropping her head and trying to make big, puppy eyes. Kyle chuckled, then sipped at his coffee and gave her a wink and a broad smile. Tanya fought back a threatening smile of her own, her defenses crumbling beneath the onslaught of his easy charm.

"I dance for money," she admitted quietly, "not revenge, and prefer not to get into the dirty side of the business, if you really MUST know!"

"Why not get into another line of work? Like a secretary, maybe? Then you wouldn't have to worry about big, mean truckers forcing you to go out to coffee with them just so you can be left alone."

"If I was a secretary, I'd need someone to keep my boss from chasing me around the desk." She muttered, half to herself, and found herself oddly pleased when Kyle chuckled again, seeming to enjoy what others had called her "quirky" sense of humor. Then he was suddenly serious, his eyes firm and steady.

"Why don't you work someplace safe to earn your money?"

Biting her lip with a frown marring her exotic features, Tanya played with the edge of her cup, betraying her discomfort at this more personal question to Kyle's watchful gaze. She finally decided that Kyle, of all the men she'd ever met, deserved to know the truth, even if she never intended to see him again after they had shared their coffee. It would hurt to tell him good-bye when he was the man she had always dreamt of meeting and marrying, but it would hurt her worse to have to tell him her terrible secret.

"Because the safe places to work don't pay that well. It's hard to make a thousand a night in the steno pool of some company where the big wigs don't even know you're alive."

Kyle grew thoughtful as he wondered why he had the feeling that he was missing part of the puzzle. What, exactly, made him feel that it wasn't just the money that prompted Tanya to dance for her living? His lady-killer smile returned again, but not full force, as he recognized a certain truthfulness despite Tanya's evasiveness, and he decided to try another angle.

"How long do you intend to be a dancer?"

Tanya's eyes darted quickly around the room, and an alarm went off in Kyle's head. It seemed she was keeping an eye out around her as if expecting someone or something to jump out of the woodwork. It wasn't until her eyes had fully scanned the almost-empty donut shop that they returned to him and her lips parted in a smile.

Her smile was real and a little wry.

"For as long as I can fight off the effects of gravity."

Kyle's eyebrow lifted and the killer grin regained its full voltage. "So that means you can dance for what, another year or maybe two? Or will you get implants to make sure you'll have a nice nest egg for retirement?"

Such teasing would normally have had Tanya dumping her coffee in his lap, but something about the cocked brow and glittering emerald eyes made his teasing enjoyable. She surprised herself by blurting out the first thing that came to mind, blushing at how corny it sounded.

"I figure it's time to quit when the only way to keep your boobs off your knees is to have surgery."

Kyle looked surprised for a moment at her response, then gave her his patented high-voltage grin as the eyebrow went up like a flag, signaling that a slightly evil thought had entered the big man's mind.

"Wouldn't you need to have awfully big boobs in order to have them bounce on your knees?"

Tanya giggled, then self-consciously looked around the room like she expected a monster to jump out at her for laughing. Kyle turned her eyes back to his by hooking one large knuckle gently under her chin. She froze while his eyes glittered into hers like gems, and he traced her jaw line with the tip of his finger, sending warm tingly sensations like she'd never felt before racing down her spine.

"I like it when you laugh!" The warmth of his voice and electric touch of his hand nearly sent her into orbit, but she took another deep breath and tried to control her body, failing miserably. Determined to change the subject to something other than herself and hopefully take Kyle's mind off the way the other dancers made extra money, she pushed his hand away and tossed out the first question that came to mind.

"So did your grandma survive your teenage years, or did you give her a heart attack?"

Kyle laughed at her obvious attempt to change the subject, but went along with it to see how far she'd go to avoid having him learn more about her. After years of holding aggressive women at bay, it was most refreshing to have a woman attempt to do the same to him.

"Gram is still alive, breaking the hearts of all the widowers in the area, having the time of her life."

"Your grandmother dates?" Tanya's surprise was obvious, as was the fact that she was no longer fully trying to hold him at bay. Some of the stiffness had left her small frame and she smiled more and more often. Kyle felt he'd scored a major victory when she leaned slightly forward as he shrugged, fully interested in what he was saying.

"Why shouldn't she? She's old, but she's not dead." He smiled softly and Tanya could almost see the love for his Gram written on his face as his voice softened. "She says it keeps her young."

"Do you visit her when you get time off?" Tanya tried not to sound overly curious, but extended families had always interested her, especially since her own family had consisted of her mother and herself for most of her early years. Kyle didn't seem to mind, though, answering her questions with a smile crinkling the corners of his eyes.

"I usually don't get more than two days at a time anywhere near home, except for Christmas and Easter." The brow raised again. "Gram says I cramp her style when I'm home, and I'd rather not cross her."

"She must be one feisty lady if you avoid going home to avoid getting her mad." Even though Tanya didn't believe that was the true reason he took so little time off, she decided to play along, hiding her smile behind the rim of her cup.

Kyle put on an overacted scared little boy face that made Tanya smile.

"I'd rather wrestle a 'gator than face Gram when she's got her wind up! All the martial arts in the world can't protect me from her revenge!"

"What kind of revenge?"

Kyle managed to pull off a dramatic shudder. "You don't want to know!"

"Oh, come on! She can't be that terrible. What could a poor old lady do to a big guy like you?" Tanya grinned and her eyes sparkled as she pictured a tiny woman with gray hair making the big muscleman whimper in fear. Kyle looked both ways as if about to tell her a tremendous secret, his face totally serious—except for the left eyebrow.

"She'd take away my allowance from my military funds!" He whispered, and nodded seriously while she covered her mouth to hold back a volley of giggles. Kyle held the serious face for several minutes before the killer grin returned, turning her mind to mush and forcing her to look away to be able to come out with anything halfway near intelligent to ask next, just to keep him from asking questions.

"What branch of the service did you join? What was your specialty?"

Kyle's eyebrow lifted, a move that Tanya already recognized as a sure sign that mischief was brewing. He snapped sharply to attention and spit out his answers as if being addressed by a drill sergeant.

"United States Navy, SIR. In their Seals unit, SIR. In layman's terms, I specialized hand-to-hand combat methods, SIR. The rest is classified, SIR."

Tanya smiled, shaking her head in both amusement and surprise. The memory of Kyle's morning mantra at the gym and calm confidence in the face of her nasty behavior lent credence to his words, but made her blush as she found herself still well warmed by even the merest thought of his firm body in next to nothing, as he had been at the gym that morning.

Kyle relaxed back, noting her blush and the shy way her eyes dropped, and took a sip of coffee with a knowing grin, certain he had caught the lady's interest before he inquired "Anything else you'd like to know?

Tanya bit her lip as she searched the gently smiling face for any sign of falseness, but found no threats in the deep green eyes that watched her. In a voice that had suddenly become slightly husky, she asked the only question that came to mind.

"Why the Navy?"

Kyle took another sip of coffee, then continued to sip at his coffee while Tanya waited. The eyebrow went up and small laugh lines appeared around his eyes as he purposefully held off answering to try to get her angry, wanting to see how long she'd wait for a reply. When she simply sat patiently watching him with a sweet smile, somehow knowing he was playing with her, he sighed and fought to keep his face serious.

"I thought my character needed improving."

"Did it?"

"Did it what?" Kyle somehow continued to keep a straight face as he baited her, looking innocent with the singular exception of his errant eyebrow.

"Did it improve?" Tanya fought for patience, suspecting that the high-flying brow meant she was being set up for something but unwilling to give up just yet.

"Did what improve?" Kyle fought a grin as Tanya sighed and rolled her eyes dramatically skyward, as if praying for help from above.

"Did your character improve?"

Kyle seemed to ponder the question, then his eyebrow went up and he flashed the killer smile. Tanya prepared herself.

"Not a bit, but I can kick butt and mean it!" Then the smile softened and he was actually serious for a change. "I learned a lot of ways to kill a man with my bare hands while I was in the service, but studied Karate and Tai Chi as a child under a master who believed in control, so I've never made use of most of what I learned in the service."

Tanya was impressed, but tried hard not to show it, enjoying their talk but still not 100% sure she wanted to encourage him. She finished off the last of her cold coffee in a gulp, then grimaced and glanced nervously around, unaware that Kyle was watching and assessing her every move, absorbing every detail for later analysis.

"So, if you joined the service to build your character and failed, how did you decide that truck driving was the next logical move? Was it the romance of the open road?"

Kyle shrugged, aping her by gulping the last of his coffee, then stared into the empty cup as if thinking about his answer. When his eyes returned to her face, they were calm, and his steady gaze went straight to her heart, stunning her momentarily. His soft bass voice washed over her like a gentle wave.

"I like seeing the country. Over the past ten years, I've been to every state in the Union." His eyebrow went up and his voice took on a definite note of bragging. "I'm going to Alaska and Hawaii, too—just as soon as I can figure out how to get my rig to float."

Tanya's face lit up and a soft giggle touched her lips, the natural beauty of her momentarily stunning Kyle. In that same instant, she found herself doing the one thing she had always sworn she would never do: throwing caution to the wind to trust the stranger who had stepped out of her dreams and into her life. Her voice was soft as she teased him back.

"So you're kinda like Bruce Wayne, huh?"

"Bruce Wayne?" Kyle repeated in surprise, at a loss for the first time since sitting down. Did she know more about him than he thought she did, or was she just guessing? Could it really be that a stripper in New York had heard about the poor little rich boy from the back woods of Maine?

"You know. Bruce Wayne." Tanya explained, enchanting Kyle with her bright, honest smile. "Batman. Lost his folks young, learned martial arts and body building and stuff, then returned home to battle evil. Do you battle evil when you go home?"

Kyle's eyes lit up, his eyebrow lifted and his voice came out with a heavy Maine twang.

"Daow. Ain't nawthin' much goin' on back in Maine. We're all too busy keepin' wahm in the wintah an' goofin' on tourists in the summah!"

Tanya laughed outright at his wit and returned to her subject, her eyes twinkling as she did her best to sound like a journalist interviewing a witness.

"So you're not a crime fighter because there's no crime back home? Is that how you have the time to run around chasing skirts?"

Pretending to be offended by the implication, Kyle pouted, but it came off so obviously faked that Tanya fought another giggle.

"But if I'm not a crime fighter, why do they call me Superman?"

"What?" Tanya's look of confusion brought back THE SMILE, the high-voltage one that threatened to melt her bones, making her pray that Kyle wouldn't notice her reaction. Heaven forbid he should figure out that she liked him!

"Not what. Who." He berated gently, his smile softening the impact. "Superman. Alias Clark Kent. The guy who flies around in red, white and blue pajamas." She smiled at the description and he explained further. "The other truckers call me Superman because I can move big loads faster than most of my peers."

Tanya imagined him moving around loads of supplies and she felt her face growing hot. The image was rather provocative, especially if she imagined him doing so without a shirt on, yet she still wasn't sure she wanted a man in her life. She was so tongue-tied it allowed Kyle to get in a question of his own.

"How about you? Did you ever join the armed forces?"

Tanya nearly choked in her effort not to burst out laughing at the thought.

"I didn't even finish high school!" she blurted out, then bit her lip while silently berated herself for revealing too much, a deep blush staining her cheeks. Kyle saw the brief flash of pain in her eyes and continued on in a voice that was soft and soothing, leaning forward slightly and finding, much to his surprise, that she didn't back away.

"But you managed to get a high paying job without an education. I think you did well."

Tanya snorted, not noticing the change in position as she was too busy studying the hand that held her coffee cup, wondering why she was being so honest with this one person after seven long years of keeping silent.

"Yeah, right. I've done great. I take my clothes off in front of a bunch of screaming lunatics." Her sarcasm was clearly evident in her voice and eyes. Kyle's eyes flashed for a moment with something that approached anger at the way she put herself down, but his voice was smoothly under control, his fingers gentle as he tipped her chin to force her to look up into his eyes.

"You could be a prostitute like some of your co-workers in their little 'private dance' arrangement, but you choose to take the money from the public act and go home alone. You're really special, and you shouldn't beat yourself up for what you do. You're keeping your act clean."

Tanya stared at him for a long moment, wondering if she could have really heard him right. He thought she was special? The sincerity in the emerald eyes was too clearly evident for her to believe he didn't mean it, but a small voice kept telling her not to believe a word. He was a MAN!

Struggling for something more to say, she looked at her watch and was truly startled to see how late it was getting.

"Wow! I really should be going." Her words were punctuated by her preparations to leave, but Kyle's hand dropped over hers, causing her to look up into his face as shock waves rolled down her arm, setting her soul on fire.

Kyle seemed totally unaware of what his touch was doing to her and appeared totally unaffected by the contact, his eyes pleading with her silently.

"At least let me buy you breakfast so you can go to bed with enough sugar in your stomach to have sweet dreams."

Tanya giggled at his odd excuse for feeding her, then looked up into his eyes, suddenly feeling as if he knew what she was hiding and wasn't bothered by the cowardly behavior she displayed by running off and hiding rather than staying to face her stepfather. The feeling of kinship was so strong that she lost all enthusiasm for leaving. She smiled at Kyle and he knew she was staying.

"I'll take something small, preferably chocolate."

Kyle grinned, the rich warmth in his voice lighting all kinds of small fires throughout her body.

"A chocoholic. At last we have something in common! We're both chocoholics!"

Tanya rolled her eyes, unable to stop the winsome smile that curved her lips.

"Heaven help me. Now that you've found something we have in common, I'll never get rid of you!"

Kyle laughed and went to place their order. Tanya watched with an odd sense of contentment, smiling softly as she wondered if he knew about the quirky eyebrow that warned her that he was teasing. Between the eyebrow and the devilish gleam that danced within the emerald orbs, he somehow seemed quite handsome to her even without being able to see his chin beneath the beard. What would he think of her if she started getting REALLY personal?

Kyle noticed the mischievous gleam in her eye as he returned to their table and wondered what she was thinking, but all that came out of Tanya's mouth at first was something complimentary about the fresh cup of coffee and the chocolate cream-filled donut that he placed in front of her. Then she frowned and bit her lip, seeming to weigh a matter for quite some time while Kyle waited, his eyes setting small fires wherever they touched.

Tanya finally broke the silence. "Are you aware that your left eyebrow goes up just before you fib, sort of like Pinocchio's nose grew?"

"You're kidding!" Kyle sounded genuinely surprised.

Tanya shook her head "no", then sighed, trying hard to keep a straight face.

"It's very—" she couldn't control the smile, "— entertaining!"

Kyle opened his mouth as if he meant to say something, the left eyebrow soaring, then tried to catch it going up, making such funny faces that Tanya found herself doing something she hadn't dared to do for several years. A volley of loud girlish giggles exploded from her and she didn't look to see if the man of her nightmares had suddenly appeared.

Sensing a victory of sorts, Kyle grinned in triumph as he leaned forward, hoping that her defenses might crumble even more.

"I was aware of that quirk," he whispered.

Heads turned their way and Tanya hid her face in her hands and fought to control herself as her fears resurfaced, worriedly looking around, expecting to see her stepfather among the many faces that turned their way. Kyle's heart sank when he saw the fear in her eyes again, and he reached forward to gently touch the backs of her hands with his fingertips, sending waves of passion racing up both arms.

Tanya was so surprised by the unexpected reaction that she didn't pull away, her fear replaced by confusion.

"Everything's fine. You've nothing to fear while I'm here." He whispered, and she gave him a shy smile, wondering if he was able to read her mind or if her emotions were just that obvious. His stroking fingertips awakened strange things in parts of her that she had never known existed as he answered her unasked question with his next comment. "Your eyes are much too beautiful to always be filled with such deep fear."

Tanya blushed, not quite sure what to say. As before, she decided that truth was the best.

"You're not at all like I expected."

Kyle's eyebrow went up and he gave her another high voltage smile.

"What did you expect? Conan the Barbarian?"

"Nope. A Neanderthal," she corrected playfully despite the remnants of fear in her eyes, and Kyle grunted like a Neanderthal, pleased to see the glow returning to her face as he gestured toward her roughly.

"Woo-man. Sexy. Goooood!"

Tanya dropped her eyes again, this time laughing softly, feeling a warm glow somewhere in the region of her heart. Never in her life had she expected to have the man of her dreams walk into her life, much less prove to be so very entertaining, and now she was too scared to let him near her. The shadow of her stepfather loomed over her and she looked again as if expecting him to be standing there, earning another thoughtful look from Kyle as her actions reminded him of a frightened rabbit.

Forcing himself to back down just in case it was him she feared, Kyle casually leaned back. Much to his disappointment, he saw her visibly relax. To relax her even more, he lifted his left eyebrow intentionally, watching her prepare herself for a wise crack, her sparkling dark eyes making her look breathtakingly, innocently beautiful to Kyle's appreciative eyes.

"I- ah…" He pretended to be confused by what he saw and even stuttered while Tanya smiled, then he faked a frown and pretended to be angry. "Don't look at me like that! You made me forget what I was going to say! What was it?"

Tanya shrugged.

"You got me!"

Kyle pounced on her innocent turning of the phrase, his eyebrow leaping upward in earnest.

"I like the sound of that! If I've got you, what am I allowed to do with you?" Kyle eyed her with much wriggling of his eyebrows, his look so comical she giggled softly again.

Before she could stop herself, she blurted out the first thing she could come up with, then blushed profusely at how pushy it sounded, much to Kyle's amusement.

"You're allowed to join me for Yoga tomorrow morning."

Kyle feigned another pout.

"I was thinking more about tonight."

Tanya crossed her arms over her chest and frowned at him in mock anger, surprised to find that she just couldn't get herself really mad at him any more and wondering what kind of magic spell he was putting on her.

"You got what you asked for tonight, so don't push your luck, buddy!"

Kyle chuckled and finished off his donut, washing it down with some coffee, then set them onto another, less sexually oriented topic, since that seemed to be what Tanya wanted. Despite her professed love of chocolate, Tanya only picked at her donut, her eyes darting around the room frequently as if she expected someone to suddenly appear. Each new face through the door was studied and analyzed, and when she wasn't looking at him, she got a haunted look that Kyle found he didn't much like.

Deciding to see if he could make her smile again, Kyle took a deep breath and purposefully made a fool of himself.

"So why would a beautiful little lady like you work in rotten dumps like BoxCars?"

Kyle pretended horror at hearing such an often-repeated come-on line come out of his mouth. Tanya responded with a sweet, honest smile that did much in the way of boosting his ego.

Choosing her words carefully, she did her very best to sound nonchalant as she cut her history down to the bare bones, once again telling him something that was almost the full truth even though she couldn't meet his eyes. "I ran away from home when I was sixteen. I didn't want to live on the streets, so I lied about my age and started waitressing at a strip joint—until I realized that the stage is where the real money is. I've been dancing ever since."

"Do you ever go back to see your family?"

The question was almost a spoken caress, his voice soft and warm. Tanya looked up into his warm gaze, then swiftly away so he wouldn't see the pain of her memories in her eyes, giving a negative shake of her head. All she could say as her voice cracked was: "I can't go back!"

Kyle tried to get her to go into detail, but she simply refused to talk, drinking her coffee and pushing at the remains of her donut between quick, fearful looks around. Something about her manner told him that something had gone very wrong with her family, so he changed the subject again, unable to bear the pain he saw on her pretty face.

He chattered on about inconsequential things, making her smile, then laugh softly as she finally started to relax again. He flirted mercilessly, amused when she blushed and shyly hung her head, the total opposite of the beast she portrayed on stage. The only thing he couldn't seem to change was the way she kept glancing nervously around, as if she were afraid of someone seeing her.

She was like a riddle that he couldn't solve, an odd blending of the jaded woman of the world and the innocent girl next door, the graceful beauty and the frightened mouse, making his mind spin with the strange mix of emotions only she seemed able to bring out in him. He wanted to take her back to his motel room and make love to her until she forgot all the pain from those who had gone before, yet there was something about her that made him feel like an old man with one foot in the grave trying to pick up a school girl—and a grade school girl at that!

Finding herself on what could probably be called her first date with a man who was both nice looking and extremely charming, Tanya found she had no idea how to act. Each time her eyes traveled around the room in an instinctual search for her enemy, she glanced back at Kyle and found it hard to believe that he was actually sitting across from her, babbling away about everything and nothing. As he talked, he slowly leaned toward her, and her eyes left his less and less frequently as she found herself mesmerized by the depth of the emerald pools.

Distracting her with the light tracing of his fingers along the back of her hand, Kyle asked her a soft question or two, questions that didn't really seem to matter and which she answered with total honesty, too dazed to notice the gentle smile that was partially hidden by his beard. Forcing herself to look away from Kyle's eyes, she looked out the window past Kyle's shoulder and saw the first red of the rising sun touch the horizon. Her gasp of surprise had Kyle turning around to see what she was looking at.

Turning back to her with his eyebrow raised, he gave her a big smile.

"Now you can tell all your friends you spent the night with me."

"Don't flatter yourself! I don't plan on telling anybody anything if I don't have to."

Her comment, delivered in what was meant to be a sarcastic tone, lacked the bite that it needed to be offensive—the bite that had come easily to Tanya's tongue at the start of their impromptu "date". Kyle hid his smile of triumph, comparing the sweet young woman in front of him to the angry vixen he left the bar with. He tried to pretend he was seriously injured by her comment, but his effort was fouled by a high-flying eyebrow.

"But why not? Didn't I rock your world?"

Tanya couldn't come up with an immediate response. She was too busy giggling, no longer caring about the eyes that turned their way or the knowing smiles on some of the faces. When Kyle stood and pulled back her chair with a brilliant smile, she threw caution to the wind and took his hand, allowing him to help her to her feet and guide her out the door.

Chapter Six

Never in her life had Tanya pictured her first date ending like this, standing in the parking lot of a donut shop in a big city while the red light of early dawn beamed down on her and cars on the nearby street roared in thebackground.

Kyle stood closer to her than she had allowed any man to stand since high school, his eyes traveling over her face as if he were trying to memorize every nuance of her exotic beauty. The soft light erased the small laugh lines from his face and lent him the youthful glow of a teenager. He reached for her hand and she allowed him to take it, watching in fascination as he brought it to his lips, catching her breath as he gently kissed her fingers, sending molten lava racing through her veins.

"The evening just past proved to be most pleasurable, my lady. I shall await, with baited breath, the chance to meet you anon." His poetic words, delivered with a softly cultured accent, would have carried a sincerer message were it not for the fact that his eyes twinkled with mischief and his left eyebrow flew high. When Tanya didn't pull free right away, he bent his head again, this time snaking out his tongue to tickle the sensitive web of flesh between her first and second fingers, sending waves of passion crashing through her most secret places as she imagined him doing the same there.

With a gasp, Tanya started to pull free, but when Kyle lifted his head and flashed a smile that almost melted her bones, she found herself powerless to do so. She was held enthralled, trapped in the depths of his green eyes like a twig caught in a spring stream, unable to speak and unable to draw away, not really sure she wanted to do either while he lifted her chin with one strong finger. His mouth angled down and she held her breath while he ever so gently brushed her lips with his own.

The kiss was so soft and sweet it was like being brushed on the lips by a butterfly's wings, but it hit Tanya with the force of a cannon ball taking her broadside. Her heart skipped a beat! Her knees went weak! The fire he had already started roared up with even greater strength, and Tanya trembled with both her first taste of real passion and a deep-seated fear of falling in love with the wrong man, thereby repeating her mother's mistake. Unable to stop her traitorous body's reaction, she felt powerless, and being powerless went against everything she had worked seven years to achieve.

Angry with herself for her inability to control her own body, she dropped her eyes and started to back away with a lame excuse.

"I have to leave before it gets too late."

"But it's early!" Kyle teased with his brow flagged, seemingly unaffected by such a simple kiss except for his smile, which grew just a little wider.

"That may be true, but I still should get some sleep before my yoga class."

Kyle sighed, but suddenly brightened.

"What kind of car do you think is the sexiest car in the world?"

Tanya stared at him in confusion, unable to fathom why he would ask such a question, especially just before they parted, but shrugged as she answered truthfully.

"Sporty ones, like red convertibles. Why?"

Kyle shrugged.

"Just wondering."

Despite his casual tone, Tanya was suspicious, but she was unable to question him before he spoke again.

"Can I ask just one more question? It's something that's been bothering me since right after we got here."

His eyes cut directly to her soul, stealing her breath away. She nodded slowly, unaware that she did so.

"How many dates have you had?"

It took Tanya a moment to realize what he had actually said. As his words sunk in, she tried not to show her fear that he had somehow discovered her darkest secrets just by looking in her eyes. She chose to try a stall tactic.

"Including this one?"

Kyle hid an amused grin under his beard and shrugged, his eyes sparkling. "If you want to consider this a date—"

Kyle left his statement hanging while Tanya bit her lip, torn between telling the truth and protecting her way of life. With an echo of her mother's voice reminding her that honesty was the best policy, she looked him straight in the eye and put her trust on the line.

"One."

Kyle was stunned, but did his best to cover it by treating her admission as a joke.

"You only went out with one other man besides me? I don't think so, Angel Face. You're too beautiful to sit at home every night."

Tanya hung her head, unwilling to admit she had chased them off, but his fingertip brushing her jaw brought her eyes back up to his face. He started to open his mouth to say something, but his eyes seemed more focused on her mouth, which began to burn long before he brushed his finger across her lips. She held her breath as he bent toward her with a devilish grin.

Kyle's lips brushed across hers again and she sighed with pleasure, too lost in the explosion of feelings to care when his fingers remained to gently cup her cheek before tracing down toward her neck. They left a trail of fire in their wake and she was unable to stop her heart from racing or her body from reacting by coming to sudden, tingling life. When he withdrew, she was mesmerized by his gaze.

"How do you do that?" she whispered, making the killer smile return.

Kyle's tattletale brow again warned of mischief, but Tanya was too dazed to care.

"Do what?"

Her voice came out on a soft sigh of pleasure.

"Make me feel like I'm on fire?"

She decided once again that his eyes were definitely his most attractive feature as they sparkled and seemed to dance with mischief.

"I didn't do anything!"

Tanya laughed at his tone, reminiscent of a child caught stealing cookies trying to plead innocent. Still smiling, she asked the only other question in her heart in a voice husky with emotions that she didn't want to feel.

"Will I see you again?"

"Only if you'll agree to go out with me again tomorrow night—or tonight, whichever you want to consider it."

One part of Tanya wanted to turn him down and return to her nice, safe existence, but another, stronger part of her was tired of hiding. It was, after all, seven years since she'd last seen her stepfather. Could it be possible that, while she was playing this game of hide and seek, he was no longer looking for her?

Kyle's killer smile intensified in wattage at her answer.

"You've got a date, but with one catch. I'd rather eat something with fewer calories and less sugar this time."

Kyle wanted to make a comment about how few calories she had actually received from the uneaten donut, but chose to keep things peaceful instead.

"Well then, I'll meet you at work."

He kissed her once more, briefly, then let her walk away with just a smile and a soft, "See you later."

Tanya could feel Kyle's eyes on her as she climbed onto her motorcycle and pulled out of the parking lot, but she didn't feel the creepy, slimy sensation that normally accompanied such looks when she was on stage. Instead of making her feel as if worms were crawling all over her, Kyle's eyeing made her feel sexy and desirable. It was a warm and wonderful feeling that accompanied her all the way back to her camper.

When she finally lay back on her bed with the door firmly locked behind her, she closed her eyes and recalled the feel of his warm lips on hers while his fingers traced a path along the side of her neck to her collarbone. Her imagination took over, and his fingers found their way slowly down to caress her breasts while his lips found their way to her throat.

Within minutes of dropping into her bed, Tanya was asleep with a gentle smile curving her lips, untouched by nightmares for a change.

Chapter Seven

It was nearly two in the afternoon when Tanya opened her eyes again. With a cry of alarm, she leapt from her bed and ran into the tiny bathroom, peeling her clothes off to take a lightning-fast shower. She brushed her hair in sharp, painful strokes to finish waking herself up, then tossed on a fresh outfit and started for the door. With a muttered oath, she turned back and opened her hidden safe, pulled cash from last night's tips out of her backpack and stuffed it inside, then resumed her flight out the door, cursing herself for oversleeping. Jimmy smiled at her as she dashed inside the bar.

"Hey there! Right on time!"

Tanya looked at her watch, sighed and slowed her pace, finding it hard to believe that she hadn't hit any traffic tie ups along the way so she could actually make it to work at her normal time despite her mistake. With a sheepish grin, she asked Jimmy for an orange juice to take backstage with her, explaining that she overslept and was dying of thirst.

Jimmy responded with a chuckle.

"Considering what you left here with, I'm surprised you can walk a straight line!" he teased, and Tanya took immediate offense.

"Since when does talking over coffee and donuts make you walk funny?" she snapped, glaring at Jimmy as he stammered out an apology, then leaning forward to pin him against the wall with her piercing gaze.

"You should be careful what you say about Kyle." Her nearly whispering voice sent more fear through Jimmy than any screaming could have, for her eyes were deadly serious. "He may well be the only real gentleman who has ever walked through that door—" She paused for effect. "—and I won't let you bad-mouth him.

Worried about what she might be capable of, Jimmy nodded slowly. He let out a sigh of relief as she turned and stomped back stage. He admitted to himself, and not for the first time, that this little gal who went by the name of Tanya was very different from the usual girls who came in to dance. Most of them would have been proud to claim the big trucker as a conquest and been bragging about his prowess, even if all they got was coffee, and to hell with the man's honor!

By the time Christi knocked on the door of Tanya's dressing room, Tanya's anger had faded to a mild frustration, but her ire resurfaced when Christi's comments followed the same train of thought as Jimmy's.

"What is it with you guys?" she railed. "I went out for coffee and donuts with the guy and everyone thinks I took him straight home and went to bed with him!"

"Well, that's what I'd do!" Christi responded, and Tanya stopped her tirade with her mouth hanging open before she grinned, then started to laugh.

"You're right. You would!" Then she sobered. "Is it considered taking him home and going to bed with him if it was just your imagination taking over?"

Christi looked surprised, then grinned back.

"So just exactly where did reality leave off?" she asked, like a teenager would to hear about a friend's first date, and Tanya bit her lip for a second as she again realized how much of her childhood was lost when she ran away. The Ice Princess image fell to pieces as, with her eyes glowing, she described the date from beginning to end.

Christi sighed, a dreamy smile on her face. Then she pouted slightly and sighed again.

"That figures. All my life I've been looking for Prince Charming and when he finally shows up, he goes for my best friend instead of me."

"Do you really think he's Prince Charming?" Tanya's obvious sincerity prompted Christi to smile and lean close.

"Honey, any man who would let you go home alone after just a couple of kisses in a parking lot when he's fully aware of what you do for a living ain't no regular old Prince Charming. He's a damned Saint!"

Tanya bit her lip again, truly worried.

"Do you think I'm crazy for going out with him after work tonight, even if it's just for breakfast?"

Christi grinned like a Cheshire Cat.

"I'd be more apt to think you were crazy if you *didn't* go!"

Hoping that she was doing the right thing, Tanya finished getting dressed and tried to step into the role of Tigré, but found it much more difficult than usual. Her thoughts kept turning to Kyle, giving her a soft, dreamy look instead of the cool animal hatred that was so much a part of Tigré. It was only when she replaced Kyle's bearded face with that of her former stepfather that she was able to regain the needed venom, gliding across the stage with her lips curled back in a vicious snarl as the beat of African drums rumbled through the building.

Kyle wasn't at the bar and didn't come up to give her a tip during the first set, but Tanya managed to continue her routine without letting her worry show on her face. Backstage, however, she frowned as she retrieved the key to her dressing room from its secret hiding place, finding Christi at her elbow. As the door clicked shut behind them, Christi looked upset.

"Didn't you say Kyle was taking you out again tonight?"

Tanya nodded, biting her lip.

"Was he planning on meeting you here?"

"That's what he said, but he may have decided to go to Yoga class like we planned."

Christi frowned, pretending to get angry.

"No, he didn't, and neither did you."

Tanya started at the sharp tone, but saw Christi's slight smile that showed she wasn't really angry. With a heavy sigh, she gave the excuse, knowing it would sound made-up.

"I'm sorry, but I overslept. I barely made it to work on time."

Christi smiled sagely, never having known her friend to oversleep before in the whole time of their acquaintance. She knew from sharing an apartment briefly with Tanya that the brunette suffered from nightmares that woke her with frightened screams.

"I'll bet he was so blown away that he's buying flowers and chocolates for you right now."

Tanya smiled, finding herself amused by the teasing tone, but continued to worry about Kyle right up until she stepped out on stage for the second set. The quick flash of his killer smile from beside the door, where he was standing with the bouncers, had her fighting not to smile in return. As it was, she stared at him long enough for the MC to take note of where her attention had become centered.

"Looks like our tiger-lady has spotted a new victim. Come up to the stage, big guy—if you dare!"

Kyle laughed as he obeyed the MC's directive, pulling a bill out of his wallet as he approached. Tanya forced herself back into character, hissing as he neared the stage, her eyes narrowing. When he held up a twenty, folded lengthwise so that it resembled a thin rectangle, she glared at him, a snarl drawing back her lips. Kyle stood at the edge of the stage, expecting her to lean out so he could put it in her g-string after their date the night before, but the tiger lady had other ideas.

Lifting the chain, she stepped almost to the edge of the catwalk, then simultaneously yanked the chain to pull the cage forward and leaned out, snatching the twenty out of his hand with her teeth, like a tiger would snatch a piece of raw meat.

"Yipes! Count your fingers, buddy!" The MC joked, and Kyle made a big production of doing just that, folding half of a middle finger down so that it looked like she'd taken it, then flipping it up with an exaggerated sigh of relief. Tigré growled audibly and flexed her claws like she planned to scratch him, but he jumped back with a wide-eyed look of fear, much to the amusement of the crowd. His quick smile and wink just before he slipped back to his place by the door were missed by all but the woman on stage, who glared at his retreating back until she could control the threatening smile.

The rest of Tigré's set was performed more perfectly than ever before as she forced herself to concentrate, so enthralling the watching men that only Kyle noticed that she avoided glancing his way. Just before the lights went out, she looked directly up into his eyes with the slightest hint of a smile. She was gone as the room went dark, leaving Kyle with the impression he'd been touched by an angel.

Kyle was still standing at the door when a short, darkly clad form slipped through the stage door. Tanya slid her hand into his and pulled him outside without a word, stopping only when they were beside her motorcycle. She looked up into the killer smile that always unhinged her knees just as his eyebrow lifted.

"Trying to kidnap me?" he teased, then bent his head closer to whisper in her ear, making her sigh as his warm breath tickled her neck. "I think you forgot the handcuffs, Angel Face."

Tanya fought back the warmer emotions and tried to sound angry, sounding like an overtired toddler instead.

"I'm hungry, and after almost ruining my act, the least you can do is watch for a cab."

Kyle ignored her tone and brushed her hair away from her neck before bending close, as if about to kiss her or share a lover's secret.

"You just don't want anyone to know you've got the hots for me," he whispered huskily, and Tanya shivered at the sensual overload, her kneecaps melting. Then his words sank in.

"Why, you conceited jerk!" she snapped in real anger, but Kyle just flashed her another grin, unperturbed. When she stomped toward her motorcycle and threatened to leave, he shrugged, sighed and pulled a key out of his pocket, flipping it so that it caught the light. Without a word, he walked over to a flashy red sports car, shutting off a car alarm by pressing a button on a small black box on the key chain. Grinning at her over the roof, his left eyebrow raised and he issued his challenge before she could ask any questions.

"Last one to the Stardust Diner on Broadway buys for us both!" Then he jumped into the sports car and raced off, lucky enough to get a break in traffic at just the right time.

Tanya grinned and shook her head in amusement as she followed at a more leisurely pace, deciding it was better to pay for breakfast than to risk getting into an accident. Kyle was leaning against the car door feigning boredom when she pulled into a parking space, so she pretended to be upset.

"If I'd known I was having breakfast with someone who cheats to win races, I wouldn't have agreed to this date!" she snapped, but Kyle lifted his head with a long, slow smile that had her blood pounding in her ears. She swallowed hard as he stepped forward, looking up at his face and promptly drowning in two pools of emerald green.

"You're just mad because you lost." He whispered, his husky voice sending passionate shivers up and down her spine. "Besides, I know you can afford two breakfasts in this place. Just find the twenty I folded into a cat face. I had Vinnie put it in the hat for me earlier."

Tanya teasingly pulled out the one he gave her during the second set and offered it to him as if he was a dancer. Kyle gave her a sizzling smile that left her breathless as his eyes traveled warmly up and down her body. Never in her life had a man made her burn with passion's flame the way Kyle could with just a look!

Trying to hide her warm cheeks, she turned toward the restaurant door, her breath catching in her throat as Kyle's large hand slipped to the small of her back. A tingling warmth shot through her and she bit her lip, fighting both passion and panic as she tried to present a calm, cool appearance.

Unaware of the thoughts that ran through her head but very aware of the troubled frown that creased her delicate brow, Kyle stopped Tanya by tipping her chin up with a gentle finger. Looking deep into her soft brown eyes, Kyle fought back the urge to kiss her and chose to try an apology instead.

"I'm sorry if my rudeness upset you earlier." he murmured, making Tanya melt at the sincere look in his eyes.

"I'm sorry that I don't know how to respond when the cute guys start flirting." she managed after a moment, making Kyle snort softly.

As he saw the admiration in the dark eyes that stared up at him, Kyle felt a powerful surge of raw emotion unlike anything he had ever felt before. He had often seen that look in his dreams when his brain tried to put his latest lover's face with his concept of the perfect woman, but never had he seen it in real life. Careful not to let Tanya see him, he pinched himself to prove he wasn't dreaming it now, then let the warmer emotions show on his own face as he continued to stare down at her.

Tanya knew nothing of what went on behind his shining eyes, drowning in two limpid green pools until an older man pushed between them to leave the restaurant. With a wry grin, Kyle held the door for her, returning his hand to the small of her back as they were greeted by the hostess and led to a table. Much to his pleasure, she didn't pull away or order him to remove his hand as she had the night before, too busy enjoying the tingling sensation that his touch produced to fight it.

Three hours later, Tanya slid into bed with a smile still curving her lips and a dreamy look in her eyes, recalling the way Kyle's eyes looked when he smiled at her and the warm, deep timbre of his voice. His lips on hers when they parted had sent her into orbit, and as shining green eyes and a lady-killer smile followed her into the land of dreams, she imagined being held gently against a rock-hard chest and kissed softly and sweetly until all resistance faded. She woke to her alarm with a smile and stretched, cat-like, in the shaft of sunlight that fell across her bed, a plan already taking shape in her mind. It was time to stop running from her past and face the future, especially if that future could involve a handsome, mild-mannered trucker. It was time to truly become the tiger for a night!

Chapter Eight

When Kyle pulled up in front of BoxCars that Labor Day afternoon, the first thing he noticed was that the black and red Kawasaki wasn't in its regular place. He had assumed Tanya would be working, and she hadn't mentioned any special plans as he kissed her good-night outside the restaurant in the wee hours of the morning, so he stepped into the bar with a worried frown creasing his forehead. His eyes flicked around the room, finding only Jimmy behind the bar to keep him company.

"Is Tanya here?"

Jimmy smiled. "Yeah, but she had engine trouble and had to take a cab to work. Good thing it's her last night!"

Kyle relaxed with a sigh and ordered a Bloody Mary, quickly amending his order to a Virgin Mary "just in case".

Jimmy served the drink, but pushed Kyle's money back over to him.

"All your drinks are free if you'll just promise me you'll take good care of Tanya tonight. I don't like the idea of her with a strange cabby."

Kyle nodded his head slowly, surprised to think that Jimmy felt the need to even ask. He, for one, had no intention of allowing her to take a cab anywhere! Settling back, he nursed the glass of seasoned tomato juice slowly while the crowd gathered.

Before long, the MC started trying to get the crowd pumped for the show, and Kyle was surprised when the man made a public announcement that it was Tigré's last night at BoxCars until November. Just the night before, she had been talking about how she had made plans to spend the winter months in "the southern half of the country" so that she could continue to ride her motorcycle to work. Making a mental note to ask her about November in New York later, he listened while the MC explained that the dancer had arranged for a very special last show, and that she would thereby be appearing for just one extra-long set at the end of the evening.

The men cheered to show that they were all for a special last set, and the show went on as if nothing unusual was happening. The only change in the routine was that, instead of seeing Tigré perform after Christi finished, the dancers started right into their second set. Watching the door, Kyle realized that no one left this evening.

After finishing her second set, Christi came back out on stage in her cheerleader outfit to claim the microphone. With a regal wave of her hand, she signaled to the waitresses, who darted around the room giving a fresh napkin to everyone at the tables. Jimmy did the same at the bar, ignoring Kyle's questioning eyes as he slid one next to the trucker's elbow. When all the waitresses had finished and were standing next to the bar, Christi brought the microphone to her lips and called for silence.

"Each of you gentlemen has been given a napkin by your waitress or bartender."

"Who told you we were gentlemen?" called a voice from the audience. Christi smiled in the heckler's direction and raised her voice to override any further interruptions.

"And on three napkins, there are numbers. Betcha can't guess which three!"

Kyle stared silently down at his napkin as the rest of the crowd cheerfully counted to three, not quite sure what the girls were planning, but having the sinking feeling he was part of it. It didn't take long for Christi, in her bounciest cheerleader voice, to let him know he was in deep trouble.

"I'll call a number, and the man who has that number will come up and take a seat on this chair that my lovely assistant is now placing." The regular MC, a scruffy-looking man with several earrings in each ear who went by the name Carlos, did the honors. "He is required to place his hands firmly on each side of the chair, as Carlos is now demonstrating, and hold on tight."

Carlos sat and grasped the sides of the seat as if preparing for liftoff, then smiled and stood up, bowing first to the raucous crowd, then to Christi.

"Thanks, Carlos," she cooed, then continued on with the rules of the game while Carlos left the stage. "Once you have a firm grip on the chair, you can't remove your hands from the sides of the chair, you can't talk to Tigré, and you can't make any suggestive facial expressions like this," she slowly licked her lips, "or this," she stuck her tongue out and wiggled it up and down while a few men moaned, "or even this," she made her eyebrows wiggle suggestively, "because the other dancers are out in the audience. Three white cards disqualify you. If any of the three contestants lasts through the end of the game, he gets a prize. Any questions?"

Several hands went up while the more bold ones yelled their question right out.

"What's the prize?"

"It's a secret. Any others?"

The room remained quiet.

"Then gentlemen, turn your napkins!" she yelled as if starting a car race, and there was a shuffle of paper as the men complied, followed by a few disappointed groans. Kyle turned his napkin over —and found his suspicions confirmed as he stared at a carefully drawn number three.

He glared suspiciously at Jimmy, who seemed to be very busy at the other end of the bar, then his glare switched to Christi, who gave him a big innocent grin. Christi called for number one just as Kyle downed half his drink, forgetting for a moment that it didn't contain vodka.

The first man up, who called himself Gary, was small and wiry, smiling with only his upper lip in a way that made him look goofy. He lasted for just the first song, losing himself in a groan when Tigré turned her back to him and bent to grab her ankles. The other dancers, scattered around the room, held up white cards to signal the foul and the lights went out.

"Number Two, where are you?" Christi called out in a singsong voice.

Kyle was in the middle of sipping his drink and promptly choked as Vinnie, his buddy from the warehouse, stood up and made his way toward the stage. Christi smiled at Vinnie as he settled himself on the chair.

"Hey there, handsome. What's your name?"

Vinnie looked out at the crowd with a broad grin, putting on his best version of a southern accent as he leaned toward the microphone, "Tex, ma'am."

Kyle's coughing fit brought Jimmy over to clap him on the back, which earned the bartender nothing but a dark look. When Kyle managed to regain his breath, he muttered an oath, but couldn't hold back a wry grin. When Christi and Tanya set a man up, they set him up in style, but oddly enough, it looked like the set up was going to turn out to be fun!

By the time his attention returned to the stage, Vinnie was seated and taking deep breaths to steady himself, then nodded his head to signal that he was ready to meet the tiger face-to-face like a rodeo cowboy signals that he's ready to have the chute opened for a ride on a bucking bronco.

The lights went out, the jungle beat began again, and the spotlight came up, trained on Vinnie in the center of the stage. A rattle of chains announced Tigré's arrival, and she stepped out to look down at Vinnie with the haughty attitude of a queen. The music changed and she moved to the rhythm as the spotlight softened and the other stage lights came up slowly in the background, moving as if she was under a spell and making many of the men in the room moan as they shared Vinnie's agony. Vinnie managed to hold out longer than Gary, but when Tigré drew her nails down just a hair's breadth from his chest during the second song, he licked his lips. Up went the cards, out went the lights, and when they came back up, Vinnie sat alone, shaking his head and looking very disappointed.

"Let's all give Tex a round of applause for trying." Christi yelled, and the crowd followed her suggestion while Vinnie returned to his seat. Without drawing attention to himself, Kyle slipped off his jacket and handed it over the bar to a grinning Jimmy with the admonition to "Watch this for me."

"Come to me Number Three!" Christi called, and Kyle held up his napkin as he started toward the stage. Christi grinned like a

Cheshire cat, eyeing him with a gleam in her eye and licking her lips in a greatly exaggerated manner, as if she'd never seen this big muscleman in the form-fitting jeans and T-shirt before in her life and was quite pleased with what she saw. "Oooo, looky what we've got here! Are you married, sweetheart?"

Kyle shook his head in the negative and gave Christi his lady-killer grin, making her fan herself dramatically with one hand and coo, "Be still my heart!"

Christi made a big show of escorting Kyle to the chair and giving him a playful wink while the crowd roared. She eyed him slowly top to toe once more to the hoots and catcalls of the crowd.

"So what's your name, gorgeous?" she asked in her sexiest voice.

"My friends call me Superman," Kyle rumbled while his quirky eyebrow flew high, flexing his muscles as if truth, justice and the American Way were being threatened. The rafters shook as the crowd roared approval, forcing Christi to retreat silently before their thunderous onslaught. When Kyle nodded, the lights went out and a hush fell over the crowd, then the drums started for the third time.

Tigré glared at Kyle from less than a foot away as the spotlight came on, looking for all the world as if she hated him. As she started to sway to the beat, Kyle took a deep breath and chose a bottle behind Jimmy's head to stare at, watching her in his peripheral vision as she went into the most provocative routine he'd ever seen. He was aware of every graceful, sinewy movement being performed up close and personal, but didn't even twitch. The only movements in his entire body were the slow rise and fall of his chest and an occasional blink of his eyes.

During the second song, Tigré warmed things up a bit more, trying to make him acknowledge her presence. She brushed his hair away from his ear with one long fingernail and blew on his neck, then lightly traced a path with another nail from the tip of his ear down to the hollow at the base of his throat. Kyle remained staring straight ahead, breathing deeply.

She stepped directly in front of him so that he had no choice but to watch while she unhooked her bra and peeled it slowly away from her firm young breasts. Kyle seemed bored, slowly blinking his eyes and counting his breaths to cool his heating blood.

By the beginning of the third song, Tigré began to look worried even as she panted from the exertion of the extra-long set.

She pulled out all the stops, doing everything she had ever seen or heard about to get Kyle to break, but to no avail. As the fourth and final song ended, she stopped beside him, snarling, then swung her leg over his so that she was almost sitting on his knee.

Grabbing two fistfuls of his long hair to tip his head back and hold him still, she placed a steamy kiss on his lips. The lights went out as the crowd went wild, and when they came back up, Kyle was still sitting as he had been, but with a shell-shocked look on his face and gold paint on his black T-shirt to show where her breasts had been. A bulge in his jeans as he stood up revealed the strain he was under.

"We have a winner!" Christi shouted while the building shook, and she sent him to his seat to await his prize. Men pressed forward to shake Kyle's hand and pat his back as he made his way back to his bar stool to down the rest of his drink with hands that trembled, once again forgetting that his drink was nothing more than seasoned tomato juice.

When Jimmy passed him his jacket, he was on the verge of ordering something with a bit more kick. Then the crowd parted, allowing Christi to lead Tigré to him.

Still in her makeup, she wore a skintight black leather dress that appeared to have been painted on and matching six-inch high stiletto heeled shoes. The gold collar was around her neck with a short chain like one usually used to walk bigger dogs attached. Christi was smiling as she ceremoniously handed him the end of the leash, then she turned and put a portable microphone to her mouth.

"Congratulations, Superman. As your prize, you get to take the tiger back to the zoo!"

Kyle sat staring at Christi in a daze as the crowd again erupted into raucous applause, then his eyes followed the chain to the face at the other end. Despite the slight snarl she affected for the sake of the crowd, the dark eyes glittered with amusement, almost daring him to let on that he knew her. His left brow lifted and he tugged gently on the leash as if seeing how willing she was to obey his directives, pretending to be scared when she growled fiercely.

"You'd better hope you're made of steel if you've gotta get in a car with her, Superman!" someone called from the crowd, sounding suspiciously like Vinnie, and Kyle nodded before responding, his eyes sparkling.

"I just hope she's not packing Kryptonite!"

He pretended to look for an odd lump under her dress, then shrugged and headed for the door with Tigré following, her look fierce. As he reached the car, Kyle draped his jacket over Tigré's shoulders before shutting off the alarm and unlocking the door. For the crowd, she gave him a glare, but pulled the jacket close when the door closed, hiding her face behind smoked glass. She smiled softly as he swaggered for the crowd, forcing herself to look angry for the sake of the watching crowd as he reached for the door handle.

Kyle climbed in and in no time, they were moving along with the rest of the traffic. At the first stop light, Kyle glanced over to find Tanya looking at him like a little kid who expected a lecture for doing something wrong. When he just grinned, she dared ask a question, sounding shy and just a little fearful.

"You aren't mad about being set up?"

Kyle only laughed and shook his head.

"Mad? When you just made it possible for us to leave together without having to wait until the crowd thinned out? Why would I be mad?"

Tanya didn't answer, heaving a sigh of relief as she pulled off her wig, shaking her hair loose around her shoulders. She snuggled into the warmth of his jacket with a wide smile on her face. So far, her evening had gone just the way she'd planned it. Now how to introduce the subject of…

"So where am I taking you for breakfast today?" Kyle interrupted her thought as they pulled up at another light.

"I was thinking we could have it at my place." Tanya sounded so nonchalant she surprised even herself, grinning as Kyle wiggled his finger in his ear as if he was having some trouble with his hearing.

"Did I just have a brain-fart or did you suggest going to your place?"

Tanya blinked, fighting back a laugh.

"Brain fart?"

"Like the other kind, only it affects your mind, whether you've been drinking or not." Kyle explained, and Tanya feigned anger.

"Well, I never!" she snorted.

"You have so!" Kyle retorted playfully, almost breaking her composure.

"If you're going to be THAT way, I'll get out and catch a cab!" She threatened, and Kyle brushed a finger along her cheek, showing her the paint on the tip if his finger.

"Not dressed like that, you won't."

Tanya grinned, suddenly glad this man had discovered her secret. He had such a wonderful sense of humor! "So, are you taking me to my place?"

Kyle responded with an eager nod, then listened carefully to her directions. In no time, he had them on the right road, heading out of the city. As he drove, he kept her busy talking and laughing, surprising her when he turned smoothly into the campground. The clock on the dash confirmed that it had taken them as long as usual, but Tanya found herself feeling oddly rushed and more than a little nervous, not quite ready to have her first house-guest despite the fact that she'd had plenty of time to prepare.

As they pulled up to the beat-up Coachman she called home, she bit her lip and worried about what Kyle might think. The used RV she'd purchased was sturdy, but not very pretty. She needn't have worried about Kyle, though. His eyes did a quick onceover, then he turned to her with a smile.

"Do you own this?"

She nodded sheepishly and his smile broadened. From the embarrassed blush on her cheeks, it was obvious that she didn't bring men home very often and Kyle found he was flattered by the distinctive honor. He found he wanted to protect her from her own discomfort as he listened to her nervous chatter.

"I paid for half of it up front after several months of saving, and just finished paying the bank off for the rest this past week. I haven't saved enough yet for a paint job, but it won't take long. Living like this is lots cheaper than doing the timeshare condo thing like the other girls do. And I don't have to waste time packing and unpacking."

Kyle bit back a laugh, amused to find yet another similarity between them. He himself hated to waste time packing and unpacking, carrying only what he absolutely needed to motel rooms and only using motels when he had one of these impromptu "vacations", sleeping the rest of the time curled up in his truck's sleeper. Brushing a finger along her jaw line, Kyle looked down into the darkness of her eyes, his deep voice coming out in a sexy whisper.

"A most interesting abode for a most interesting lady."

His breath touched her lips with the last word, then his lips followed suit, making her heart melt like a chocolate bar on a radiator. Tanya found herself quite certain she was making the right decision, no matter what her conscience screamed at her. Kyle was a dream come true and she didn't want to wake up!

Nervousness assailed her as she unlocked the door, and she did a quick check to make sure the place was still as clean as she'd left it. Her voice shook slightly as she tried to sound confident in her own actions.

"If you'll excuse me, I'll wipe off this paint and be right back to make coffee."

Kyle nodded, his eyes busily taking in the small bunk to his right, neatly piled with wigs and bits of costumes, the tidy little kitchen and eating area with it's booth-style table, and the tiny bathroom whose door was just sliding shut. He thought about the bedroom that probably resided on the other side of the bathroom and smiled. If his luck held, his evening would end on the other side of the bathroom.

While he waited, Kyle found the bag of coffee and carefully opened it. He pulled out the basket on the coffee maker, but couldn't locate a filter anywhere. He was still looking when Tanya stepped back out and realized her mistake. She blushed furiously and covered her hot face, mortified to discover that even with all her careful planning, she would have to reveal her plot.

"I borrowed the machine from Christi. I forgot about it needing filters."

Kyle frowned. "How do you usually make coffee?"

"I don't usually drink coffee or tea. I drink a lot of juice," she confessed, peeking up at him with a shy smile. Kyle ran the tip of one long finger over her lips, his sparkling eyes as dazzling as his brilliant smile.

"Well, you shouldn't change your routine just for me!" He murmured, mesmerizing her with his gaze as he bent slightly to kiss her. Tanya sighed as reality fled. There was only this time, this man, and the heavenly way he made her feel. Her body arched closer to his and she welcomed the strong fingers that brushed lightly along her neck and over the curve of her breast before slipping around to her back to pull her closer. Moments later, when Kyle drew back with his eyes smoky with desire, she could do nothing but stare at him in amazement, shaking with her first taste of an all-consuming sensual hunger.

"If you expect me to leave before morning, now is the time to send me away." He whispered, but Tanya shook her head while her lips curved in a sweet, sexy smile.

"Please stay," she whispered back, and Kyle echoed her smile as he reclaimed her lips. When his hands slid down to fondle the soft yet firm roundness of her buttocks, she moaned against his lips. She gasped, wrapping her arms around his neck for balance, as he lifted her feet off the floor and headed toward the bed. Her shoes slipped off along the way, but Tanya didn't notice, lost in the swirling joy of their passion.

Kyle set her back on her feet in the bedroom and slowly pulled down the zipper of her dress, kissing each section of silky flesh as soon as it cleared the fabric. Tanya moaned softly, closing her eyes to enjoy the wonderful sensations he created, gripping his shoulders to keep from falling as her knees trembled and threatened to buckle.

The dress fell to pool around her feet and she was suddenly airborne again, pulled close to a rock-hard chest and laid gently onto the mattress by strong hands. Kyle pulled his T-shirt off over his head and dropped it on the floor before joining her, exposing the firm muscles of his chest with the crisp matting of hair that started just below his shoulders and tapered down his abdomen in a "v" that disappeared into the waistband of his jeans. She ran her fingers through the dark, curling fluff, following its path toward his manhood, pleasantly surprised when her touch made him close his eyes and moan as if she awoke the same feeling in him as he awoke in her. A feeling of power possessed her and she ran her finger back up toward his chin while his eyes opened and he gave her another smoky eyed smile.

His lips returned to possess hers and his fingers returned to stroke her bare flesh, slowly building up the fire that he had already started within her young body. Instinct took over where her lack of experience left off and she arched her body toward his touch, moaning out his name as his caresses grew bolder. His mouth followed the path of his fingers, making her writhe in an agony of wanting, despite being unable to name what she wanted. The damp warmth of his mouth and tongue combined with the tickle of his beard to send a tingling heat racing from the top of her head to the tip of her toes, making her gasp as sensations unlike anything she had ever felt before shook her. A small voice in the back of her head whispered that she should see what his pants were hiding, but when she touched his waist, he pulled away with a throaty laugh and a raised eyebrow.

"Not so fast, Angel Face. I seem to recall a certain young lady who thought it amusing to tempt me this evening in public."

"But Kyle," she groaned, trying to reach for him. He easily kept her from her goal by catching her hands in his, then laughed again, a deep, sexy chuckle that fanned the flames even more.

"Sorry Angel, but I don't get mad, I get even. We're not anywhere near even yet."

Tanya groaned and turned her face away from his kiss, so Kyle kissed her throat, pushing her hair aside to nuzzle her neck beneath her ear.

"Just lay back, relax and enjoy it," he advised. "I know what I'm doing."

"You're making me crazy!" she groaned, gritting her teeth as he repeated that incredibly sexy laugh.

"Exactly!"

Tanya lay back and bit her lip as she tried to obey his directive, but it was hard to relax when her blood was flowing through her system like lava, hot and steaming. Her hands seemed to move on their own, running over his body to draw him closer, then slipping again and again to the waistband of his jeans. Each time she touched the snap that held his jeans closed, Kyle patiently and gently pushed her hands away, continuing to tease her until she thought she would burst with pleasure.

She was pleading with him in a husky voice that she didn't recognize as her own before he finally stood and popped the snap open while she watched, then ever so slowly, like a stripper in front of a hot crowd, he pulled the zipper down. Tanya held her breath as he slid the jeans past his hips, then groaned yet again as he revealed nothing more than a pair of under shorts styled like a Speedo bathing suit. Kyle's grin was positively devilish as he slipped out of his cowboy boots and left his jeans on the floor next to their other discarded clothing, his sparkling eyes drawing her gaze like a magnet.

"What's wrong, Angel? Can't stand having your own tricks played on you?"

"But I didn't pay for a private dance," she argued, loving him and hating him at the same time, wishing she knew how to drive him this crazy even as he flashed her another sexy grin.

"Let's just say I'm living by my own version of the Golden Rule. I'm doing unto you as you did unto me."

Tanya groaned again as Kyle dropped to his knees beside the bed, catching one slim ankle in his large hand and holding it still. With a quick nip on her captured ankle, he began to kiss his way up the inside of her calf, continuing up her thigh to run his tongue up and down the soft flesh of her womanhood through her panties, then working his way down the opposite thigh to her other ankle. He turned back and did the same in the opposite direction, this time gently nipping at her secret place and making her arch up instinctively to meet his touch. On the third pass, he stopped and pulled at the elastic waistband of her panties with his teeth. When

Tanya arched upward, he pulled back, dragging her panties part-way down before slipping his hands in to help with the task.

Kyle returned to her ankle and started over, caressing her feminine flesh with his tongue on the first pass, then nipping her gently on the second. Instead of continuing on to her ankle after the nip, though, he snaked his tongue out and smiled to himself at the soft, mewling cry that came from deep in Tanya's chest to betray the depth of her arousal.

Thinking he should test to make sure she was truly ready for him before pausing to put on a condom, he slid a finger into her most private space—and heard her gasp of pain as his finger broke the resisting flesh.

Kyle reared back in surprise, staring at the blood that coated his finger and trickled down to stain the sheets. His shocked gaze slowly lifted to Tanya's face, but she was unable to meet his eyes, biting her lip and looking frightened, hurt—and deeply ashamed of herself. Finding his voice, Kyle rumbled gruffly, "You're a virgin?"

Tears filled Tanya's eyes and she nodded, feeling miserable. She hadn't realized her lack of experience would be so obvious, expecting the whole interlude to go by with Kyle none the wiser. Instead, he was staring at her with a frown darkening his brow, the proof of her deception already growing tacky on his hand. Shamed beyond belief, she stumbled into an explanation.

"I'm so sorry, but I didn't know it would be so—I didn't think you would need to—" She gave up when tears choked off her voice.

"You didn't want me to know I was the first?" His soft, husky voice sent a shiver down her spine and she dared a glance up at him. He pretended to be upset with her, frowning sternly despite the gleam in his eyes. "I hate to tell you this, but I would have known, even if I hadn't seen the blood. I've been with a virgin before."

Tanya blushed at his candid admission, then gave him a shy smile. "You don't find it odd that an exotic dancer is a virgin?"

Kyle sighed, a smile slowly growing as he stroked a hand along her cheek. "I should have been able to put two and two together just from our talks over coffee, but I didn't want to believe what my brain was telling me."

"How could you have done that when I haven't given you the twos to put together?" Tanya's soft smile was as wry as her voice, making Kyle laugh softly.

"You gave me a lot more than you know just from a comment here and a comment there. In fact," he gently kissed her lips, "you seem able to say quite a lot when you aren't even talking."

"What's that supposed to mean?" Tanya asked with a frown, and Kyle's eyebrow rose.

"How about if I show you?!" His sexy whisper matched the warm look in his eyes as he bent his head to gently caress her throat with his lips and tongue, making her sigh as her blood rushed through her veins and her body responded by instinctively arching upward in an invitation as old as time itself. Kyle gave that sexy laugh yet again, making her groan as he whispered in her ear, his warm breath sending shivers down her spine. "You're an open book."

Tanya would never be able to explain later how he managed to slip out of his under shorts and into a condom without her being fully aware of what he was doing, but when he finally allowed her to see his manhood, he was just finishing the project of sliding the latex sheath over it.

Tanya gulped aloud, biting her lip to fight down the sudden onslaught of fear as she realized how large he was. Kyle's finger had hurt her earlier, and his male member appeared to be much longer and wider than his finger. Surely there would be pain instead of the pleasure Christi had always described!

Kyle saw fear warring with the desire in her eyes, once again using all his knowledge of the feminine form to make the desire overwhelmingly powerful. Keeping his own lust at bay while he aroused her proved to be painful, but he was rewarded for his trouble when Tanya again arched toward him, her fear forgotten as she ran her fingers along his sheathed length and gently urged him toward her. Her legs opened in an instinctive gesture of welcome and Kyle shook with the effort of keeping his passion reined in as he drew ever closer.

"Oh, my sweet Angel," he moaned as he slowly slid into her, hearing her breath hiss through her teeth as she fought the urge to cry out while her body stretched to accommodate him. When he could go no deeper, he stopped, kissing her and holding her close to allow her to get used to the foreign brand within her. Knowing he had stopped, but not understanding why, Tanya tried to pull back, thinking the finale much less satisfying than the passion that had built up to it. Kyle stopped her with a hoarse whisper that hinted of the strain he was under.

"Don't move, darlin'. If you move now I won't be able to stop myself, and I don't want to hurt you more than I already have."

Tanya relaxed beneath him as his lips moved from her ear to her throat, tracing a path to the hollow of her neck, sending shock waves hurtling through her body. When he began to move, slowly at first, she felt the sharp pain fade to a tingling ache, which in turn faded away as the passion began to build again. Before long, she began to writhe beneath him as instinct again took over, helping to turn the fire Kyle had started into a raging inferno that threatened to burn them both alive.

Together, they climbed higher and higher, their bodies moving as one in a dance of love. Kyle whispered hoarse words of encouragement as the dance became more frenzied, urging her onward as their passion continued to build. Just when she thought she would surely go insane with longing, Tanya was possessed by a strange rapture that exploded around her as Kyle bellowed his release and shuddered to a halt, rolling her with him so that their bodies were still joined, but she lay on top of him instead of being crushed beneath his greater weight. With a sigh of satisfaction, she relaxed against him, nearly falling asleep before the rapid beat of his heart beneath her cheek slowed to a normal rate.

Kyle sighed, completely satisfied in both mind and body for the first time in his life. That he had found such ecstasy with a virginal young lady who worked in a strip joint caused such a sense of wonder that he purposefully pinched himself, hard, just to prove that it wasn't some alcohol-induced dream from which he would awake at any moment. He brushed his fingers across her cheek and thought of all the women who'd come before, most of whom had made him feel like they were doing him a favor, faking their lust because they liked the idea of being seen around town with a nice man who seemed to have no problem getting money to spend on them.

But Tanya was different. She had all but pushed him away at first as if he was carrying a fatal disease that she didn't wish to catch, clearly unmoved by either his looks or his charm, which had never failed him before. By her own words and actions, she had confirmed time and again that she wasn't the type to get into casual sexual relationships. Then he had kissed her while the sun came up over the city and saw her eyes go soft and smoky, heard her breath catch in her throat, and felt for the first time that his soul had touched another's.

Her reaction then had been nothing compared to what he had so recently experienced here in her bed. Past experience told him that her quivering flesh beneath his inquisitive fingers could not be faked, nor had he ever felt a woman's vagina pulse in the way hers had, which had resulted in an orgasm like nothing that Kyle had ever experienced before. No, the sweet young woman who lay so obviously satiated on his chest had not faked her arousal any more than he had.

The dual gift of her virginity and her honest reaction to his touch left Kyle feeling doubly honored, his only regret centering around the condom that he had donned. He had made love without one only once in his life, and the experience had proven that, despite the thin latex material that was used to make the sheath, it took away a lot in the way of friction between male and female, thereby making a sexual encounter much less satisfying for both parties.

He didn't want to expose Tanya to a social disease or unwanted pregnancy by not wearing one, but never had he felt so sorry for stopping to pull one on. As incredible as their encounter had been, he couldn't help wondering what it would have been like with bare flesh against bare flesh—and swore to himself that he would find out before he let this sweet young thing slip out of his grasp!

As his thoughts centered on the condom, he suddenly became aware that he and Tanya were still joined at the hips—and that the condom might possibly leak, thereby removing any benefit to its use. Sighing deeply, he tried to think of a diplomatic way to excuse himself, but his mind was too lost in the ecstasy of moments past to enable him to think very clearly, so he chose to simply state fact and hope for the best.

"Excuse me, Angel. I have to get up," he murmured against her hair. Tanya didn't move, but her voice came from somewhere in the region of his throat, sounding muffled and very groggy.

"Why?"

A slow smile creased Kyle's face and he pressed his lips to her hair before his deep, slightly hoarse whisper came again. "I have to get rid of something in the nearest trash can, but you need to move so I can get up."

"Trash can's in the bathroom," she muttered, but made no effort to move until Kyle flipped her onto her back and rolled over on top of her, holding most his weight on his arms as he kissed her soft lips.

"Sorry, Angel, but if I don't get rid of this condom, we'll have trouble of the kind it was meant to ward off. I'll be right back"

At Tanya's embarrassed blush, Kyle gave that soft, sexy laugh again and pressed one last quick kiss to her lips as he slipped out of bed. He was still grinning as he stepped into the bathroom and slid the door shut behind him. Tanya settled back in the bed to await his return, but found that she couldn't keep her eyes open, so she settled herself on the bed with her back against the wall, as was her custom, and dozed off. As had happened so often in the past few years, her dreams were soon invaded by a slim man with a long bony nose and big front teeth that gave him a ratty look when he smiled. The only difference was that this time, she felt as if she could find a protector if she only ran fast enough.

Kyle was cleaning up in the tiny bathroom sink when he noticed the gray hairs in his dark beard. Staring solemnly at his reflection, he tried to discern what it was about his face or form that made Tanya trust him to be her first lover, but could see nothing in his outward appearance that would encourage such trust. He looked, to his own eyes, like an aging biker, even without the leather jacket and jeans. What in the world did Tanya see in him?

His frown of concentration made him look fierce, and he experimented with a few other faces before reaching for the door. He wore a bright sunny smile, but it quickly faded as he realized that the object of his attention had fallen asleep. He slipped up beside the bed on silent feet to stand staring down at her, enchanted by the delicate beauty of her exotic face in repose.

The cat-like tilt to her eyes was less pronounced without her makeup, but her high-set cheekbones and the deep hollows beneath were even more so. Against the thick, deep chocolate-brown curls, the lightly tanned skin of her heart shaped face was as pure and delicate as the porcelain used to make the china dolls that sat on his grandmother's dresser. He searched for a word to describe such a fine beauty, but his mind was stuck on the one he already used so often: angelic. She was an angel who had for some unknown reason come down to earth, and a certain pride washed through him at the thought that he had been granted the privilege of introducing her to her sensuality.

Tanya stirred in her sleep and moaned as the nightmare man from her past chased her through the dark, shadowy streets of an unknown city, suddenly sitting upright with a muffled scream as she felt a presence beside her bed. Her wild eyes took in the familiar surroundings of her trailer, then finally settled on the startled green eyes that watched her from the edge of the bed. Still quaking with fear, she wrapped her arms around Kyle's neck, holding tightly to him as if her life depended on it. Feeling her fear in her shivering frame, Kyle wrapped his arms around Tanya and held her gently, whispering soft, soothing words against her hair as her shivering slowly faded away, giving her time to get over whatever fear had possessed her.

"Easy, Angel," he teased. "I'm willing to help, but I have to be able to breathe."

Tanya relaxed her grip with a self-conscious giggle, blushing as she allowed Kyle to push her back enough to look into her eyes. Biting her lip and feeling extremely foolish, she dropped her gaze and struggled to explain her actions.

"I— um—I had a bad dream," she finally managed to stutter, and closed her eyes as Kyle's gentle fingers brushed her hair away from her face.

"Happens to all of us." His soft, almost cheerful tone and easy smile made her relax even more, and she took a deep breath to shake off the last traces of fear.

"I still feel like an idiot, jumping up and half-throttling you." Her smile was shy and she avoided his gaze, still blushing deeply.

Holding her on his lap while he murmured unintelligible words against her hair, Kyle tried to ignore the pressure building within him as the urge to make love to her again overtook him. He felt like a lecherous fiend when Tanya felt the throbbing warmth of his manhood against her buttocks and giggled softly.

"I guess I didn't throttle you too much if your mind is already on other things," she teased, and felt Kyle's responding chuckle through the breast that brushed against his chest.

"It would take a lot more than a little squeeze to hurt me." He joked back despite the painful pressure in his loins. "I'm Superman, remember?"

Tanya reached up and brushed a lock of auburn hair off his face, her smile so soft and trusting that it took Kyle's breath away.

"Then I'll depend on you to protect me from pushy fans and bad dreams," she murmured, lifting herself a little higher so she could kiss him. Catching her chin in one large hand, Kyle deepened the kiss, pressing her back slowly onto the mattress as he tried to remember which pocket held his extra condoms.

Chapter Nine

Tanya was sleeping soundly, the nightmare man's face replaced by smoky emerald eyes and a sexy, high-voltage smile, when Kyle slipped back into bed after disposing of the second condom. As his arm slipped around her waist, she sighed softly and snuggled closer to his warmth, a peaceful expression on her sleeping face and her body totally relaxed. Smiling himself at the feel of her soft flesh pressed against him, Kyle dropped a light kiss on the top of her head and slowly relaxed, drifting off to sleep in the strange bed as if he always slept there.

His internal alarm woke him shortly after 7 a.m., and his first thought was of calling Jack. He was unexpectedly in no rush to leave New York and wanted to make sure any load Jack had set up could be picked up by another driver.

As soon as he could find out where Tanya planned to appear next, he'd try to get a load going the same direction, even if he had to ship something himself! Moving as quietly as a mouse, he slipped back into his clothes and was tiptoeing through the kitchen toward the door when he spotted her keys on the table.

With a grin, Kyle pocketed them to let himself in again without having to wake her, then caught the notation on the calendar that sat on the table right under the keys. The grin widened as Kyle read the notation twice more, just to be sure he had seen it right. There it was in front of him, bold as brass— the date and next location for her next job. The notation for that Friday read only "Asia— Bubba's—Atlanta", but it was enough to tell him all he needed to know. Looking in at the pretty lady asleep in the bed one more time, Kyle slipped silently out of the trailer with a gleam in his eye, already eager to find out what "Asia" would be like.

Tanya woke up about an hour later, rubbing her eyes as she stumbled to the bathroom, yawning as she dropped to the seat before becoming aware enough to realize that she was naked. Her sleep-fogged brain tried to recall why she was in bed naked—and clarity suddenly dawned as her body reminded her of the passionate kisses Kyle had pressed to her soft flesh and the resulting loss of her last semblance of innocence. Her cheeks flamed as she realized how wanton she must seem despite her lack of experience, and she stepped out of the bathroom with an apology on her lips only to be disappointed when she found the trailer empty.

Wondering if it had all been a very vivid wet dream, she looked at the bed, seeing the stains on the sheet proving the loss of her virginity at the same time as she spotted his jacket where it had been kicked under the edge of the bed.

With the same reverence usually reserved for religious relics, she picked up the fine leather piece and hugged it to her chest, smelling the mingled scents of leather, cigarettes and Kyle's own manly fragrance. With a smile, she slipped into it, laughing at the way the lower edge barely covered her hips and the sleeves dangled almost to her knees before pushing the sleeves back to open a drawer for a pair of clean underwear.

The rattling of keys outside the door made her jump and spin around, and she was standing there, frozen, holding a pair of silky underpants in one small hand and keeping his jacket closed with the other, when Kyle opened the door and stepped inside. Kyle's eyes set her on fire as they traveled the length of her, from the top of her head to the tip of her toes and back. A slow, lazy smile stole across his face and his eyebrow went up.

"Love the outfit!" His deep, warm tone was accompanied by the suggestive dip of his eyes and Tanya unexpectedly blushed. Dropping her head in an effort to hide it, she spun around to put on her underpants, smiling at Kyle's exaggerated groan. Unable to resist the urge to tease him, she made a show of removing the jacket while working her way toward her tiny closet. She did a playful reverse striptease, putting her clothes on in the same manner she used to take them off for the nightly patrons while Kyle sat at her table and watched it all with his eyes sparkling, occasionally laughing softly. When she finished and brought him his jacket, he caught her hand and pulled her to his lap, kissing her gently and brushing his knuckles along her jaw.

"Nobody ever did that for me before!" He murmured, and Tanya tried to tell her body to stop melting beneath his touch. It didn't listen.

"I've never done that before, either." She returned softly, knowing she should pull away but finding that her body refused to do that, either.

"Will you be my little private dancer tonight and take your clothes off again for me?"

His warm kisses along her neck were most distracting, and Tanya fought to remember why she wouldn't be able to see him. Then she sat bolt upright, white as a sheet, when it suddenly struck her.

"I have to leave for Atlanta this afternoon," she moaned softly, half to herself. Kyle feigned surprise.

"Atlanta?"

Tanya nodded, looking more miserable by the minute.

"I have a gig there starting Friday night, so to get the trailer settled into a campground and all…," her voice, already soft and sad, gave out on her entirely and she turned away in confusion as a tear traced a path down her cheek.

Kyle hid a satisfied smile under his beard and tipped Tanya's chin back with one long finger.

"I have a load that I have to deliver to Atlanta by Friday afternoon. We can drive down in a convoy if you're willing to wait until tomorrow to head out. If we don't have time to get you set up before you have to report to work, I can get the camper settled, then pick you up and drive you home."

Tanya stared at him for a moment as if she couldn't understand plain English, then wiggled her finger in her ear like Kyle did when she proposed coffee at her place.

"You'd set up my camper in a campground for me?"

The killer smile returned to Kyle's face.

"I'd do anything to make sure I can spend more time with you." He kissed her, then drew back with a sigh. "Unfortunately, it won't be much time. I have a load going to California on Monday."

Monday seemed like a long way off to Tanya, especially since Tuesday had barely begun, so she placed a kiss on Kyle's lips with a happy smile curving her own.

"I'll take any time you're willing to give me," she whispered, but Kyle didn't hear her. He was too busy fighting down the urge to carry her to the bed and make love to her while the sun shone on her face.

Chapter Ten

Evening found Kyle and Tanya watching the sunset from a horse-drawn carriage in Central Park. To avoid the temptation to stay in bed all day, Kyle had insisted on taking Tanya sight-seeing for their last day in New York, and they had seen everything he could think of. But now, Tanya was so tired she was almost dozing as she cuddled against his side, a contented smile on her face, and the soft warmth of her was sending him into orbit. Just when he thought he had himself under control, the wind shifted, bringing him the scent of her perfume. In an instant, his mind brought him back to the night before, when he had smelled that same soft fragrance each time he kissed her.

Tanya came fully awake as Kyle shifted in his seat, clearing his throat as he changed position. Tanya looked up for a moment at his tense, almost pained face, then dropped her eyes to his lap, smiling as the reason for his discomfort became obvious even to her inexperienced eyes. She pulled herself as close to his ear as she could and whispered to draw him closer.

"Would you mind taking me home after this? I didn't get much sleep last night."

Kyle looked down into her dancing eyes, smiling at the obvious invitation, but sighed deeply and shook his head, faking a disappointed pout.

"I have to stop at my motel first. Can you stay awake that long?"

Tanya didn't answer, at least not in a way that anyone could hear, but from the look in her eyes, he felt quite sure that neither of them would make it out of the motel room. His fingertips brushed across Tanya's lips, then traced the path down her neck that his lips had explored the night before, and her eyes closed as the flames leapt up within her in response to his touch. Kyle gave her one kiss, as light as a butterfly's wings, then asked the driver to return them to their starting point.

Kyle's premonition proved correct, because he barely made it through the door of his motel room before he was overcome with his need and wrapped Tanya in his arms, smothering any protests she may have made with his smoldering kisses. For her part, Tanya lost all control over her body's response to Kyle from the moment he touched her. Whatever spell he wove around her, she was powerless to resist, responding to his kiss by wrapping her arms around him and kissing him back. Her conscience screamed at her, in a voice remarkably like her stepfather's, that such behavior made her a slut, but instead of listening, she forced the voice into a deep, dark closet and locked the door, choosing to listen to her wildly beating heart rather than her too-sensible head for a change. When Kyle lifted her up and carried her to the bed, she didn't protest.

Sometime later, as Kyle slid back in beside a drowsy Tanya after taking care of his post-sex business, he couldn't resist kissing the swan-like curve of her neck where her hair had left it bare any more than he could resist the urge to bare his soul to her. His tender words caused her to stiffen.

"I love you, Angel Face."

Tanya pushed away from him, sliding toward the side of the bed with wide eyes.

"You can't love me!" she argued, her eyes wild. "You barely know me."

Kyle stared at her in confusion. "What do you mean? I know plenty about you."

Tanya scoffed.

"Like what?"

"I know that what you told me about your reasons for dancing are the truth, because I don't think you could look anyone in the eye and lie without it showing in those beautiful eyes of yours." His lips curved as his frown softened and he pinned her with his gaze, "And I know that you usually don't bring your customers home, so you must feel you can trust me, at least a little."

"That's not what I meant!" Tanya snapped, then tried to slide off the bed, but Kyle stopped her by gently wrapping an arm around her and drawing her back. She looked up into his eyes for only a moment, but in that moment, he saw the pain she was trying to hide. Then the mask of anger dropped firmly into place and she snarled at him like the tiger she portrayed on stage as she struggled to pull free of his restraining arm. With a snort, Kyle released her, his eyes revealing his frustration at the way she continued to keep him at arm's length despite the softer emotions he sensed in her.

"Oh, I get it. You wanted to find out what sex was like, so you led me on. Now you're going to humiliate me by throwing me out on my ear for saying something you didn't command me to say."

"What?"

"You heard me!" He snapped, venting his frustration by pretending to be mad at her for something else entirely. "You used me for your sexual pleasure while fully intending on breaking my heart! Admit it!"

When Tanya could do nothing but stutter, Kyle bit back a smile that threatened to ruin the game and pretended to start crying, hiding his face behind his hands and howling like housewives were always stereotyped as doing.

"I work, and I slave, and what thanks do I get? Nothing, that's what! Just once it would be nice to hear 'Thank you for a wonderful time' instead of 'Move over, lard butt, I'm trying to get some sleep.' "

Tanya gaped at him before it dawned on her that he was teasing. His quirky eyebrow and playful eyes were hidden behind his fingers. When she finally cracked a smile, he dropped his hands and reached out to brush her cheek with one long, strong finger, sending shivers of pleasure racing through her.

"Why should I have to know everything about you before I can love you? I've loved you from the moment you looked into my eyes at the bar."

Tanya frowned. "But how can you be sure there isn't something in my past that will come out and ruin our future together? For all you know, I could be an ax murderer or a pickpocket or have a police file a mile deep. How can you be so sure that you love me?"

Kyle laughed quietly at the image of Tanya the ax murderer, then grew thoughtful, his eyes assessing her carefully before he decided to trust her with the whole truth.

"Ever since I was a teenager, I've been thinking about the attributes that the woman I loved would have to have. At first, I concentrated on things like a big bust and a sexy rear view, if you get my meaning. I found a few who matched the physical dream woman, but they wanted to be nothing more than a bit of pampered arm dressing. As I got older, I started concentrating more on the inner woman, looking for the street urchin with a heart of gold, the diamond in the rough who I could take home to Gram and show off with pride. Someone who could warm both my bed and my heart through the long, cold winter nights."

The thought of spending long winter nights in a snow swept cabin with nothing but a fireplace and Kyle to keep her warm made Tanya close her eyes for a moment with a feeling of ecstasy, but it didn't take long for a rat-faced shadow of a man to force her mind back to the present.

She couldn't pretend he wasn't out there, and her constant fear of him finding her would eventually force her to move on, breaking both their hearts at a later date.

"But what if, in a month or two, you find out I'm not the woman you think I am?" She persisted, but her feeble protest only brought a smile to Kyle's lips.

"In a month or two, I may decide that I love you too much to care that you're not my image of perfection. Even a perfect woman is human, so there are bound to be a few flaws, but nothing I'm not willing to work around."

"But I—"

Kyle silenced Tanya by placing a single finger over her lips, which he soon replaced with his mouth. Tanya forgot all her protests as his kisses started the lava flowing in her veins again, and much later, when he kissed her tousled hair and murmured again of his love for her, she simply cuddled closer to his warmth with a sleepy sigh.

Kyle lay awake for quite some time, staring at the ceiling while he wondered if he'd made a mistake. He suspected that her strong reaction to his proclamation of love had something to do with her estranged family, but what could they have done to her? A million possibilities flashed through his head, so many that he finally sighed and rubbed at his forehead to ease the ache of trying to decide which one might be closest to the truth.

Curling protectively around Tanya's smaller body, Kyle drifted slowly off to sleep, breathing in her soft fragrance as he settled his cheek against her hair. In his dreams, he picked her up and flew off, like Superman, to his handmade Fortress of Solitude, where they made love again and again. In his dreams, when he whispered words of love to her, she responded in kind, her love shining in the depths of her dark brown eyes....

Chapter Eleven

Tanya opened her eyes the next morning to the sound of running water and a radio that was tuned to a country station. As she groaned and tried to bury her head under the pillow, a deep, rich baritone voice took up the melody and Tanya paused to listen, enthralled. Despite the fact that she abhorred country music, she found herself enjoying the impromptu serenade, closing her eyes and letting the warm tone of Kyle's voice wash over her.

The sound of running water reminded her body that she hadn't seen the inside of a bathroom for several hours, and when she could wait no longer, Tanya slipped out of bed and pulled on her panties and shirt from the night before. Just before she knocked on the bathroom door, however, it popped open and Kyle grinned at her, a towel held modestly around his waist and water dripping off the ends of his too-long hair.

"Good morning, Angel!"

He gave her a quick peck on the cheek as he slipped past her, giving her a gentle push in the right direction when it seemed she forgot where she was going, staring up at him with a slightly dazed smile. Tanya sighed as she watched the most perfect male body she had ever had the pleasure to ogle saunter away, almost wishing he wasn't wearing a towel. Shocked at the turnings of her mind, Tanya slid into the bathroom and shut the door, coming out only when she had regained control of her senses.

She promptly felt herself losing control again when she found Kyle, dressed only in form-fitting jeans, scrubbing his head vigorously with the towel. His muscles rippled beneath his skin, and when he turned the killer smile her way, she sighed, trying hard to tell herself that she felt nothing for the man but lust, plain and simple.

"I'm not in love," she kept telling herself again and again as Kyle sauntered back over to her, trying to turn that simple statement into her private mantra. Her heart didn't believe her as Kyle's fingers slid along her cheek and his vibrant green eyes caught hers. Their lips met and clung in a silent communication that she wouldn't be able to deny for long, and Kyle's look was knowing as he pulled back.

"You can grab a shower here, if you'd like, then I'll drive you home." His softly spoken words made her feel as giddy as a schoolgirl with her first crush, forcing Tanya to think fast in order to cover her flushed cheeks.

"I don't have any clean clothes with me," she murmured, as if embarrassed at having to make the admission. Kyle gave a quick snort of laughter, then apologized for his reaction with a merry twinkle in his eyes.

"There's no need to fear. Superman is here."

Tanya couldn't resist smiling at his playful tone, but tried hard to remain at least partially serious.

"Even you can't fly clear out to my trailer and back before I get out of the shower," she insisted, but Kyle continued to grin, unperturbed.

"Who said anything about flying out to your trailer? I only have to go a few feet down the street to find a store and buy you something new."

"But you've already spent a ton of money on me. I can wait until I get home for my shower." Her argument sounded lame, but she stuck to her guns, determined to regain control.

Kyle sighed and shook his head, starting to get sincerely frustrated by the continued battle.

"I've already told you, money isn't a problem. I don't have many expenses on the road, especially since I seldom stay in motels, and I only spend money on family at Christmas. Buying you a new set of clothes won't even make a dent in my bank account."

"But—" Tanya began, but her protest was but off as Kyle placed a finger on her lips to silence her.

"But we're never going to get on the road if you keep this up," he intoned quietly, and Tanya found herself being gently herded back into the bathroom as Kyle added. "Enjoy your shower. I'll be back before you know it."

The bathroom door closed and Tanya listened for a moment as Kyle finished dressing. When she heard the outside door close behind him, she heaved a sigh and frowned at her reflection in the mirror.

"Stubborn man," she snorted, then couldn't resist grinning as her mind brought back the image of his firm body covered only by a damp towel. "But what a body!"

The grin remained on her face as she climbed into the shower and let the soap and hot water wash Kyle's scent from her skin. The small aches left behind by the unaccustomed sexual activity also eased, and as she shut off the shower, she felt like a new woman. She had dried off and was thinking about pulling Kyle's brush through her hair when she heard the outside door open and Kyle call to her to let her know he was back. She was wrapping a towel around herself before going out to greet him when the bathroom door opened a crack and Kyle's arm appeared, holding a shopping bag.

"Thank you," she said as she took the bag out of his hand, then was surprised when he withdrew and closed the door, allowing her the privacy to get dressed. Had he realized that the reason for the playful reverse-striptease in her trailer was to hide her odd discomfort at being naked in front of him when they were alone in broad daylight?

She bit her lip, worrying about the impression she was making, and absentmindedly reached into the bag, gasping as she pulled out everything she needed from underwear to hair ribbons, even special travel-sized toiletry items. She frowned, wondering how Kyle could possibly afford to spend so much money on a whim as well as wondering about his reason why. Then she remembered what he'd said while they were making love.

"I love you," he'd whispered, over and over.

Tears sprang to her eyes as she found herself at a complete loss, unable to recall exactly when she had lost control of the situation. When she first agreed to go out for coffee with Kyle, it was to keep her secret identity a secret. When she decided to invite him into her bed, it had been to satisfy her curiosity about sex with a man who should have been nothing more than a one-night stand. Now he was showering her with gifts and offering to escort her to Atlanta while casually telling her that he had somehow fallen madly in love with her!

Turning to stare at the face in the mirror, Tanya tried to discern what Kyle could have seen to make him fall in love.

Had it been her exotic almond-shaped eyes? Her small, thin nose? Her thick, softly curling chocolate-brown hair? Or if it was something else, what could it possibly be that had made him fall in love?

"What am I doing here?" she whispered aloud to her reflection, then listened to find out if Kyle had possibly overheard.

She was caught on the horns of a dilemma. If she followed her heart and allowed Kyle to become a more permanent fixture in her life, she would probably let down her guard, giving him the chance to prove himself to be like her stepfather. If she chased Kyle away because of a man whom she hadn't seen for the better part of seven years, she would be forced to chase away the kind of man she had been waiting for all her life. It seemed she was destined to be hurt one way or another, either by knowing she'd hurt Kyle or by hurting herself.

Kyle's admission of love had made the whole affair much more complicated, for she had counted on him having a track record as a "love-'em-and-leave-'em" type. Now, with the knowledge of his deeper emotions, she felt guilty about the pain she had already caused him and would continue to cause if she didn't tell him about her past. Yet there were doubts running through her head. If she told him all about her sordid past, would he understand why she lived this way, or would he be disgusted at her display of cowardice?

How could she ever explain that she hadn't been in touch with her mother in seven years out of fear that her stepfather would be able to trace the call and somehow be there before she could hang up the phone? That is, if her mother had ever come out of the coma she was in when Tanya's whole run for her life had begun...

Tanya was still thinking about her dilemma as she pulled up the zipper on a pair of jeans that fit like a second skin and tugged a soft, lightweight sweatshirt down over her head, then brushed her hair into a ponytail and tied a bright ribbon around it. As she opened the door to watch Kyle putting the last of his things into his overnight bag, she sighed, more confused than ever. How could she ever bear to say good-bye to the only man who had ever made her kneecaps melt with a smile?

Feeling her eyes upon him, Kyle looked directly into Tanya's thoughtful face and gave her his big, lady-killer smile. No matter how much she tried to deny it, her heart had already made the decision, and when he opened his arms, she walked into his embrace before she could think about turning away.

Chapter Twelve

"You're being awful quiet!"

Kyle's comment came as they turned into the campground where Tanya's trailer was parked.

"Sorry. Just going into my normal pre-move concentration mode, trying to make sure I don't forget to do anything." Tanya told him, but her voice lacked the sincerity needed to convince Kyle that she was telling the truth. Instead, he had the feeling that she was deep in thought about something concerning him, considering the dark, thoughtful frowns she kept throwing his way, thinking he didn't see her.

"Is there anything I can do to help?"

Kyle's soft-spoken question brought Tanya's head around with an almost audible snap, the guilty look in her eyes confirming Kyle's suspicion. There was something on her mind, all right, but it had little to do with the move to Atlanta. His quirky brow hidden by a pair of mirrored sunglasses, Kyle hid a smile under his beard and decided to see if he could catch Tanya mentally napping, maybe even enough to admit what was bothering her. He started off by pretending to get mad.

"Okay, fine!" he snapped. "So you've got your little routine all mapped out and you don't need my help. You don't have to insult me by looking at me like I suddenly grew another head or something!"

Tanya's jaw dropped open and she tried to come up with something to explain her actions, but Kyle snorted as he pulled in beside the trailer and slammed the car into park, then continued on before she could do more than stutter.

"I know you don't love me like I love you, but if you want me to get lost, just say so. Don't sit there trying to come up with ways to lose me once we get on the road."

Tanya just sat staring at Kyle with her mouth hanging open. A part of her wanted to do just that, to go back to the way she'd been living and let Kyle get on with his life without ever having to reveal the truth about her past. But when she opened her mouth, it was another part of her that responded, the part that was already falling for Kyle despite her best intentions.

"It's not that I don't care about you," she began, then her eyes dropped to her hands folded in her lap and she sighed deeply. Sometimes this truth business was very painful! "I— " She looked out the window, unable to finish the original thought, for it wouldn't sound right. "My mother…made a mistake and trusted the wrong man."

Kyle watched as her face contorted with the pain of her thoughts as she tried to find the words to speak, hurting because he was unable to ease her pain, and it clicked about the way she looked around in the donut shop.

"I just don't want to make the same mistake," she finally finished in a voice barely above a whisper, and her eyes brimmed with unshed tears as she willed herself not to cry in front of Kyle.

Kyle found himself at a loss. He had expected a little fire, a denial of any form of emotion save anger. In short, he expected the tiger to surface and do battle, either for or against his staying. Instead, he stared at a sad little waif who looked like she'd lost her last friend and was totally alone in the world. His heart almost breaking, he dropped his large hand over her folded ones and squeezed gently.

"I'm sorry, Angel. I didn't mean to make you sad."

Tanya shook her head as a single tear slipped past her guard and dropped onto their hands.

"It's not you. I just—I feel so...." She sighed heavily. "Oh, I don't know what I feel."

Kyle smiled as her voice tapered off.

"Sounds like you might be feeling the first pangs of love yourself, Angel Face," he teased.

"I'm not in love!" Tanya snapped, but Kyle just continued to smile knowingly, making her even angrier, and the blushing beauty it brought forth made Kyle's eyes sparkle all the more. "I'm not, so stop looking at me that way!"

"Now this is more like the Tanya I know! Welcome back, Tiger Lady!"

Tanya opened her mouth to snap off another rude comment, but ended up smiling instead. She still wasn't willing to admit that she might be feeling anything more than lust for Kyle, but he certainly knew how to push her buttons, and there were some buttons that she really enjoyed having pushed! Feeling like a total idiot, Tanya decided that she should try to mend a few fences.

"I'm sorry, Kyle. I think I got up on the wrong side of the bed. Maybe I should climb back in for a while and start the day over."

Kyle's smile turned slightly lecherous and Tanya could picture the curve of the quirky eyebrow behind the mirrored sunglasses.

"I thought you might need a little rest after two nights of love-making, but if you really want to start over in bed…?"

"That's not what I meant!" Tanya growled, a blush staining everything from her hairline to the collar of her sweatshirt. Kyle's long, lean finger brushed along her jaw line so softly that it felt like a feather against her tender skin, followed by a thumb that caressed her lips. She tried to resist, but Kyle's touch was so soft and sweet. She closed her eyes to enjoy the sensation.

"Why don't we take this inside?"

Tanya's eyes popped open and she realized that they were still in the car outside her trailer. Kyle was smiling at her and she had to swallow hard to force herself to think of all she needed to do to get one her way.

"I'd like to invite you in—" she began, but Kyle interrupted with a laugh, deep and sexy.

"Worried about what I'll do?" he teased, and Tanya shook her head and leaned forward, as if about to reveal a deep, dark secret.

"Worried about what my new boss would do if I don't show up in Georgia," she whispered, then planted a kiss on his cheek and started to slide out of the car. Kyle stopped her with a gentle hand on her wrist.

"I have to go return the car, pick up my truck, and collect the load. Would you rather have me meet you back here or at a site south of the city?" Tanya tried to figure how long Kyle's errands would take and decided she wouldn't be that long, so she voted for the latter. Kyle pulled down his glasses so she could see the sincerity in his eyes.

"Meet me at the first rest stop after you cross into New Jersey on I-95. If there are other people there who make you nervous, just lock up until I get there."

Tanya smiled and nodded. Simple and direct. Just her kind of instructions! Then her smile faded as Kyle leaned toward her.

"See you soon, Angel Face," he whispered just before his lips touched hers. The kiss was both sweetly gentle and passionately searing, letting Tanya know that there could be no mistake. Kyle felt both love and lust for her and wasn't about to let her slip back out of his life.

As she somehow slid out of the car and floated to her door, Tanya tried to remind herself that she didn't love Kyle, and that she should be upset by his persistence, but there were wires down somewhere in her head. Instead of looking at this parting as a way to slip quietly out of Kyle's life, she was in a hurry to get everything stored away and tied down for the road so she could be at the rest area when he pulled in with his load in tow.

Stopping for just a moment to look into the mirror, she was surprised at the face that looked back at her. The high cheekbones were flushed to a becoming pink, the dark, almond-shaped eyes glowed with an inner light, and even the curly hair seemed to have more life and bounce than ever before. Was this what love looked like? Had Kyle seen himself looking this way and realized his love for her or was there more to it that she just wasn't aware of?

With a troubled frown creasing her brow, Tanya turned back to her duties, her heart heavy in her chest. What was it about Kyle Benton that drove her to break every vow she had ever made to herself? She had made a vow to avoid romantic entanglements and remain virginal until she either died or was properly married, yet she had given herself to him in guilt-free abandon. She swore that she would never let her emotions blind her to the true man, yet she found herself trusting Kyle unconditionally when she knew almost nothing about him. Was this what love did to a person?

When everything had been battened down, Tanya got behind the wheel, determined to end her confusion by simply continuing on past their meeting place. Once again, her body betrayed her while her mind was elsewhere and she found herself pulling to a stop in the rest area even as she muttered curses at herself under her breath. Before she could do more than unbuckle her seat belt, a big black Mack truck pulled in behind her, its air brakes hissing as it slowed to a stop. Gold letters on the driver's door caught the morning sun and Tanya read them out loud as the door opened and a tall, lean form slid out.

"Jack & Benny Trucking, Inc, Greenville, Maine"

The trucker turned to face her and Tanya felt her heart stop as white teeth gleamed at her through a dark beard while sunlight reflected off mirrored sunglasses. With a baseball cap pulled over the ponytail he'd made of his too-long hair, she hadn't recognized Kyle at first, and couldn't stop herself from taking another look at the door as it swung shut.

It suddenly fully registered that he was from Maine, and she grinned. That certainly explained some of his archaic manners, as she had heard that Maine was a rather backwards state. With such thoughts on her mind, she gave him a sweet smile as she opened her window. Kyle ran a finger along the curve of her lips, his deep voice rumbling up from somewhere around his toes.

"Hi, Angel. Guess what I'm hauling!"

Tanya looked over his shoulder, wondering at his game, but decided to answer dryly. "I'd guess a flat bed. Am I supposed to be impressed?"

Kyle's grin turned mischievous as he shrugged.

"I don't know. Is the thought of saving all your gas and toll money impressive enough?"

Confused, Tanya looked at the trailer again, then at Kyle, trying hard to figure out what he meant. Kyle pulled down his glasses and peeked at her over the top, reminding Tanya of a mischievous elf in a movie she'd seen as a girl as she looked into the gleaming eyes. He explained simply.

"If we load your trailer onto the flat bed, you won't use any gas and won't have to pay any tolls, because that will all get charged to J & B, which the company would have had to pay anyway. Just outside of Atlanta, I'll drop you off and you can find a campground and get settled while I drop off the trailer."

"Won't the guy who bought the flat bed object?"

Kyle's grin only got wider.

"It's already been cleared with him."

Tanya stared at him aghast for a moment, then fought back a smile, managing to sound and look grumpy just long enough to lodge one complaint. "You really should have checked with me before you set it all up! I'm not at all sure I like the idea of being at your mercy."

Kyle produced an exaggerated pout, and seeing such a childish expression on such a firm, manly face struck Tanya as being extremely amusing. She giggled, and Kyle bit his lip to keep from moaning as his body reacted to her innate sensuality. His tight jeans gave him away, but he gave Tanya a quick kiss, buying himself a minute to regain control.

Forcing a smile, he made himself think about what needed to be done to get them rolling again.

"How about if I get this loaded up while you get settled in the truck."

"But don't you need help?"

Kyle sighed and pretended annoyance about having to explain the obvious. "This is my job, Angel. I know what I'm doing."

Tanya shrugged and collected the few things she needed for an overnighter, but stayed off to one side watching while Kyle prepared the flat bed, meant for transporting construction equipment, for its load. It was a fairly simple matter of letting down ramps and double checking that they were in the proper place. Then he climbed into the camper and backed it onto the trailer with an ease that Tanya had yet to master.

Tanya almost giggled as he climbed around on the flat bed and her camper like a monkey, hooking safety chains onto the camper. Turning to see her grinning, he exaggerated his movements even more, swinging from the motorcycle carrier on the back of the camper with one arm while he mimed scratching his armpit with the other and pulled up his knees, grunting to complete the image of a gorilla. Tanya shook her head and smiled while Kyle's warm laugh echoed across the parking lot, but she nearly swallowed her tongue when a male voice came from almost at her shoulder.

"I thought Tarzan was the one that was brought up by apes and Superman was a farm boy!"

Kyle looked up, then gave a wave and a smile to the hulk of a man the voice belonged to. Tanya relaxed slightly, offering just the smallest hint of a smile to the stranger before returning her attention to Kyle, who hopped down off the flat bed and strode toward them, pulling off his work gloves as he came.

"Hey Bear! How's it hanging?" Kyle clasped the big mitt Bear offered and thumped a beefy shoulder. Bear did the same, grinning broadly.

"Same as always."

"Clear to China," both men said in unison, then laughed while Tanya rolled her eyes and feigned disgust, thinking they were behaving like a pair of high school kids. In the next instant, Kyle claimed her as his by grabbing her hand and pulling her close.

"This is my girlfriend," he began, but Bear jumped in while Tanya offered her hand.

"Lois Lane! I thought you'd be too busy reporting for the Daily Planet to go on the road with your boyfriend!"

All three laughed while Tanya's hand disappeared into Bear's ham-sized fist.

"I'm writing a piece on truckers and getting a little on the road experience," Tanya returned playfully, and the jovial joking went on as Bear helped Kyle with the last few safety chains. When the load was deemed road-worthy, he went on his way with a cheerful grin and a wave, leaving Tanya with a feeling of warm camaraderie. Riding with a trucker wouldn't be bad at all if the other truckers were like Bear.

"That Bear. He's a special breed." Kyle commented, and Tanya started, looking at him as if he'd suddenly grown a horn on his forehead.

"How did you know I was just wondering if the other truckers are like him?" she asked with a heavy frown marring her brow.

Kyle's eyes sparkled as he gave her a quick kiss, laughing softly as he drew back.

"See? That's how I know I love you. We think a lot alike," he whispered without actually answering her question, then turned toward the truck with a briskly stated "Let's get this show on the road!"

Tanya looked up at the door handle high above her head, then at the tall steps she had to climb to reach it. Chewing her lip in concentration, she started to lift her leg, but Kyle moved her aside and stepped up himself, turning to offer her one large hand after popping the door open.

"Just put both of your hands in mine and I'll pull you up."

Biting her lip, Tanya did as she was told, giving a squeak of surprise as Kyle lifted her easily to a place on his knee, where she wrapped her arms around his neck with wide eyes. Kyle then swung her easily into the passenger seat, grinning as she pulled her arms back and blushed. His payment for his assistance was exacted in the form of a stolen kiss that made her heart sing.

Tanya waited until Kyle started around the trailer for one last safety check before she smiled, then sighed as she realized that, whether she wanted to admit it or not, Kyle was starting to get under her skin. The animal magnetism he exuded was something she could probably have ignored if not for the boyish charm that came along with it. She thought ahead to their arrival in Georgia, and the smile faded as she considered the thought of Kyle going back on the road. For some strange reason, the thought sent a feeling of loneliness surging through her.

Kyle climbed into the driver's seat to find Tanya staring out the windshield with a slight frown marring her delicate features. He stared at her a moment, reading a slight sadness in the look, then softly cleared his throat.

"Something wrong, Angel?"

Tanya's eyes showed surprise when they turned his way, then she blushed and stammered out an explanation, trying to come up with something that wouldn't reveal the true turning of her thoughts.

"I—ah—I was just...ah—thinking about something."

Hidden by his sunglasses, his eyebrow lifted as did one corner of his mouth, which was hidden by his beard.

"You shouldn't be thinking, Angel," he said in a serious, reprimanding tone. "It will put premature wrinkles in your forehead."

Tanya tried to be angry with him for his teasing, but found that she couldn't seem to be very convincing. Instead, she sighed and gave him a quick kiss on the cheek.

"Thank you for your concern, but now, as you so bluntly put it earlier, we should get this show on the road."

Grinning to himself, Kyle started up the truck, missing the look of horror that crossed Tanya's face as country music came blaring out of his radio. Biting her lip, Tanya said nothing, staring out the window as they pulled back out onto the Interstate and headed south, missing the concerned looks Kyle threw her way every few miles as she tried to control her impulse to reach out and change the station.

After driving in near silence for half an hour, Kyle started singing softly to the songs on the radio, unaware of Tanya's eyes on him as she admired the deep, rich tone of his voice, even if the music style grated on her nerves. About halfway through the second song, he looked over to find her staring at him.

"Sorry, Angel. I like to sing, but I'm really not that good."

"You sing beautifully," she returned with a smile, "but I'm just not into country music."

Kyle brought her hand to his lips as a thank you for the compliment, then let her go so that he could reach for a button on the radio panel. In moments, rock music poured over them and he began to sing along with the rock tune with the same abandon as when he'd been singing country.

Shaking her head, unable to believe he had actually changed radio stations to please her, Tanya suddenly smiled and joined in, her own soft soprano harmonizing beautifully with his deep baritone as the big rig ate up the miles between New York and Atlanta.

Chapter Thirteen

It was nearly midnight when Kyle yawned, stretched as much as his seat would allow, and started watching for the off ramp to the motel he sometimes used on this run. The day had been quite uneventful and Kyle was pleased by his truck's performance, with the only stops his scheduled ones for fuel for both the big machine and its human cargo.

Tanya, who now dozed lightly in her seat, had adjusted to Kyle's rather strict schedule without difficulty or complaint, quietly easing her needs during the scheduled stops as if they had always traveled together. It helped that Kyle kept his New York to Atlanta schedule posted on a clipboard in plain sight, and so long as the big rig ran well, he had his runs timed out almost to the minute, leaving no need for her to ask when the next stop would be. She had even smiled to herself as he filled the big rig's tanks, checking his watch as he cleaned the windows and getting back to the hose seconds before it automatically clicked off.

As he glanced her way, Kyle felt a warm glow in the region of his heart, then sighed and returned his gaze to the road. It almost hurt to admit that, whether she liked it or not, he was falling more and more in love with Tanya with each passing minute, and he didn't want to think about how she might react if he admitted it to her. In his own mind, he knew that they were made for each other, but how could he get her to see that without scaring her away?

Tanya woke as a turn of the wheel upset her balance and blinked sleepily at the street lights. Kyle greeted her with a red-eyed smile, and she found herself on the verge of a giggle as he did his best to stifle a yawn, resulting in a comical, teary-eyed expression just before he turned his head slightly to yawn into his fist. Yawning as if to mimic him, Tanya tried to make sense of the passing road signs, frowning as she realized that they had turned onto Route 85 at some point that she was not readily able to remember, but was totally baffled as to where they were.

"We just crossed the border into South Carolina. If we get up early, we should be able to get you to Bubba's a day early." Kyle told her in response to her question. She was too tired to question how he knew where she was working, as she couldn't recall telling him, but remembered chattering at him just shortly before she dozed off. Maybe she had mentioned it without realizing she had.

She snapped fully awake as she realized they were pulling into a motel, remembering clearly that Kyle had told her he almost never slept in one as they chatted over lunch. He gave her another sleepy smile as he explained.

"My sleeper's too small for both of us,"—he winked and his smile became a mischievous smirk—"and for some reason, I haven't slept real well for the past couple of nights, so I'm too tired to climb up to your bed."

"I take it you already figured out that I can't carry you up there." Tanya's wry comment caught Kyle napping, so it took a moment for him to realize what she'd said. Their laughter mingled as they both pictured Tanya trying to pick Kyle up, then Kyle sobered enough to add his own comment.

"I figured this would save us money on the medical bills."

"Well then, I want to pay for the room, since your boss is picking up the tab for gas and tolls."

"Why?"

"Because I don't feel right about charging off a motel room that you wouldn't normally have used if you didn't have me along." Then it was her turn to wear a mischievous grin. "Besides, some of my money used to belong to your boss!"

"How do you figure that?"

"Well, you gave me money you earned from driving, right? So the money you gave me used to belong to your boss, at least until you got paid."

Letting out a quick burst of warm laughter, Kyle didn't offer to argue with her logic, nor did he want to explain anything about his "boss". Instead, he took the cash she passed him and quietly slipped from the truck. When he returned with a receipt and handed her "change", she didn't bother to count it, stuffing it back into her bag with a satisfied grin, missing the twinkle in Kyle's eyes and therefore was unaware that he gave her back exactly the same amount as she gave him, just broken into smaller bills.

Tanya watched Kyle's almost graceful movements as he put the truck into gear for the last time that day, pulling it along the edge of the parking lot where it was out of the way. He flipped switches, pushed buttons and turned dials, then gave her a grin in the glow of a streetlight.

"Ready when you are, Angel Face."

Tanya gave him a wink and opened her door, sliding out onto the high steps with a confidence she hadn't felt when setting out that morning. Kyle waited until she closed the door, then locked it, making sure she had her overnight bag before sliding out to close and lock his. Tanya watched from a few steps away, feigning impatience.

"Come on, Grampa," she teased, laughing when Kyle started toward her walking like an old man, wheezing and holding a hand to his back.

"These old bones just ain't what they use ta be," he chided in a quivery voice, then elicited a squeal from her when he suddenly swooped down on her like a bird of prey.

Kyle scooped her up while Tanya giggled merrily, then they both fell silent as their eyes met. A gentle kiss followed, a kiss that deepened as Kyle sought a response from Tanya— and got just the response he was after. He was grinning as he let her slide back to the ground, his left brow flying high over twinkling eyes, and Tanya bit her lip as she waited for him to say whatever was on his mind. True to form, he didn't make her wait long.

"I don't know about the other bones, but you just made one feel a lot better." The quirky brow was joined by the other as he wiggled them suggestively and Tanya giggled again.

"Pervert," she muttered, trying to pretend that she was disgusted by his behavior, but failing miserably when unable to wipe the grin off her face. Kyle sighed.

"It's a tough job, but somebody's got to do it!"

"That's right." Tanya offered helpfully. "If not for the perverts, we wouldn't know who the really nice ones are."

Kyle pretended to take offense by faking another big pout, making Tanya giggle again, then he became serious, brushing his thumb along her cheek. His smile was almost sad, making Tanya's heart ache, as his voice fell softly from his lips.

"I love listening to you laugh."

Tears came to Tanya's eyes, but she was still unable to get the words past her throat, feeling torn between the fear from her past and the softer emotions that she couldn't push away. Kyle seemed to understand, his eyes gentle as he cradled her cheek against one large palm and brushed his thumb across her lips.

"I know there's something in your past that you aren't ready to share with me,"— Tanya's alarmed eyes shot up to Kyle's face, but he pretended not to notice—"but that doesn't mean I'll avoid saying what I feel. I love you, Tanya, and I'll keep saying it until you either tell me the same or tell me to go jump off a bridge."

Tanya own smile was touched by sadness.

"But would you jump just because I told you to?"

Kyle saw the way her smile didn't touch the dark eyes and tried to bring her back from whatever thoughts were causing her pain with a small joke.

"I'd even kill for you, if that's what you want."

The warmth in his eyes sent a warm glow racing through Tanya, but she still didn't feel comfortable with the thought of him claiming to be so deeply in love with her. A memory intruded, one that involved a man who had beaten her severely for daring to defend her mother, then claimed to love her when he visited her in the hospital the next day.

Even though Tanya didn't say anything, a wall of tension seemed to form between her and Kyle as she recalled the reason she didn't trust a man who said he loved her.

Kyle attempted to tease Tanya as they headed for the room, hoping that she'd relax once they got inside. Much to his dismay, the tension was still there, thick enough to cut with a knife despite Tanya's obvious attempts at relaxing. When she came out of the bathroom and slid under the covers, she could only stare at the ceiling, again wondering if she was making a mistake by listening to her heart.

Kyle lay silently on his back beside her, unable to come up with a reason for Tanya's abrupt withdrawal. He sighed deeply and was about to ask if it was something he'd said or done when she cleared her throat and wet her lips, then spoke in a small, slightly shaky voice.

"I want so badly to trust you, but I—" she hunted for what to say, "—I just can't."

Kyle looked over in time to see Tanya brush away a tear, her face more miserable than he'd ever seen it. Without a word, he slipped his arms around her and pulled her close, feeling her tears as she cuddled against his bare chest, almost crying himself as a feeling of helplessness washed over him at her silent tears. He whispered words of comfort and held her until she regained control, brushing his fingers through her hair as she slowly relaxed and drifted off into an exhausted sleep, her head resting lightly against his shoulder.

It was a long time before Kyle's mind slowed down enough for him to join her, mulling over the few tidbits about her past that she had let slip and wondering why she left her family. Could her family be why she felt she couldn't trust him? Could she have been brought up in one of those dysfunctional families where love meant pain? Or was it just that she was hurt badly by a man she thought she could trust and now didn't dare to trust any man?

A thoughtful frown remained on his face even after his eyes closed, softening only when his dreams took him from thoughts of dark secrets and dysfunctional families to memories of sexual enjoyment with the soft, feminine form that he held so gently in his arms.

Chapter Fourteen

Kyle's internal alarm woke him up at the same time as always the next morning, and he opened his eyes to find Tanya just sliding off the edge of the bed. He watched as she stumbled off to the bathroom and was still laying there, watching the door, when she came back out. Stopping to bite her lip, a habit Kyle had come to associate with her nervousness, Tanya took a deep breath and pushed each word out as if it hurt.

"About last night," she began, but Kyle interrupted her by shaking his head.

"You have nothing to explain. I've been trying to rush you in a situation that you think needs time and a lot of thought. I'm sorry, Angel."

"But—" she began again, and again Kyle interrupted with a simple shake of his head, his manner and face displaying both his complete understanding and a deep pain.

"Angel, we only have 'til Monday, and then I'm back on the road. I can't promise when my next load to Atlanta will be, but if you're still here when I come through, can I at least come see you, even if it's just on stage? I promise that I won't say that nasty 'L' word you hate so much."

Touched by what was so obviously a sacrifice on his part, Tanya nodded her head. Tears threatened at the thought that Kyle was much more than she deserved, and she dropped her head until a silly thought came to her, enabling her to look up into Kyle's face with a mischievous grin and dancing brown eyes.

"Since you're Superman, will you be able to fly to my rescue at the speed of light when I need you?"

Kyle pretended not to understand what she was getting at.

"Need me to what?"

Tanya tried to come up with the right words, but when she could only blush and stammer, Kyle laughed in the way Tanya found so irresistibly sexy.

"Maybe to satisfy any unforeseen desires that might overcome you due to our little encounter?" Kyle offered, and Tanya nodded and gave him a shy smile.

"Thank you. I was wondering how to say that."

Kyle's warm laughter served to lighten her mood even more and before long, they were back in the truck, teasing each other and singing along with the radio as they had the day before. It was only as they neared Atlanta that Tanya seemed to withdraw back into herself, as if preparing for Kyle to leave her right away. Kyle pretended not to notice, his mellow baritone filling the cab with rich sound as he continued to sing along with the rock station.

True to his word, Kyle pulled into a little campground just outside of Atlanta shortly after noon and unloaded Tanya's camper, driving it like it was made of glass. As he got out, he gave Tanya a quick grin, then grew somber.

"Well, you're here."

"Yup." Tanya's brilliant conversation gave no hint of the activity going on in her head as she tried to decide whether to be pushy and ask if Kyle intended on coming back to sleep in the camper or simply wait and see what he might suggest.

"What are your plans for this afternoon?" Kyle's brain was also working faster than his words indicated as he tried to decide in advance whether or not she would turn him down if he suggested they go out on a real date for her last night free before starting at Bubba's.

"I figure it'll take a couple of hours to get all signed in and set up, then I need to stop in and let the manager at Bubba's know that I'm here. Beyond that—" Tanya shrugged.

Taking a deep breath, Kyle put his head on the block, still unsure whether he would feel the bite of the headsman's ax or hear that he had a temporary stay of execution.

"We could go out for a little dinner and dancing this evening, if you're interested."

Tanya almost smiled at the undercurrent of uncertainty in Kyle's tone. It was as if she was his first girlfriend and he didn't quite know how to proceed, and for some reason she chose not to investigate too closely, the thought of being his first real love gave her a warm, fuzzy feeling deep inside.

"Are you sure? I mean, we've spent an awful lot of time together the past few days. Are you sure you don't want a little time to yourself?"

Kyle's snort gave her the answer even before the words left his lips.

"Why should I want time to myself now? I'll have plenty of time to be alone over the next few weeks."

Tanya's smile was as bright as the sun that beamed down on them and she gave up the battle entirely as she moved closer to him, unwilling to worry about her past when the future she desired was within touching distance.

"What time will you be coming by?"

Kyle's easy grin was accompanied by the disarming sparkle of his eyes and Tanya felt her kneecaps melting yet again as his warm voice assailed her senses just before his fingertips brushed her lips.

"What time will you be ready?"

The only answer Tanya was able to give at first was a soft moan of pleasure.

Chapter Fifteen

Kyle arrived promptly at the agreed-upon time of 5:00, running his fingers down his trimmed-back beard and over his slicked-down hair, which he'd tied in a ponytail at the base of his neck, to make sure he looked his best as he walked to the door. When Tanya answered his knock, he held out a single red rose and gave her a soft, sexy smile.

"Oh, Kyle. It's beautiful." Tanya breathed, and Kyle was quite content with the delighted look on her face as she gingerly took the rose from him.

"Like the lady I bought it for." He murmured gallantly.

Tanya's eyes plumbed the depth of the emerald orbs that watched her so closely, then a smile warmed her expression in the same way that her subdued humor warmed her voice.

"Flattery will get you everywhere."

Kyle's answering smile was followed by a light kiss that sent a tingle racing all the way down to Tanya's toes, making her sigh as he drew back. His eyes took in everything about her present appearance, from the shining brown hair to the toe of her high heeled boots, then traveled back up again, twinkling with mischief as he returned his gaze to her eyes.

"I hate to point this out to you, what with promising not to push the relationship issue, but do you realize that we also share the same taste in clothes?"

Tanya took in his outfit with a feigned gasp. They were both wearing a T-shirt and blue jeans tucked into western styled boots and topped with a leather jacket. The biggest difference was that Tanya's boots sported high, stiletto heels while Kyle's were the low-heeled cowboy style. Nonetheless, there was no denying his observation, and Tanya's eyes twinkled as she sighed and dramatically threw up her hands, not wanting to admit that she had noticed that he wore a lot of T-shirts and jeans and had dressed herself to match his style.

"I give up trying to figure any of this out. It's too weird. It looks like fate's thrown us together, and who am I to try to fight fate?"

Kyle bent close, whispering as if telling her a deep, dark secret. "You wouldn't win, anyway. I hear fate is a big guy with muscles out to here."

Tanya looked from one outstretched hand to another before looking into Kyle's face, failing miserably when she tried to give him a chilling look.

"This fate guy. He wouldn't have green eyes would he?"

Her voice fairly dripped with sarcasm, but when Kyle laughed, she joined in.

They painted the town red in Kyle's rented car, this one a blue convertible. They made love until almost dawn in Tanya's camper, and when Kyle's internal alarm woke him promptly at seven, they made love again and slept until Tanya had to get ready for work.

As they drove into the red-light district, Kyle told Tanya that he had a few things to get done and promised to return for her at closing time. Disappointed, but unwilling to let Kyle see how attached she was becoming to him, Tanya gave him a quick kiss and got out, swinging into the place like she owned it.

She was so lost in the splendor of first love that she didn't see the man sitting off by himself in a dark corner of the bar, his gray beard covering the thin lines of his face and making his nose look a little less long and thin. She missed the look of surprise that crossed his face as he recognized her and the smile that followed, his prominent front teeth giving him a rat-like appearance.

Kyle arrived just before the last set of the night, slipping into the partially-filled bar to stand near the door, where Tanya would be sure to see him. To his extreme pleasure, the last act of the night just happened to be the new dancer, Asia, and his eyes glowed with suppressed amusement as she made her way out onto the stage, a blue silk kimono with elegant, hand-painted birds clinging to her small form.

White face paint and a long red wig, styled in the traditional knot on her head, completed the look of the Geisha Girl, emphasizing the exotic tilt of her eyes, which she had artfully made up to make the look even more pronounced. Beginning with feathered fans and a shy demeanor, she went through a set that ran the gamut from sweet innocence to steamy sensuality, leaving the crowd screaming for an encore. When the MC suggested that any who wanted more should return the next night and wished them all a safe journey home, there was nearly a riot, but Kyle and the bouncers managed to regain control of the situation and get everyone out the door and heading for home without incident.

By the time Tanya stepped through the stage door, only her co-workers and Kyle remained in the bar. She slipped up beside the big trucker as the bartender, Bobby, was making one last attempt to give him a drink for his volunteered assistance.

"Sorry, but he's my sober ride home," she told him, and felt Kyle's large hand squeeze her shoulder lightly. She tipped her head back to meet the green eyes that smiled down at her, oblivious to the impression she gave to those who watched of a woman who was deeply in love with the man at her side.

Kyle saw the warmth in her eyes and thought only of the bed that awaited them, eager to taste again of the sweetness of Tanya's charms. As he looked back up into the knowing faces of her co-workers, he couldn't resist smiling.

"It's a tough job, but someone's gotta do it!" He rumbled, and there were chuckles a-plenty as one of the bouncers, a hefty fellow with more fat than muscle who went by the name Terry, sighed in feigned pity.

"I feel sorry for you, man," he intoned, causing even more laughter to which Kyle's rich baritone was added while Tanya smiled and blushed, then the pair said their farewells and slipped out the door hand-in-hand. Neither saw the beat-up brown Chevy of a bygone era nor the little man who sat behind the wheel, watching with both rage and lust vying for space in his cold heart. As the blue convertible pulled away, his lips peeled back from his prominent front teeth in a snarl.

"I found you, Teresanna." He growled to the retreating taillights. "I found you at last."

Chapter Sixteen

Two mornings later, Kyle kissed Tanya and climbed into the car, trying to smile as he waved good-bye. Despite the fact that he had left her with his planned route and schedule of stops, he had a nagging sense of foreboding. Tanya had tenaciously refused to admit to the softer emotions he saw mirrored in her eyes and given him no hope that she would call him at any point in the near future, so Kyle was almost positive that his sense of doom was nothing more than his subconscious mind trying to prepare him for the heartache of her loss.

Tanya, for her part, was doing her best to pretend that she hadn't become totally dependent on Kyle in the short time since she had first spotted the big trucker in the crowded bar in New York. She counted back again and again, unable to believe she could become so attached to anyone in just ten days, and kept her softer feelings to herself rather than let Kyle know how much it would hurt if she had to disappear again before his return. It was much better, she reasoned, to have him think her a cruel, heartless witch who had used him for her own needs and cast him aside than to be there to see his face when she burst his image of her as the perfect woman by admitting to him that she was a coward, forever running from her past.

Tanya walked into Bubba's that afternoon with her helmet under her arm and a heavy frown marring the beauty of her face. Bobby's greeting from behind the bar got only a wan smile in response, and Tanya was once again too preoccupied to take note of the shadowy figure in a dark corner. In the dressing room backstage, she stared listlessly at her face in the mirror and tried hard to smile, but failed miserably.

The addition of her costume didn't help Tanya's mood, and her act that night had a bittersweet quality that the men seemed to respond to. More than one offered a larger bill than was customary to try to get a real smile out of the melancholy dancer, but the most they got in return was a sad little twist of her lips. As Tanya spread cold cream over her face, the manager came in with a smile, ignoring the blank face that turned his way.

"Great show, doll face. The melancholy routine has everyone convinced that Asia is in need of a little romantic interlude to make her forget whatever it is that's bothering her. Drinks are selling like hot cakes while they all wait for you to make an appearance."

Tanya's smile came across as something more like a grimace of pain and she picked up a wash cloth to scrub at her face before trusting her voice enough to respond.

"I'm glad you're making a profit, but how am I supposed to sneak out with a crowd here and no bodyguard?"

The manager shrugged, his good humor untouched by this unexpected development, and offered to have Terry escort her to the door. Tanya accepted the offer with a sigh and returned to the removal of her makeup and costume.

A short time later, Tanya finally made an appearance, her dark hair hidden under a blonde wig she'd borrowed from another dancer and her exotically tilted eyes hidden behind a pair of dark glasses. Pretending to be blind, she put her hand on Terry's elbow and, when he bent his head to hear her over the noise of the crowd, asked him to go along with the charade.

Terry and Kyle had become fast friends over the past three nights while Kyle waited at the door to take Tanya home, so Terry felt a certain pride at being asked to act as a stand-in during the trucker's absence. With the same kind of tender care he had seen displayed by the trucker, he led Tanya through the crowd as if she couldn't see where she was going, stepping outside and loudly offering to call her a cab for the benefit of a customer who followed them out, then hiding her in his shadow while she pulled off the wig and glasses. When she had the disguise safely hidden in her bag and her helmet in her hand, he bid her goodnight and stepped back into the bar, leaving her alone to take the half-dozen steps to her motorcycle.

Tanya had put her key in the ignition and was fumbling with the buckle of her helmet when a scuffing noise made her raise her head. There was a bright flash of light accompanied by blinding pain as a fist shot out and broke her nose, making Tanya stumble back a step. Shaking her head to force herself to maintain consciousness, she looked up—and directly into the rat-like smile of her stepfather.

"Thought you got out from me, didn't ya?" he taunted in the odd jargon that Tanya always associated with his lack of education. "I done seen ya with that big boyfriend a yers, but don't think just 'cause ya gave him what was mine that I won't still get a piece a yer sweet tail 'fore I send ya to live with yer Ma."

"I'm not going back home! You can't make me!" Tanya's brave words were accompanied by a step back toward the bar, but her stepfather moved to intercept her escape, placing himself firmly between her and her nearest source of help while he laughed coldly.

"I never said nothin' about you goin' home. I'm jus' sendin' ya to live with yer Mama, but I can't honestly say whether that might be Heaven or Hell. Guess that depends on whether or not you been a good girl while I ain't been around to make ya mind."

Looking around for another means of escape, Tanya heard Kyle's voice in her head as if he was whispering in her ear, reminding her of what they had discussed just the day before as he taught her a few moves that she could use to defend herself. "It's not the move itself that's important as much as the element of surprise."

Suddenly aware of the helmet in her hand, Tanya tightened her grip on the strap, the jammed buckle forgotten, and picked her chin up in feigned bravado, her taunting voice wiping the smile off her stepfather's face. "I haven't done anything that I'm ashamed of, so why should I worry about going to Hell? I think that privilege is being reserved solely for bullies like you, Big Daddy Long."

Her words had the desired effect, and Mark took a step forward with a growl rumbling in his chest. Tanya swung the helmet with deadly intent and heard a satisfying crack as it connected solidly with the side of Mark's face. The man collapsed on the ground with a howl of pain and Tanya saw her chance. With a sudden burst of speed, she leapt onto her motorcycle and turned the key, letting the helmet hang off her elbow like a purse rather than take the time to undo the stubborn buckle and risk being caught again. Terry opened the door to see what all the howling was about as Tanya roared off down the street, but before he could get close enough to catch the man who lurched to his feet in her wake, Mark Long stumbled to the door of his beat-up Chevy and took up the chase. Racing back inside, Terry called 911 and gave the police a description of both Tanya's motorcycle and the brown car that followed her.

Trying hard to see past the tears of pain that still clouded her vision, Tanya became aware of the pursuit when Mark cut off a car and the driver blared his horn. A twist of her wrist sent the powerful motorcycle roaring down the street at a breakneck pace, and Tanya soon found her vision further hindered by the tears that were produced by the wind screaming past her unprotected face.

Recalling a police station they'd passed the night Kyle took her out on the town, Tanya squealed around corners and wove dangerously in and out between cars on both sides of the road, hitting the final turn that would take her in sight of the police station at just shy of 50 miles per hour.

Her tires screamed in protest as she squeezed the brakes and her voice screamed in harmony as she lost control of the big machine.

A police officer was just stepping out of the precinct house in response to Terry's call when he heard the squeal of Tanya's tires and looked up just in time to see the motorcycle start to go over. Just as he realized the girl's helmet wasn't on her head, she hit the ground on her side and rolled to within inches of his feet. The motorcycle, as badly shattered as its erstwhile rider, came to a rest a few feet away, almost groaning its pain.

He looked back up just as the second reported vehicle, a brown Chevy, roared around the corner and headed toward the curb. His gun materialized in one hand and his radio appeared in the other as he put himself between the car and the injured woman, determined to prevent the driver of the car from causing further damage. His quick action worked, and the driver turned his wheel sharply, making the tires squeal. The car sideswiped a police car just a few feet from the wrecked motorcycle and roared off into the night as the officer added a license plate number to the car's description and called for an ambulance.

Looking up into the face of a uniformed police officer, Tanya fought back the encroaching darkness long enough to reach into her jacket pocket and pull out a business card that had "Jack & Benny Trucking, Inc" etched on the front in fine gold letters. With the last of her fading strength, she pressed the card into the officer's hand and breathed the name of the one person she had a message for should she prove to be fatally injured.

"Kyle."

The officer tried to ask her who Kyle was, but found that Tanya was unable to answer. She was unconscious, her blood blending with the gas and oil that was leaking out of her damaged motorcycle to run into the nearby sewer.

Chapter Seventeen

Kyle had delivered a load to Nashville, picked up another, and made it as far as the Southfork Truck Stop between Little Rock and Texarkana before stopping for the night. After eating his fill of the best chicken fried steak he'd ever found, he curled up in his sleeper and spent the night dreaming about a warm, sexy lady with exotic brown eyes.

He woke the next morning with her still on his mind and wasn't at all surprised to find a message waiting for him, but was disappointed when he recognized the familiar number for J & B's home office, as he had carefully given Southfork's number to Tanya in hopes she would call.

Strolling to the bank of phones, Kyle dialed the number and gave Jack a cheerful greeting. His smile slowly faded as his face went pale under his tan, and he welcomed a chair brought to him by an attentive waitress with a murmur of thanks. Dropping onto the seat, his silence broken only by short, sharp questions, he looked alternately furious and pained.

Kyle hung up the phone and sat staring out into space, the lost look on his face so obvious that the waitress returned, her concern written in her eyes. When she asked if she could do anything to help, Kyle looked up with a start, too lost in his thoughts to have noticed her approach.

"I need a plane to Atlanta. My girlfriend's been in an accident."

The waitress, a rather plain woman who recognized Kyle from the many trips he'd made coast to coast that had involved stops at Southfork, made the offer to find him a ride without a second's hesitation. She knew from the pain in the green eyes that Kyle was in no condition to worry about his load, and after a quick phone call to her husband, was able to assure him that the replacement driver from Jack & Benny Trucking would be met by the same man who was dropping Kyle at the airport.

Lost in his worried thoughts, Kyle was vaguely aware of being brought to the airport and placed on a flight to Atlanta. He responded to the stewardess in monosyllables while he stared out the window during the flight, and only became fully aware of his surroundings when greeted at the airport by a uniformed policeman who had been sent to escort him to the hospital.

The officer answered Kyle's anxious questions to the best of his ability, but it was the doctor who greeted them at the door of the intensive care unit who was able to give Kyle the answers he sought. He insisted that Kyle have a seat, then proceeded to list out Tanya's injuries in a cool, detached tone that hid his concern behind a mask of professionalism.

"I'm going to start at her toes and work my way up, because otherwise I'll miss something," he began, and Kyle found himself thankful that the doctor had had the foresight to make him sit down. When the list was completed, it included 15 breaks, 32 fractures, a ruptured lung, a severe concussion—and in particular, a broken nose.

"Since the blood on her face was already somewhat dry when the officer bent over her, we can only assume that her nose was broken before the accident that caused the rest of the damage," the doctor added, and Kyle felt rage bubble up from deep inside him. The evidence suggested that someone had hit Tanya, but who had hit her hard enough to break her nose and why?

With the doctor's permission, Kyle followed a nurse into the room where a small form, wrapped almost entirely in what appeared to be Plaster of Paris and gauze, was surrounded by various machines. The only parts left open to his gaze were her bruised, swollen eyes, a small section of her left cheek, and her left arm. Plastic tubes were everywhere, and Kyle bit his lip as he gingerly lifted the left hand, which had two tubes running into the back of it, and slid his hand under to find a stiff brace taped to her wrist. Clearing his throat, he tried to force himself to sound cheerful, but only succeeded in sounding strained.

"Hey, Angel. It's Superman. I came flying to your rescue as fast as I could."

There was no response from the figure on the bed, and the nurse turned away to avoid seeing the pain on the big man's face. She checked the readouts on several of the machines, making minor adjustments where necessary, then took her leave after extracting a promise that Kyle would press the call button if Tanya showed any sign of reviving.

Kyle stayed a while at Tanya's side, talking softly to her as he held her hand, hoping to have some sign that she was fighting for her life. Long hours passed as he watched and waited, and whenever a doctor or a nurse made him leave her side, he wandered down to the cafeteria and had cup after cup of steaming coffee until the allotted time they had bade him to stay away was gone and he could return to her side. He lost all sense of time as the minutes became hours and the hours became days, starting in surprise as a familiar voice hailed him during one of his forays to the cafeteria.

"Hey, Kyle! Wait up."

He turned to find that his ears weren't deceiving him as his best friend and dispatcher, a short, pleasantly plump man with a cherubic face, came puffing up to him, sweat dappling the scalp under his curly blonde hair. Pulling off his gold wire-rimmed glasses, Jack ran a handkerchief across his pale blue eyes, looking Kyle over from head to toe as soon as the glasses were back in place.

"Jack? What are you doing here? I thought Kathleen wasn't due back for two days." Jack shook his head and sighed at Kyle's obvious confusion.

"That was three days ago, buddy. The doctor was right. You haven't slept yet."

Kyle frowned, too tired to follow Jack's train of thought, and Jack sighed again.

"Come on, buddy. You and I need to talk."

Jack headed for the door to the outside world, but Kyle refused to leave. His eyes were bloodshot from lack of sleep, but Kyle was still determined to stay until Tanya woke up. His thunderous scowl only served to make Jack scowl back, unafraid of the taller man's dark mood.

"You're not going to do her any good if she wakes up to find you looking like you crawled out of a dumpster." Jack snapped, furious with Kyle for not being his usual, sensible self. "Trust me on this, Kyle. She needs you strong and in control. You need to get some sleep or you won't be."

"But I can't. What if she wakes up and I'm not here? She'll think I deserted her."

Jack heard the whiny tone in Kyle's voice and was strongly reminded of his five-year-old daughter at home.

"Tell you what. The nurse is going to watch her while I take you to a hotel. As soon as I get you settled, I'll come back and sit right by her side. The minute she even twitches, I'll be on the phone. Okay?"

Kyle frowned, but sullenly agreed to do as his friend asked.

"I want her bills taken care of," Kyle ordered like a petulant child as they passed through the doors.

"You've got it," Jack murmured, nodding his head and doing his best to keep the exhausted man moving in a straight line. True to his word, Jack brought Kyle to a hotel that was within walking distance of the hospital and made sure the big trucker climbed into bed before heading for the door. Kyle was asleep before Jack's hand touched the doorknob.

Several hours later, his hair still wet from his shower, Kyle returned to the hospital with his eyes and thoughts clear. He was waiting for the elevator when he overhead a man at the reception desk who seemed to be quite distraught.

"She was brought here three days ago after a motorcycle accident, I tell ya!" the man was yelling, ignoring the receptionist's repeated requests to lower his voice. "Teresanna Montesallo. I oughta know my own stepdaughter, and I saw her get brought here!"

"I'm sorry, sir. We have no one by that name registered. There's nothing I can do for you!"

Kyle watched as the angry man with the strangely rat-like grimace turned and stomped out, then climbed onto the elevator that opened in front of him. It wasn't until Kyle was pushing open the door to the intensive care unit that a portion of the man's tirade echoed in his mind: "She was brought here three days ago after a motorcycle accident."

Something tickled at Kyle's brain, but there were pieces to the puzzle missing, so when Jack stepped to the door of Tanya's room with a smile on his face and signaled for Kyle to hurry, Kyle forgot all about the rat-faced man. He stepped through the door just as the doctor was saying, "There's someone who's been waiting to see you."

Tanya's bruised, bloodshot eyes moved to his face, and Kyle was at her side with no knowledge of how he had managed to cross the room. Her hand lifted and he slipped his underneath, responding to the squeeze of her fingers with a gentle one of his own.

"Hey, Angel. How do you feel?"

The edges of Tanya's lips twitched as she tried to smile, but a tear came to her eye. Kyle dabbed at it gently with the edge of a tissue, his voice catching in his throat. "Don't cry, sweetheart. You'll clog a tube or somethin'."

Once again, there was the twitch at the corners of her mouth, then her eyes closed, her grip on Kyle's hand relaxing slightly. The doctor checked his instruments and smiled.

"She's asleep, but at least she's out of the coma. In a couple more days, we might be able to move her out of the ICU."

Closing his eyes in a prayer of thanks, Kyle kissed Tanya's fingers and sat staring at her battered, yet peaceful face.

Jack watched his friend and a slow smile brought out the cherubic qualities of his chubby face. Jack found he enjoyed seeing a tenderness in the big man's gaze that he never thought he'd see.

Shaking himself out of his reverie with a sigh, he flagged down a nurse and got directions to the billing office to make an arrangement about Tanya's bills. It was obvious that the couple in the room had other things to deal with without worrying about the cost of anything.

Chapter Eighteen

The nurses introduced a system for getting answers to yes or no questions through a code of blinking. Tanya would blink once for yes and twice for no. Over several days and with an officer in the room to serve as a witness, Kyle asked her the carefully phrased questions that the police needed answered and Tanya answered them with yes or no. It was during one such session on the second day after Tanya awoke from the coma that Kyle suddenly remembered the rat-faced man. He had already confirmed that Tanya's nose was broken in front of the bar, a fact corroborated in that Terry saw her assailant leave the scene in his brown Chevy, which the police had found abandoned at a rest area at the edge of the city. Kyle was trying to think of what to ask next when the angry man's tirade came to mind. Watching Tanya closely, he spoke as gently as possible.

"Was the man who hurt you your stepfather?"

Tanya's wide eyes went to Kyle's face and tears welled up as a look of shame filled the bloodshot brown orbs. When she slowly blinked her eyes once, understanding flooded Kyle as all the pieces of the puzzle suddenly dropped into place. He turned to the police officer.

"She told me that she ran away from home, but not why. I think I know what happened now."

The officer drew closer, wanting to hear every word.

Taking a deep breath and steeling himself for the answers he suspected would come, Kyle rubbed his thumb across Tanya's knuckles, trying to give her some of his strength. The nurse, standing by to insure they didn't push her too hard, wiped away Tanya's tears and whispered a word of encouragement.

"Did your stepfather beat you until you ran away from home?"

She blinked once.

"Is he why you became a dancer, so you could move around often enough to keep ahead of him?"

Another single blink. Remembering the name the rat-faced man had screamed at the receptionist, Kyle's voice dropped to a husky whisper.

"Is your real name Teresanna Montesallo?"

Tanya's face went ghostly pale, but she looked directly into Kyle's eyes to blink just once, certain he would turn away in hatred as the depth of her lies was revealed.

Instead, he sighed and tried to appear stern as the errant eyebrow curved upward.

"Is this the deep, dark secret you didn't want to tell me?"

Tanya blinked once, not quite daring to hope for a miracle.

Kyle gave another deep sigh, then leaned forward until their noses were almost touching, looking deep into her eyes as if searching for signs of more secrets. His smile brought a sparkle to his emerald eyes and his husky whisper made her heart skip a beat.

"I still love you, Angel Face, so quit trying to get rid of me, okay?"

The nurse smiled as she looked around at the readings. If the doctor asked, she would be able to show him just where the questions about her stepfather had made the patient's breath stop for a moment in surprise—and where the tender looks she got from a certain trucker made her heart beat a little faster. If the girl was suffering from low spirits, the nurse knew just who to call.

Chapter Nineteen

Two days after finding out Tanya's dark secret, Kyle met with a police officer, a private detective and Jack in a room just down the hall from the private room Tanya had been moved to. The officer spread the faxed contents of a file across the bed and Kyle felt his heart drop down to his   toes as he looked at picture after picture of a girl named Teresanna Montesallo. The pictures documented repeated abuse from the time she was thirteen until she disappeared at the age of sixteen. In each case, the charges had been dropped by her mother after her release from the hospital.

Next came a file that showed similar pictures of an older woman, one who had the same curly dark hair and high cheekbones, but whose eyes lacked the exotic tilt and were listed as being blue. The reports identified the woman as Linda Montesallo Long and Kyle took a long, hard look at the mother of the woman he loved. A death certificate listing cause of death as "spousal abuse" sent shivers racing up and down Kyle's spine as horror stories about obsessive, abusive men becoming stalkers filled his mind. The private detective, who had been given the job of finding out about the stepfather, offered information about a man who had called himself Mark Long at the time Linda Montesallo Long was murdered — and Marcus Longley when his wife and stepdaughter were beaten to death in Nebraska just five years earlier. Fingerprints from both crime scenes had been compared, offering proof that the same man had been at both places, but he hadn't turned up under either alias since the murder in California.

Wrapped up in their discussion, they didn't see the strange man in hospital scrubs slip past the door of the room they were in. With no one at the door to stop him, he slipped quietly into the room with the temporary nameplate that read, "T. LaMonte".

Marcus Longley, a.k.a. Mark "Big Daddy" Long, looked at the small figure in the bed and let his lips curl back over his prominent front teeth. For seven long years, he had sought the one witness who could name him as the aggressor in a certain house in California on a certain night, and he almost rubbed his hands together in glee to see her finally here before him, virtually helpless despite her return from near death, the only one who could tell police what he looked like.

The only thing keeping him from rubbing his hands together was the syringe that he carried, the same one he'd used seven years ago in a hospital room on the other side of the continent. Linda Montesallo had finally had enough of the beatings and was planning to take Teresanna out of his reach before he could taste her sweet virgin flesh. To prevent the girl from getting away, he had given Linda no chance to warn her, not knowing she had already run away.

His lips curled back even further in a grimace as he remembered how this little slip of a girl had first managed to disappear without a trace, then elude him for seven long years. It was pure luck that he found her, and he wasn't going to give her the chance to get away again.

As he slipped up beside the bed, his lecherous eyes took in every detail of her sweet young form, hungering for just a little taste of her softer feminine parts, but knowing he didn't have the time. That man of hers was just a couple of rooms away and could return at any moment. Longley reached for the call button by her left hand, holding his breath, letting it out only when he succeeded in moving the button out of her reach, quite sure that his victim would be at his mercy. When the brown eyes opened and she cringed back in fear, he was feeling quite proud of himself and couldn't resist the chance to brag.

"Bet you an' yer boyfriend thought I wouldn't figure out that you was usin' another name." The odd nasal quality of his tone made Tanya's skin crawl even as his grin made the ratty quality of his face more prominent. Tanya was forcibly reminded of the Christmas ballet about the Nutcracker and prayed her prince would come dashing to her rescue. Mark Long let out a short, snorting laugh and advanced slowly, feeling the power that always surged through him at the thought of making a woman do exactly what he wanted.

"A-course, neither one of ya knowed I seen him fer three whole nights at the bar, so it was just a matter a waitin' in the lobby 'til he come by. I oughta thank ya fer gettin' such a uncommon lookin' fella, 'cause it made my job a lot easier."

Tanya longed to make a snide comment, but because of her punctured lung, she still needed a breathing tube, and because of her broken nose, the tube had to go down her throat, blocking her vocal chords. She had to be satisfied with letting her eyes show her hatred of the man. Seeing her look, Mark sighed and pretended to be sad even as his sharp eyes glittered in ill-concealed excitement and he drew air into the syringe.

"I do have one regret over this whole thing, ya know. I really wanted ta get me a bit of that cute tail a yers while ya looked up at me with them Chinee eyes all wide, just ta see if it was different from what yer Mama give me. 'Course, ya probably got some disease by now, either from the man ya got now or some other fella ya had before, but I don't guess that matters now, does it?" He picked up the IV tube and poised the needle above it, smiling as Tanya tried to pull it out of his grasp. "'Cause I'm a little pressed for time, I gotta make this short 'n' sweet, so I gotta send ya to the next world without knowin' what that sexy piece a' ass feels like."

"And what makes you think I'd let you lay a hand on her?"

The deep voice coming from the doorway made Mark falter, and in the next instant, Tanya managed to yank the IV tube hard enough to rip it free of the drip bag, sending saline solution spraying across the hospital scrubs her stepfather wore and onto the floor at his feet. The man who had insisted that this girl call him "Big Daddy Long" had only time to yelp in surprise before Kyle's massive fist was gathering up the front of the green shirt, then he was fighting with everything he had to pull away. Remembering the syringe full of air, he stabbed it into Kyle's arm, gaining his release but losing his grip on the cylinder before he could squeeze the plunger.

Kyle roared as the needle jabbed him, slamming the little man with the rat-like face against the wall before yanking the syringe out of his arm. In a fit of temper, he pitched it away, sending it skittering under the bed, and went after Mark Long with a vengeance. Seeing death looking him in the eye, the little man fled, knocking down the police officer who was racing toward the room and setting off a fire alarm as he escaped down the nearest stairwell.

Kyle started for the door, ready to give chase, but a sound from the room behind him made him pause. As he turned back, his eyes widened and his next bellow brought doctors and nurses on the run. Tanya gasped for air on the bed, the machine that had been helping her breathe lying on its side on the floor with a blood-dappled length of plastic tube still attached to it.

Chapter Twenty

"It's not your fault, Kyle!"

Jack had been repeating the same thing for the whole hour since they had been forced to retreat to the hallway, but Kyle still showed no sign of listening.

"I lost control. Years and years of martial arts to learn how to control my temper and I lost it just when I needed control the most."

Kyle paced up and down the hallway, stopping each time the door to Tanya's room opened and resuming agitated movement when no one stopped to give him any word of her. His fist opened and closed repeatedly as he saw the rat-like face before him again and again, and Jack started in surprise when Kyle growled an oath and swung his fist to punch a cement wall. Spinning away with barely a grimace, he resumed his pacing as if nothing had happened, ignoring the bruising on his knuckles that attested to his outburst.

Jack, not wishing to have the knuckles tested against his face or form, wisely remained quiet.

Half an hour after Kyle's outburst, he stood staring out the window at the parking lot, finally calm, but far from relaxed. The hand that he'd smashed against the wall resembled an odd-shaped purple balloon, but he refused to have it tended until he got word about Tanya. It was with some relief that Jack accompanied the doctor to his friend's side.

"Sorry it took us so long, Mr. Benton. We wanted to make sure the blood wasn't from her lungs before we put the tubes back in."

Kyle said nothing, his brooding eyes fixed on the doctor's face, so Jack asked the question that plagued them both.

"Is she going to be all right?"

The doctor smiled and nodded.

"There was no permanent damage, although she did get scared for a little while when she had a hard time drawing a full breath."

Kyle closed his eyes and sighed in relief, missing the silent signal Jack made to get the doctor to look down at Kyle's hand. When he opened his eyes again, the doctor was staring at his bruised hand with wide eyes.

"Looks like my work isn't finished yet! We need to get you down to x-ray and have that checked out."

"Can I see Tanya first?"

The plaintive note in Kyle's voice brought an understanding smile to the doctor's face. It was obvious how much the petite woman meant to the big trucker, and the physician could see no reason to deny the request, especially if it meant they would get Kyle's full cooperation in x-ray for the price of a five-minute delay.

Kyle stepped into the room with his heart in his throat.

The small, well-wrapped form was still on the bed and the breathing tube had been restored, but all that caught his gaze was the soft glow in the dark eyes. Carefully hiding his injured hand, he took her fingers in his and kissed them gently.

"Are you all right?"

Tanya's eyes closed once, deliberately. Kyle smiled at her and brushed an errant curl out of her eyes. His eyes were sad as he whispered his soft message to her, not afraid of her reaction.

"I love you more than my life. I'm going to see that you're kept safe."

Tanya stared at his face, wishing she could tell him of her love for him, wanting nothing more than to lie safely in his arms as she drifted off to sleep and knowing that she would not be allowed to do so until she left the hospital. Unaware of her thoughts, Kyle held her hand until she drifted off to sleep, then brought the police officer into her room to protect her while his hand was taken care of. When he returned, he sat down with Jack, the doctor, the officer, and the private detective in her room, where they plotted strategy while Tanya slept in complete safety, surrounded by big, strong men.

Chapter Twenty-One

The plan was quite simple and went into effect the very next morning. A "Code Blue" was called for Tanya's room, and hospital personnel rushed to her side. The assembled team was given instructions and they went into action just as if the girl was in danger of dying. In moments, she was on her way to the operating room while a sedative took effect, then she was hooked up to a portable oxygen tank and further sedated to the point that she would be unable to move and would barely even be breathing for a short period of time.

Mournfully, the nurses talked in front of the door, blocking the view of anyone looking in through the window while a sheet was draped over the still form, then the "body" was rolled out and down the hall toward the morgue. In the waiting room, the doctor had pulled Kyle aside and was delivering the news that, at 8:00 a.m. Eastern Standard Time, Miss Tanya LaMonte, exotic dancer, passed away as the result of the injuries she had suffered in a motorcycle accident. Kyle sank into a chair with shock clearly written on his face while in the stairwell next to the waiting room a small man with a rat-like smile sat slowly down against the wall and sighed deeply. Finally, after seven long years of searching, Mark Long had managed to put an end to the one witness to the beating of Linda Montesallo. He was just starting to relax when he heard the doctor speak to the trucker who had been Teresanna's latest consort.

"What do you intend to do now?" the doctor asked, his concern evident in his soft, slightly accented voice. Kyle's anger rumbled in his voice.

"Find the man who snuck in here and caused her death. If I can't bring her back at least I can avenge her death."

Playing along with a carefully planned script, the doctor shook his head and laid a hand on Kyle's arm.

"But that's impossible. It would be like looking for a needle in a haystack!"

"But I know just what he looks like. I saw him in her room."

In the stairwell, Mark Long stiffened, remembering the look of death in the green eyes of his stepdaughter's boyfriend. He began to sweat.

"There must be a million men who answer his description. How will the police ever catch him?"

"The police will get their chance only when I give up the search myself. I don't want this guy going into the justice system. I want to pound him into dust myself."

In the stairwell, Mark Long paled, then suddenly smiled at the thought of doing away with a man. It shouldn't be hard, if he planned carefully enough, but he would have to keep the trucker in his sight while he made his plan.

Kyle and the doctor continued to argue while Tanya, hidden under a sheet, was taken to the morgue. As planned, she was rolled down the restricted access corridor and into the big main room. There, several stretchers lay in wait, some with real bodies in body bags, some with mannequins in body bags, and some with bodies or mannequins under sheets. Tanya was rolled into the middle of these and left.

At various times over the next half hour, workers came in and out to move the bodies around, pulling one out here and another there and shuffling the rest around until the only way to tell one body from another was to be able to read the toe tags. At one point, Tanya was rolled out into a preparation room, slipped into a body bag, and brought out through a dark, little-used corridor to a waiting ambulance. At the same time as the ambulance rolled, several hearses from various funeral homes left as well, all taking different routes out of the city.

The ambulance carrying Tanya stopped at a fire station and carefully backed in as if returning from a long stint at the hospital. In the fire station, paramedics checked the girl's vital signs while firemen and policemen checked the streets from various hiding places to insure that the ambulance had not been followed. Tanya was loaded back inside and the rescue unit went out as if it had been called out to an accident, but turned and raced toward the airport instead, its red lights flashing and its siren wailing. At the airport, Tanya was hurried into a Medivac chopper, where a familiar-looking man with gold-rimmed glasses and a cheerful, cherubic smile waited to greet her as the sedatives she'd been given wore off.

"Hi! Remember me? I'm Kyle's friend, Jack."

Tanya blinked her eyes once, but couldn't understand what she was doing here instead of lying in the hospital with Kyle at her side. As if he could read her mind, Jack explained the situation.

"Kyle wanted to make sure you were protected, so we faked your death and did the old switcheroo on your stepfather. For all intents and purposes, Tanya LaMonte is officially dead, so we've created a new identity for you complete with all the necessary documentation, courtesy of the Atlanta Police Department and Jack & Benny Trucking."

While the helicopter lifted off from the airport, Tanya was given all the information she would need to take on a new identity in a faraway state called Maine.

Chapter Twenty-Two

On a sunny September morning, Kyle solemnly followed a shiny white coffin to its final resting place in a beautifully landscaped cemetery on the outskirts of Atlanta. In a pair of black chinos, with a black T-shirt under his leather jacket, he was the picture of the mourning lover. His long hair covered the wire that ran from his ear to a transmitter that was hidden under his arm, and not even Tanya's coworkers, who had attended the funeral truly believing she had died from injuries suffered in the accident, knew that he was wired and listening for a warning from one of the many police officers stationed around the cemetery.

The only sound coming from the earphone was static, and behind his mirrored sunglasses, Kyle's eyes studied the trees that he could see without becoming obvious. He saw one of the plainclothes officers kneeling next to a tombstone as if praying for her deceased loved one, but nothing else moved except for a few flowers that were being gently rocked by a slight breeze. The minister read a few verses from the bible, and then Kyle stepped forward and placed a single rose on the top of the casket, which had been sealed with the excuse that she had been too severely injured to allow for an open-casket funeral. Terry was next to step up, weeping openly, and placed a rose on the casket next to Kyle's. The bouncer shook hands with Kyle while apologizing profusely for not walking Tanya to her motorcycle.

Feeling like a heel for keeping the truth from Terry, Kyle accepted his condolences and uncomfortably accepted similar sympathies from each of the others as they first placed a rose on the casket, then turned to the "grieving lover". The earphone continued to broadcast nothing but static, and it wasn't until Kyle was seated in the car and driving away from the cemetery that a report was made about a gray-haired man with rat-like features. Oddly enough, although the rat-faced man stepped up close for a good look at the beautiful stone Kyle had purchased to mark the grave, he seemed much more interested in the direction Kyle's car had gone.

A short time later, while gathering his gear at the hotel he'd been staying in, Kyle was startled by another transmission. The suspect had again been spotted within Kyle's vicinity, and Kyle prepared himself for a visitor, expecting that the man would try to kill the one witness to the attempt on Tanya's life. He was disappointed, as the strange, vicious man seemed to realize what they were doing and disappeared again before the net could be dropped. Scowling, wanting nothing more than to board a plane for Maine and rejoin the woman who had stolen his heart, Kyle finished packing and vowed not to return to her side until he was assured that the maniac who had tried to kill her was locked up, safe and sound.

Book Two:

Teran

Chapter One

October 10, 1995

In a room in the Eastern Maine Medical Center in Bangor, Maine, Teran Hodges stared out at the Penobscot River from her wheelchair, wishing for a way to scratch the millions of places that itched under her casts. Her lung had finally healed enough for the removal of the oxygen tube just one week before, so her doctor had finally given the go-ahead for her to go home. Her only fear as she waited for her cousin Jack and his wife Kathleen to arrive was that they would be forced to take her into their home and tend her until the casts came off in November. The dull, gray sky overhead did nothing to boost her sagging spirits.

Somewhere down the hall in an area of the hospital she hadn't seen in almost a month, the elevator doors slid open and she heard two familiar voices coming her way. Using her good hand on the button of the electric wheelchair that Jack had rented for her, she turned herself to face the door, looking up with a smile as Kathleen stepped into her line of vision.

"Hiya, cousin. Ready to split this Popsicle stand?"

Kathleen's bright green eyes gleamed happily under her cap of bleached blonde hair as she took a look around the room and found Teran's belongings piled on the bed. Her sparkling white teeth made an appearance as she stepped into the room and settled her trim figure comfortably in a chair, explaining, "Jack is getting the nurse to check you out of here, so it should only be a few more minutes."

An hour later, in a van Jack had rented from the facility that the hospital suggested for such short-term handicaps, the trio pulled out of the parking lot. Jack and Kathleen shared an amused glance as Teran gave a deep, heartfelt sigh of sheer pleasure and commented, "It is so good to see something other than four white walls!"

Teran watched, fascinated, as the colors of a typical Maine fall slid past the windows. Having always gone south after Labor Day, Teran had never seen the changing leaves, and her first experience left her almost breathless. Turning to check on the invalid, Kathleen saw the awe in her gaze and leaned forward to catch her attention.

"You should see the leaves on a sunny day. The colors come right out at you." Kathleen's soft voice brought a brighter glow to Teran's dark eyes as her imagination brought brightness to the leaves that passed by. Uphill and down, through small towns and farmlands, the van made its way to the northwest, but from her chair in the back of the van, Teran was too lost in her thoughts to pay much attention to details. It was only as the van pulled to a stop in the dooryard of a white farmhouse that Teran raised herself from her doldrums. Jack slid out of the van while Kathleen turned to her with a quick grin.

"Jack arranged for you to stay at a friend's place just up the road, but promised to let his Gram have a look at you before we take you up to Benny's."

Curious, Teran trained her eyes to the open porch that formed the front of the house in time to see Jack step out with a small gray-haired lady following close behind. Pulling a gray sweater close about her bone-thin form, the elder woman stepped off the porch with an agility that belied her years. As she neared the van, faded green eyes peered through the bifocals that were perched on her nose and her wrinkled face held a stern look of concentration that faded to a smile as she got her first look at the invalid through Kathleen's open window.

"Hello there. I understand you're to stay at my grandson's for a bit." The old woman's voice, seasoned with just a touch of a Maine accent, was smooth and cultured, hinting of a higher-than-average education level.

Teran nodded slowly, wishing she could extend a hand far enough to give a proper greeting. Instead, she could only blush as the elder took in every detail of her damaged form, her nerves as tight as a bowstring by the time the old woman gave her a wink.

"I'm Helen Godfried, but everyone around here calls me Gram. I understand you go by the name Teran?"

Once again, the younger woman nodded, then self-consciously cleared her throat, blushing even more as her voice came out as a croak.

"I'm pleased to meet you, Mrs. Godfried."

The elder frowned sternly, her voice soft, but her disapproval plain.

"I'm glad your Momma taught you proper manners, but when I said everyone calls me Gram, I meant you should, too."

Kathleen turned and gave Teran an encouraging wink.

"Don't let Gram scare you, sweetie. Her bark is worse than her bite."

The elder woman's eyes flipped to the blonde and a wry grin crossed her face.

"You just don't remember how hard I can bite," she teased, and Kathleen laughed softly as she leaned out to give the old woman a kiss on the cheek.

"Actually, I do, but I don't want you to scare the poor girl. It's bad enough to be forcibly hauled out into the boonies without finding out that your nearest neighbor is a crotchety old woman."

Gram took the insult with a good-natured grin, brushing the blonde woman's cheek lovingly before turning to give Jack a quick hug. As she turned back to Teran, her eyes glittered joyfully.

"Don't you worry about a thing, little miss. These two will take real good care of you and if there's anything they forget, you just give me a call. My phone number is right beside the phone."

Teran promised she would, a warm glow deep in her heart giving her shy smile a special light that brought a feeling of peace to the old woman. In that moment, a close bond was formed between the two women, and Teran knew without a doubt that she would enjoy her stay at Benny's house, whoever Benny might be.

After promising to stop by "once you're settled", Gram turned and made her way back onto the porch while Jack climbed back into the driver's seat and started the van. At the door, she turned to watch them pull out of the circular drive, her wise old eyes gleaming as her left eyebrow lifted.

"My grandson's taste is improving," she murmured to herself, then slipped inside with a grin still creasing her wrinkled face.

In the van, Jack was chattering nonstop about Benny, who had inherited a piece of land with the remains of an old farm several years before.

"He's a little eccentric, I guess you'd say. When he saw what was left of the original farm buildings after a fire, he decided to do little more than strengthen the existing structure and do most of the remodeling on the interior."

It was at about this time that the thick woods to each side of the dirt road they were driving along started to thin, and Teran gasped as she began to get glimpses of a building through the trees. The last trees gave way to a cleared field and the sun chose that precise instant to peek out through the clouds; its light touched the house at the top of the hill as if spotlighting it for the awestruck young woman.

The huge building, painted in the traditional red and white commonly associated with New England barns, still had a very barn-like appearance, but the twinkle of a multitude of windows in its facade served to explain Jack's words. It was immediately apparent that Benny had been left with the barn after the fire had destroyed the old farmhouse and had turned the barn into a very unique house. As they drew nearer, Teran's eyes got wider, taking in the details of the remodeling. The big front door of the old barn had been nailed into place, then a smaller front door had been cut in its center. Just under the peak of the roof, a huge, triangular window had been cut, nearly as tall at its center as Teran when she was able to stand. The old silo, still attached to the barn with its lower half hidden behind an attached shed, sported tall, thin windows that gave it the appearance of a castle tower, making Teran smile, but it was the view that appeared behind the barn/house that really brought Teran's breath to a halt.

Sitting at the top of the hill, the place commanded a breathtaking view of the surrounding mountains covered with the multicolored glory of the changing leaves. The drive curved back around just before it reached the house, and Teran gasped again as she looked over Jack's shoulder to see the way the ground dropped rapidly on the other side of the house. A long screened porch, supported by tall, stilt-like metal posts, stretched out along the west side of the house, and Teran's smile grew as she realized that Benny was a man after her own heart. The porch obviously had a most magnificent view of the sun setting over the mountains and would no doubt be quite a comfortable place to sit come summer.

Jack pulled up to the front door and honked his horn twice before getting out of the van. By the time he made his way around the vehicle to begin the process of unloading his fragile cargo, the front door had opened and an older couple stepped out. It didn't take Teran long to decide who at least one of the people could be, because the woman was obviously an older, feminine version of Jack. The man, who had the weather-beaten features so common to the area, touched the woman with a hint of intimacy as they drew close to the van, so Teran swiftly concluded, and quite correctly, that he was Jack's father.

"This is your Uncle Junior and Aunt Emma," Jack informed her as he rolled her out onto the electric chair-lift to lower her to the ground. "They'll be staying until the nurse I hired gets here."

Like Gram, they both gave her a quick once-over, then smiled at her warmly. While the men each grabbed a side of the wheelchair, Emma started to chatter, making Teran giggle as she realized that Jack took after the woman in more ways than just his looks. Unaffected by the girl's humor, Emma continued on right up until Teran was set ceremoniously past the threshold, getting her first look at the interior of Benny's house.

Like the outside, the barn was still clearly visible in the lines of the room, especially since the central part had been left open all the way to the roof, some three stories over Teran's head. Skylights cut in the roof gave the room a light, airy feeling, and four fans set in the peak forced warm air back down from the lofty heights. The rich, darkly stained wood that paneled the tall, thin room added a feeling of understated elegance, and Teran had to remind herself to breathe. Kathleen, at Teran's side, observed her reaction with a giggle.

"Benny may be a bit eccentric, but he sure has great taste, doesn't he?"

Teran nodded her agreement, still taking in the detail of the room. Her eyes passed almost lovingly along the balcony railing that ran along the edge of the second floor, then followed the flowing lines of the elegant staircase with its short, wide steps that ran along the back wall, first to the left, then to the right, with a beautiful grandfather clock resting on the landing where the staircase changed directions. Watching her eyes, Jack felt inclined to add more detail to his tale about Benny.

"Most of what you see here was done by the local high school's shop class. Benny paid for the wood and the shop teacher used his classes to teach the kids how to cut parts for stairs, do lathe turnings, and put together simple pieces of furniture, like bookcases. If you look really close, you'll find some places where the kids made some mistakes, but we all think it adds a certain character."

"You mean kids did all this?"

Jack grinned.

"Actually, the kids just did the prep work. Benny, Dad and I, along with a few other friends who chipped in from time to time, did all the actual remodeling."

Teran barely had time to acknowledge Jack's words with the appropriate amount of awe before Emma took over the conversation.

"We won't make you take the tour, as I'm sure you must be tired, but I'll give you an idea of the general layout. Off here to the left, where the cows used to be, there's a kitchen with the laundry room out where the milk room used to be. Then there's the dining room tucked back in the corner. Straight back through that door at the end of the stairs is the family room, and you can get to the first floor of the library in there—that's what Benny turned the silo into, a three-story, round library with a spiral staircase going right up through the middle all the way to the reading room at the top. Then, on this side, you've got Benny's office through that first door, a bathroom, and the back side of the furnace room, which you have to go down a little hallway off the family room to get to. Also down that hallway is an exercise room, so when you get to the point of losing those casts and needing physical therapy, you won't have to go anywhere. We'll just get a therapist to come a couple of times a week to work with you and you can lift weights, if you want to, in between times."

Teran released her held breath as Emma finished her tirade and started toward the living room

door. Halfway there, she stopped and turned, looking at Teran as if the girl had missed something important.

"Well, you gonna sit there or are you gonna follow me to the guest room?"

Biting back an amused giggle, Teran pushed the button that sent the wheelchair after the stout woman while Emma continued on her way. Just past the door, Teran stopped with another gasp of surprise, finding herself in another room that spoke of the simple, elegant style of the eccentric Benny. A large fieldstone fireplace took up most of the outer wall with well-built rectangular windows to each side to let in the light. Like the other room, it was paneled in tongue-and-grove wood stained to a rich, warm brown. In the corner where the silo/library met the edge of the screened porch, an antique-looking elevator had been put in, its metalwork embellished with a vine and leaf pattern that added to the understated elegance of the room.

"Benny's Granddad had a stroke that put him in a wheelchair while they were redoing this room, so Benny put in the elevator. The old guy used to come up here and help out by supervising some of the less-skilled guys."

"Benny must be a really nice guy," Teran murmured, and Emma grinned.

"You got that right, honey!"

Emma loaded Teran into the elevator, flipped the switch that started it moving, and hurried up the stairs to meet her at the top. Teran found herself in a small alcove between the library wall and the wall of the master bedroom, or at least that was what Emma identified the straight wall to the right as. Following the direction of Emma's short, fat finger as she pointed to the right, Teran took note of the three closed doors across the way while Emma explained that there were two bedrooms with a shared bathroom to that side of the upstairs. The door to Teran's left was opened as she looked down at the empty entrance down below, then Emma directed her through into the guest suite.

Like the rooms downstairs, the small grouping of bedroom, sitting room and bathroom had a certain understated elegance. The sunlight that streamed through big windows was reflected by cream colored wallpaper that was designed to resemble a fine moiré cloth. Curtains of a soft blue shade hung at the windows and scatter rugs of the same soft blue lay casually about on the hardwood floor.

The bedroom boasted a huge four-poster bed with a thick patchwork quilt that made Teran want to yawn, thinking how nice it would be to cuddle up under that downy softness and take a long nap. Seeing where the girl's eyes rested, Emma smiled and patted her charge's hand.

"I'll go get the boys up here to hoist you into bed so you can have a nap. You must be exhausted after that long ride!"

Smiling her gratitude, Teran covered her mouth and let the yawn come as soon as Emma's back was turned, then sat smiling as a sense of peace came stealing over her. Wherever and whoever this Benny was, she would have to thank him for his generous hospitality just as soon as she got the chance.

Chapter Two

When Teran awoke from her nap some time later, a private nurse was bustling about the room, setting up various pieces of equipment that would make Teran's time as an invalid much easier on all involved. When Teran admitted her curiosity, each piece was shown to her while the nurse explained its use. Teran's favorite of all the gadgets was a monitor like the kind used by new parents to listen to their baby when they had to do chores in another room.

With the transmitter in the pocket of her chair, she could call for assistance no matter where she roamed—and roam she did, learning quickly how best to maneuver her chair into the elevator so that she could investigate the house whenever the mood struck her.

The mood to investigate struck her often during her first few days, so she began where Emma did and worked her way through each room, slowly studying the details of Benny's simple, yet elegant styling. The kitchen was aglow with white tile walls, wooden cabinets (the upper berth of which had spotless glass doors) and a red tile floor. Just off to one side, the former milk room, with its flat cement floor and tall cement walls, made the perfect laundry, with plenty of room on the wall closest to the outside door to hang dirty clothes, should one do nasty chores like gardening or vehicle repairs, without tracking dirt through the rest of the house.

The dining room, with sliding glass doors that led out onto the L-shaped screened porch, was almost completely filled by a long, formal dining table with a full dozen chairs arranged around it. The walls were covered by a textured wallpaper of a soft tan color that complimented the deep burgundy velvet chair seats and the matching placemats, giving the room the feeling that it was simply lying in wait for the beginning of a formal dinner party.

Louvered doors that could fold back, accordion-like, against the wall separated the dining room from the family room with its fieldstone fireplace, and Teran smiled each time she wheeled through the opening. Of all the doors in the house, it was the only place she felt certain she could breeze through without worrying that she would mar Benny's careful work.

Next came the first floor of the library, and it was with a mild disappointment that Teran discovered that, although the tall shelves held great possibilities, they held very few books. Most of those available were Sherlock Holmes mysteries, and because they reminded Teran of a certain trucker, she shunned them. It wasn't long, though, before Kathleen started bringing over stacks of books that she purchased in order to support libraries, church groups, and other such local charitable organizations. Before the first month was out, the first floor was starting to look like a true library.

The downstairs bathroom, actually nothing more than a toilet, sink and shower stall, was tastefully small and neat. Finding nothing important there, Teran moved on, peeping in the study to find a massive oak desk, a file cabinet, and a big desk chair with a high back. Nothing in the room hinted that it was ever used, and Teran withdrew with a frown marring her features.

She rolled down the short hallway off the living room to check out the exercise room—and gasped as she rolled down the ramp that had been installed for her use. It wasn't so much the weight-lifting setup, complete as it was, that made her gasp. Instead, her eyes were fixed on the swimming pool just beyond a set of glass doors, with its tall, stockade fence. It was there that Emma found her at lunch time, and as they rolled back toward the dining room, Emma told about how Benny had taken the rock-lined cellar hole for the old house and dug it deeper at one end, using the removed debris to fill in the shallow end, then poured fresh concrete over the whole to make the surface smooth and watertight, turning an eyesore from a bygone era into yet another special addition to his eccentric house.

"But why the barn? Why didn't he just build a new house?" Teran's plaintive question brought a smile to Emma's face.

"Have you ever been asked if you were brought up in a barn for leaving the door open?" Teran nodded as she remembered many times that her mother had asked her that very question.

Emma's grin broadened.

"Well, Benny figures his kids should be able to answer that question with a resounding yes."

Teran's mouth hung open in shock for a moment, then she giggled, finally starting to understand the true depth of Benny's eccentric behavior. Still, one couldn't put a man down for reusing the existing structures instead of destroying the site, especially when the results were so magnificent!

On investigating the upstairs, Teran discovered one other thing about Benny—he wasn't finished with his house. The guest quarters she was using and the master bedroom, which had a stone fireplace and glass doors that opened out to a balcony on the roof of the screened porch, were both completely finished and furnished with good taste, but the other two bedrooms still needed work. The one that was furthest from the stairs had wallboard only on the walls that were insulated and the one that bordered on the master bedroom had all the wallboard up, but needed to have paint or wallpaper added to finish it's look.

Like the downstairs level, the second floor portion of the library had plenty of shelf space, but no books. A closer examination showed that a couple of mysteries were on one long shelf, almost as if they had somehow migrated up from the downstairs level. Making a full circle around the spiral staircase, Teran looked up, longing for the day when she would be able to go to the top and see what it held. The narrow windows of the first two floors gave off less light than she could see at the top of the stairs, hinting that there might be a view to be had.

Curious as to what the view could possibly hold, Teran went around again, stopping beside one of the tall, narrow windows to look out, stretching herself up taller when she could only see sky, but unable to get high enough to see anything else. Frustrated, she dropped back into her seat with a snort—and nearly came out of her skin when Jack's cheerful voice came from the doorway!

"You can get the same view by going out onto Benny's balcony."

Teran blushed in embarrassment at having been caught and her voice was soft as she argued. "But I don't want to intrude into his room."

Jack smiled, but shot down her argument without allowing any humor to touch his voice. "Since Benny's not in there, no one will care. Besides, he gave you free run of the place, and didn't specify that you couldn't check out the view from his balcony."

Tempted, Teran bit her lip, trying to come up with another reason for not going through a strange man's room, but when Jack started egging her on in a tone that sounded like he may have picked it up from one of his kids, she sighed and gave in. Moments later, she was glad she had, despite the cool breeze that was chasing across the upper part of the house.

From the balcony, it seemed the sky went on forever, and by looking almost straight up, she got a better look at the top of the former silo. Short, slightly bowed windows like the kind used in lighthouses formed a band around the top just under the edge of the silo's slightly rounded roof, but would have only been clearly visible from the road if it had been very early in the morning or very late in the afternoon, so squat were they. Jack saw the direction of her gaze and smiled, recognizing her curiosity.

"Those were specially made by a friend of Benny's who does glass blowing and sculptures and such. He was initially brought in just as a consultant, but when he saw our problem with the windows around the top, he came up with a way of making the glass curve so it matched the curve of the wall, then made them short so there could be some wall left under them instead of having windows that went all the way to the floor of the reading room. The view is a little distorted, but it gives plenty of light for a little quiet reading where you won't get disturbed by random noises."

Teran gave Jack a sideways glance, hearing no "random noises" that had to be escaped from. Seeing the look in her eyes, Jack laughed.

"I think Benny built that room for when he has a bunch of kids tearing around the place."

As they passed back through the master bedroom, Teran glanced up to see what kind of ceiling the master bedroom had—and stopped with a gasp, staring up through a decorative arrangement of beams at the roof of the structure, a good 18 feet over her head. Like at the other end of the building, there was a tall, triangular window that let in sunlight to brighten up the room below, and the same rich brown stain that had been used throughout the building gave the light a warmth that was breathtaking. For just a moment, she imagined lying with Kyle in the big bed, staring up at the high ceiling while they made love with the golden glow of the setting sun burnishing the rich tone of the wood.

Shaking herself out of her dream, she rolled out into the hall, missing the amused glow in Jack's blue eyes as he observed the odd flush of color in her cheeks. As her eyes had done, his traveled from the ceiling to the big bed that took up most of the available floor space, and a knowing smile curved his lips as he followed his young charge.

Chapter Three

Time moves on at a regular, measured pace, but for Teran, the time spent in Benny's house often seemed to move at a snail's pace when she was alone with her thoughts, then race off at the speed of light the moment a visitor stepped through the door. It wasn't until Halloween, when Gram stepped through the door with a big bowl of candy in her hands, that she came to the shocking revelation that three weeks had slipped by without her being fully aware of the fact.

"It's hard to believe that next week, I'll be able to find out how tall you really are." Gram teased, but Teran was too preoccupied with her shock to notice the lifted eyebrow that preceded the statement. Her dark eyes grew sad as she tried not to think about the fact that it had been almost two months since she'd last seen Kyle—and she had received no word from or about him!

Seeing the melancholy look on the pretty face, Gram frowned heavily. Having had a full explanation of the girl's situation from Jack, the older woman was fully aware of the need to protect the girl from any contact with the outside world, but she simply couldn't bear to see Teran hurting so. Her quick brain came up with a notion, and before she had time to get second thoughts, the words were tumbling off her tongue.

"Jack tells me you know one of the guys who drives for J & B." Teran's head snapped up in surprise and the old woman continued, trying her best to keep her tone and manner casual. "Do I know him?"

"I don't know. Do you know Kyle Benton?"

Gram seemed to think a minute, then nodded.

"I seem to recall that he grew up around here, but I can't say as I know much about his daily comings or goings. Is he your boyfriend?"

"I hope he still wants to be," the girl murmured fervently while hope lit the dark eyes, and Gram was hard pressed to keep her pleased smile from touching her face. Instead, she frowned and tried to sound surprised.

"Well, good heavens, dear. What could a sweet girl like you do that would chase him away?"

Biting her lip while a blush stained her cheeks, Teran decided that Gram, like Kyle, deserved a certain amount of honesty if they were to respect each other. Taking a deep breath, she started with telling the old woman about their meeting, their strange semi-courtship (leaving out only the sexual nature of their nights), the trip to Atlanta—and the man from her past who had forced her to change her name and hide in Benny's secluded house in order to save her from certain death. As the flood of words dried up, Gram gave the girl a look of such sympathy that Teran was unable to hold the spectacled gaze, tipping her head to hide her tears.

"And Jack hasn't given you any word of him since you've been here?"

Teran's slow, silent negative response, made without lifting her head, brought a heavy frown to the old woman's face. Half to herself, she muttered "I see no reason at all for that."

"I think Jack believes that he's protecting me, but I worry about Kyle," came Teran's wistful answer, revealing a wisdom beyond her years. Gram offered a tissue, still frowning heavily. The girl's emotional ties to her erstwhile suitor were evident to the older woman, and she silently swore to have a private talk with Jack as Teran wiped at her moist eyes and gave a forlorn sniff.

"I'm sure your boyfriend will be back just as soon as he can, sweetheart. I'll see if maybe I can't find out if he's all right so you can quit worrying."

The smile of gratitude that brightened Teran's eyes was mirrored by a more self-satisfied one on Gram's. Ever since this slip of a girl had been brought to Benny's in the rented van, she had wanted to find out whether or not the girl meant anything to her grandson. The girl obviously thought well of him, and all it would take was dialing a phone number and putting in a special digital code to find out for sure.

Excusing herself to go use the phone in the office behind a closed door, Gram left Teran alone. Teran sadly looked around the airy entry hall, wondering if Kyle could ever be comfortable in such a place as this. It seemed she could almost see him standing at the railing in front of the master bedroom, giving her a smile.

Sighing softly, she closed her eyes and pictured him as she knew him best—within touching range with his eyes soft and emerald green, like a deep mountain pool she had seen once in a travel brochure. She opened her eyes to find Gram smiling at her, the ancient eyes behind the color distorting bifocals twinkling merrily.

The moment was interrupted by the ringing of a doorbell, and Teran nearly jumped out of her skin. No one had used the doorbell for the entire length of her stay, and the acoustics of the entry hall proved to be surprisingly good.

Gram gave a soft chuckle and went to the door while Teran placed her hand over her racing heart, feeling like a total idiot. She turned her chair to face the door just as Gram pulled the door open to admit four trick-or-treaters, who were followed in by a haggard-looking Kathleen.

It took Teran only a moment to identify Princess Leia (who appeared to have ducked her head in a bucket of bleach), Chewbacca (whose bright blue eyes in the furry full-head mask were so much like Jack's it was startling), and Han Solo and Luke Skywalker (who stood exactly the same height and wore the same face, but different clothes).

They all smiled after giving the invalid the once-over and Kathleen introduced them as they came forward.

"The fur rug is J.J., the oldest at eleven. The twins are Chris and Danny, good luck telling them apart any other time than now, and they're nine. Then there's Kitty. She's five."

"And Daddy's little sweetheart," chimed in J.J., muffled by the fur. Teran giggled while Kathleen threw him a "Mommy frown".

"I'm sure she is." Teran's soft voice and gentle smile brought all the kids over to gently shake her good hand with a polite "pleased to meet you", then they were off with yells, whoops, and squeals. Kathleen rolled her eyes and shook her head.

"Benny's gonna rue the day he let those kids get away with all this running around in the house." She sighed, turning away to set down her coat and purse. Gram frowned a moment, then her eyes gleamed as they dropped to Teran.

"He'll understand some day, when he has kids of his own."

Teran accepted the squeeze of Kathleen's hand in greeting, then turned to watch the kids run, pretending to be in a fight with invisible Stormtroopers. Kathleen gave another dramatic sigh.

"I shoulda known it was a mistake to rent that movie for 'em." Her exaggerated Maine drawl made Teran giggle, then Kathleen tipped her head toward the kitchen. "We'll let the kids wear themselves out some and have a little woman talk. You with me, Gram?"

In no time, Teran forgot her previous blues, as Kathleen and Gram started swapping gossip, so it seemed, about some of the locals. At first, the tales were fairly believable, but soon they were such tall tales that all Teran could do was laugh until her sides ached.

In her bed some time later, with her eyes slowly sinking shut, Teran couldn't hold back the smile that softly creased her face. If this was what it was like to belong to a real family, she wanted to be in one for the rest of her life!

Chapter Four

The removal of Teran's casts the week after Halloween was given holiday status by her small family group, and the affair was celebrated with dinner at Greenville's finest restaurant. After an evening of laughter that included the hired nurse who had been with Teran every night since her arrival at Benny's, Teran was tucked up in bed with a happy smile on her face, scratching all the places that had itched for weeks with no relief.

The next morning, the hard part was begun as soon as the physical therapist walked through the door. Teran's muscles, weakened from the weeks of inactivity, had to be gently stretched and then exercised in order to regain their former strength. All through November, Teran saw the therapist twice a week and worked with either Gram or Kathleen as spotters on the weight machine the other days. Shortly before Thanksgiving, Teran was almost her old self again and generously offered to have the traditional feast at Benny's, where they would have plenty of room at the big dining room table.

Early Thanksgiving morning, after putting the turkey in the oven and preparing all the side dishes so that the rest of the dinner would be a matter of turning on a few burners, Teran and Gram lit a fire in the big fieldstone fireplace. They had just settled down to enjoy a little relaxation when the phone rang. Gram picked it up and, with a strange smile lighting her face, handed the receiver to Teran with a slightly surprised sounding "It's for you".

"Hi, Angel Face," said a deep voice at the far end of the line. "How're you doing?"

Teran's eyes lit up and Gram found a quick excuse to leave the room. She didn't return until Teran had placed the receiver back on the cradle and sat staring off at the distant mountains with a bright, happy smile. Seeing the dreamy look in the dark eyes, Gram allowed herself a very smug smile, then schooled her features into a look of vague disinterest before she brought the girl back to the real world.

"Was it something good?"

Teran's happiness was very nearly contagious as she turned her glowing gaze to the older woman.

"It was Kyle," she said, her voice fairly vibrating with the depth of her emotion. "He said he might be able to get some time off around Christmas to come see me."

"Well, that's wonderful!" Gram exclaimed, her own voice revealing a wealth of emotion that spoke of her pleasure that her grandson's house guest was so obviously in love. "You make sure you bring him by and introduce us, okay?"

Teran nodded happily, then jumped to her feet and did a fair imitation of skipping out to the door in response to the doorbell. Emma and Junior, closely followed by Jack and Kathleen with all four kids in tow, carried in the portions of the meal that they had promised to bring, and the silence of Benny's house was destroyed by the cheerful whoops and yells of the playing children. Even Teran joined in the game from time to time, sneaking up on an unsuspecting child and attacking with tickles from behind, hiding behind a door to pop out and scare someone, or simply sitting in a chair as if taking a break and suddenly hooking a finger into a belt loop as a child went by to hinder a planned escape.

Jack, used to seeing the quiet, almost melancholy Teran who had inhabited the wheelchair, seemed startled at first, turning to Gram with a question in his eyes. The old woman's smile was sly as she answered his unvoiced question in her best "oh, by the way" voice.

"Her boyfriend called this morning to wish her a Happy Thanksgiving. Seems to have perked up her spirits a little."

Jack's surprised face even got a laugh out of Kathleen as she leaned toward him and whispered in his ear, "You didn't really expect him to avoid contact forever, did you?"

Jack sighed and appeared very disgruntled, then finally growled, "I just hope he doesn't get her killed."

Teran, totally unaware of the conversation, placed a kiss on Kitty's cheek and laughed as the little girl pretended at first to be disgusted, then gave a pert little grin and winked one bright blue eye. Her first Thanksgiving with a real family was going to be the best Thanksgiving ever!

Chapter Five

Teran looked at the calendar one bright morning on her way to the exercise room and came to a stop with a gasp. It was one week before Christmas and she didn't have a single present to give, nor any money to get anything with! A frown marred her pretty face as she stepped down the two steps that had been under the ramp and set her towel down on the weight bench. There didn't seem to be any help for it! She would have to ask Jack to let her borrow some money and provide a way into town so that she could have something under the tree for each member of her "adopted" family!

Deep in thought, she started doing her morning stretch routine, closing her eyes in relief as a particularly sore spot suddenly released in her lower back, unaware as she stretched her legs apart in an inverted "V" and bent her head toward the floor that she had gained a very interested audience of one.

"Now there's a sight that's worth coming home to," rasped a deep bass voice, and Teran's eyes popped open to see the man who stood at the top of the stairs upside-down.

Her eyes widened in surprise and she sprang upright with a snap, turning to stare as a name came to her lips.

"Kyle?" she whispered, and an all too familiar smile appeared in the dark auburn beard. In the next instant, she was in his arms, her squeal of joy echoing in the exercise room, and Kyle was kissing her deeply, holding her like he'd never let her go again. Teran came slowly down to earth as her feet came into contact with the step leading to the main house, drawing away from Kyle to look at his dear face, tears streaming unnoticed down her cheeks.

She brushed a hand along his cheek as he did the same to her, smiling as he whispered, "God, I missed you, Angel."

Her response had a bittersweet quality that made Kyle's heart jump.

"I missed you, too." Her eyes caught his and she smiled. "I love you, Kyle. I think I always have."

Kyle couldn't come up with anything to say, so he told her how happy he was in his kiss. The kiss deepened as passions flared, and before he could think, Kyle had Teran in his arms and was heading for the stairs. As he shouldered open the door at the top of the stairs, Teran suddenly pulled back with a gasp.

"No, Kyle, not in here! This is Benny's room!" At her words, Kyle stopped for a moment, confused.

"But—," he began, but she kissed him and pointed toward the guest room.

"My bed is down there."

"Well my bed is much closer," he growled in return, and cut off any questions with a searing kiss that set her soul aflame. The door closed softly behind them as he bore her to the bed and lay her across it. Like on their first night, he undressed her with great tenderness, but soon he was shaking with the effort of holding his towering passion in check. With a sweet smile, Teran took over, making quick work of his remaining clothes and pressing warmly against him, her own body aching with desire.

The first round was over almost before it began, but Kyle soon initiated a second, growing hard again before he withdrew from her. Teran found herself hopelessly adrift, clinging to Kyle's strong form as a drowning swimmer clings to a life preserver. Again they climbed to the loftiest heights, and it was only when they were laying together in the ashes of the flame that she realized something was different.

"Kyle?"

"Hmmm." He was almost asleep, having driven all night to get home to his beloved.

"Why is there something sticky on my thigh?"

Kyle's eyes popped open and his muscles stiffened beneath her. Furiously, he searched his memory and couldn't recall stopping to pull out a foil packet for either time that they had just made love! Like a child caught doing something wrong, he gave her a sidelong glance, his voice soft and vaguely apologetic.

"Oops?"

Teran pretended to be angry even as she saw the opening to spring her surprise, her voice coming out in a gruff growl like Kyle often used.

"Boy, I don't know about you. Here I thought I could trust you. It's a darn good thing I decided to go on the Pill anyway!"

Kyle laughed softly, relaxing again.

"So do I still need to show you the results of the STD tests I had done in Atlanta?"

Her eyes sparkling, Teran continued to pretend to be angry.

"Why, do you got chirpies or something? I hear it's untweetable."

With a playful growl, Kyle dove for her throat, tickling her neck with his beard until she begged for mercy. Ending his game with a loving kiss, he cuddled up close to her smaller form and was soon asleep. A pair of fans at the peak of the roof clicked on as a heat sensor did its job, and it was to their soft hum and Kyle's even breathing against her neck that Teran dozed off.

Chapter Six

Teran awoke some time later, disoriented for a moment as she looked up at the high ceiling and thought she heard bees. As she lifted her head, it seemed the sound was coming from the bathroom, so she pulled Kyle's shirt off the floor and tugged it over her head as she padded in to investigate.

She stopped at the door with a gasp of shock.

Kyle stood with his back to her, dressed in nothing but a towel, which was wrapped around his waist. He was looking in the mirror as he ran an electric razor over his face, and his bare feet were covered with the short curls from an earlier trimming of his beard. As she moved forward to peek at his face in the mirror, Kyle caught sight of her and his image in the mirror gave her a wink.

As she moved forward, he noticed the slight limp that remained as a reminder of the accident that had almost taken her life.

As the black stubble was shorn away, a face emerged beneath the high cheekbones that Teran had always been able to see, a face with a firm, square jaw. It was a movie star face, etched by time and ruggedly handsome, and it was only as he set the razor aside that she noticed the scar on his chin that formed a crooked cleft.

"How did you get that?" she asked, touching it as he turned to face her. "Was it over a woman?"

Kyle grinned.

"It was over Gram's piano. She put me in karate classes because I kept tripping over my own two feet."

"Did karate make you less clumsy?"

Kyle's eyes twinkled as he executed a graceful bow.

"You tell me."

He turned back to the mirror and fluffed up his still damp hair as if trying to decide what to do with it, then picked up a pair of scissors and bit his lip in concentration as he tried to judge how long his hair should be.

"What are you doing?"

Kyle turned at Teran's question and looked at her as if she'd gone crazy.

"If I want to visit Gram on our way to Bangor, I have to get this mop to a reasonable length or I'll never hear the end of it."

Teran took the scissors from his hand and pulled around a chair that rested against the wall. Settling himself into the chair, Kyle put his trust in Teran's able fingers, and got up some time later sporting a much shorter style. The back would still brush his shirt collar, but the feathery layering along the sides and back gave him an air of sophistication.

Watching his face carefully to catch his reaction, Teran was rewarded by a bright smile.

"Not bad at all. Gram will probably still think it's too long, but I like it. Thanks, Angel."

His gentle kiss touched off warmer emotions, but Kyle withdrew with a wry smile twitching at the corners of his mouth, making deep dimples appear in his cheeks. Teran gave a blissful sigh and decided she liked this beardless look, too, for it allowed her to see the tiny nuances of expression that she had missed before. She followed him into the bedroom, and when he went straight to the closet and swung it open, she found herself suddenly frowning, unable to put two and two together.

"I thought this place belonged to a guy named Benny," she began, and Kyle looked up, a pair of chinos over one arm and his hand on a nice knit sport shirt.

"Who told you that?" he rumbled, releasing the shirt and taking a cream pullover sweater from a shelf in the closet instead.

Teran answered with one word.

"Everybody."

Kyle frowned as he turned around, then understanding of a sort brightened his look slightly. He rubbed his chin in thoughtful consideration.

"I wonder...." He thought for a moment more, then a question came to his lips. "Has Jack ever told you his full name?"

It was Teran's turn to look thoughtful before she shook her head.

"No. The only last name I've heard is Gram's."

Kyle shook his head as another wry smile touched his features. Teran watched, fascinated by the newly revealed expressions of his handsome face. Settling on the bed and pulling her down on his lap, Kyle began to explain.

"Well, Jack's full name is Jeffrey Michael Jackson III. Since his grandfather was Jeff and his father was Junior, they started off calling him Michael. Then the Jackson Five got famous and since he didn't like being teased about being a black singer, he started using Jack."

Teran giggled, enjoying the tale.

"When I moved in with Gram after my folks died, Jack and I both had this thing about Jack Benny, so since my last name was Benton, which could be shortened to Ben—"

"You went around as Jack and Benny!" Teran finished, suddenly seeing the light. She looked around and saw the house as she'd never seen it before. "So you're the eccentric friend who built this house with his bare hands!"

Kyle grinned.

"Well, I did have plenty of help."

Chapter Seven

Gram opened the door that afternoon with a beaming smile for the pair she found on her porch. In the sweater and chinos, with his hair shortened and his beard trimmed away, Kyle looked like some seaman of old just come back from the sea. At his side, in a nice dress under her coat and with her dark hair pulled back in a ponytail, Teran was femininity personified, her petite beauty the perfect accent to his tall, handsome frame. Gram gave the big man a once-over glance and, for the first time, Teran saw her left eyebrow lift behind the frame of the bifocals.

"Well, hello young man. You must be this Kyle Benton this young lady has told me about."

Kyle gave an exaggerated sigh.

"Et tu, Gram?" he teasingly quoted, and the old woman's eyes twinkled merrily, knowing full well without being told that the cat was finally out of the bag. She turned and took both of Teran's hands in hers, her green gaze apologetic as she drew the girl into the house.

"Don't judge me too harshly, little one. Jack didn't want you to get too attached to the place, just in case you had to be moved again before your stepfather was caught." She bent a critical eye on her grandson. "He has been caught, hasn't he?"

Kyle smiled and nodded, closing the inside door behind him.

"We set a trap for him in Northern Colorado just a couple of weeks ago. I stuck around until he was extradited to Nebraska to stand trial, then drove home as fast as the law allows."

Teran looked up at Kyle in some confusion.

"Why would he stand trial in Nebraska? My mother died in California."

Taking her shoulders and gently guiding her toward the couch in Gram's living room, Kyle sounded almost apologetic. "Angel, I think you'd better sit down."

Looking from Gram to Kyle and back again, seeing them exchange a look that spoke volumes, Teran prepared herself for the worst. Settling beside her on the couch and taking her hands in his, Kyle explained all he'd learned about her stepfather—and the woman and girl he had beaten to death in Nebraska before moving to California.

Teran's face went deathly pale, which sent Gram scurrying out to the kitchen to make a bracing cup of tea. When the older woman returned, she sat close to the girl and kept a critical eye on Teran as she slowly sipped the tea and regained her color. Then the spectacled green eyes traveled the full length of Kyle's form and her observation came out as a wry comment.

"Seems you didn't suffer any from the chase."

Teran smiled softly.

"Of course not. He's Superman."

Gram snorted.

"That's what he thinks!" She grumbled, her tirade softened by a slight smile and a gleam of mischief in the ancient eyes. "Just let him keep his hair long like this and I'll show him that this old woman can still make it hard for him to sit down, Superman or no Superman."

Kyle rolled his eyes at the thinly veiled insult to his hair style while Teran giggled joyfully, enjoying this interaction between the pair. It was easy to see that they cared about each other despite the insults, and there was a warmth in the room that had nothing to do with the temperature the furnace kept the place at. Teran decided once again that she really enjoyed being part of this extended family.

Chapter Eight

Kyle and Teran went on a massive Christmas buying spree on reaching Bangor, purchasing presents for all the relatives on a seemingly never-ending supply of credit cards from Kyle's wallet. When Teran finally got up the nerve to ask about them, Kyle shrugged.

"My Dad left me an inheritance that I gained control of when I turned twenty-five. So did my Grampa Godfried and my Grampa Benton. My trust funds all fell into my lap the year after I got out of the service. Gram and Jack suggested investing, so I gave them power of attorney over the investment money, and Jack got me all these cards to use whenever I need anything. He just takes care of the bills when they come in and I'm usually careful not to spend too much."

Teran grinned, imagining Jack's face when he got next month's bills.

"At least you can be honest and say all this spending was for the holiday."

Kyle's return grin, with his whole face open to Teran's gaze, revealed a charmingly devilish side to his nature as he, too, imagined the look on Jack's face on seeing how much had been spent. Never before had Kyle gone quite so crazy on Christmas, but then, he'd never had Teran at his side, looking thoroughly enchanted as she wandered through the stores. It was when he noticed that her limp was becoming more pronounced as she tired that he had an idea. Perhaps he should add one more unexpected expense.

"Do you want to stay in a motel instead of driving back to Greenville tonight?" Kyle asked, then waited while memories of the last time they had been in a motel room together brought a sensual smokiness to Teran's eyes. At her answering nod, the lady-killer smile made an appearance, turning Teran's knees to rubber. Devastating enough when most of his face was hidden by the heavy beard, it was sheer poison when she could see the way small dimples appeared at the corners of his mouth as those corners curved slowly upward. His gentle kiss as he led her to the bank of phones was quick, yet filled with promise of things to come.

As soon as he had the name of a motel that still had vacancies, Kyle drove them to it, his hand riding protectively at Teran's waist as they went in to register as Mr. and Mrs. Benton. Giggling like kids, they hauled all their purchases up to the room and spread them out across one double bed, going over their shopping list and noting who they had left. Each tried to ignore the other bed for as long as possible, but it wasn't long before a chance glance became a gaze, a chance touch became a caress. It was Teran who initiated the first kiss, prompting Kyle to lift her slim form and bear her gently to the empty bed as if she was nothing more than thistle down.

Christmas was forgotten as they soared on the wings of love, and they fell asleep still entwined, not caring that neither had clean clothes to start the morning in.

Chapter Nine

Late the next night, sitting next to Kyle on the sofa in front of the living room fireplace, Teran found that she couldn't help but enjoy the view as she stared at her handsome lover. When they met in New York, he had been nice enough to look at, but nothing like the way he looked now. Before, he had looked like an aging biker. Now, he looked like a businessman on vacation.

Turning to find her staring at him with a soft smile playing across her face, Kyle gave her a tender smile of his own, then had a sudden brainstorm. Without a word, he took her hand and pulled her off the sofa. She tried to ask where they were going, but Kyle shushed her with a finger on his lips, then gave her a devilish grin. He led the way to the library, where he popped open a hidden panel and flipped a switch.

Teran gasped as small lights, built into a recessed groove along the edge of each step on the spiral staircase, lit up.

The lights were of such a small wattage that they only revealed the steps, leaving the rest of the room in darkness, and the effect was like something out of a fairy tale. The airy, ethereal spiral rose out of the center of the darkness until it disappeared into more darkness. Still holding Teran's hand, Kyle started moving forward again, putting her in front of him when they reached the stairs so that she would see what awaited them at the top of the second flight without anything to block her view.

Kyle knew immediately when Teran was able to see into the top of the former silo, because she stopped on the stairs with a gasp. Grinning to himself, he gave her a light slap on the rump to get her started again and did his best to sound grumpy.

"Come on, get moving. Haven't got all day!"

Teran moved, climbing the last few steps so she could gaze up at the stars that seemed close enough to touch. It seemed that the whole rounded roof had opened to allow her an unimpeded view of the major constellations. Kyle smiled at her obvious awe, gently moving her over to where a huge beanbag waited for them and pulling her down on it with him.

"That's the North Star." He said, pointing. Then he named off other constellations for her, pointing them out and telling tales about some of his favorites. When he got to Orion, he frowned, then sighed deeply.

"Darn. A light's out on Orion's belt!"

It took a moment for Teran to fully understand what Kyle had said. When she did, she sat up and took a closer look at the "stars". Tiny lights set in the ceiling, each blinking to its own beat, made up the "star-filled sky" she had been gazing at. She wanted to be angry at having been tricked, but when she thought of how much time it must have taken Kyle to place each light in just the right place, she could only feel awe at his patience. She leaned back against him with a giggle.

"When Jack and Kathleen called you eccentric, I didn't know what they meant. I think I'm starting to understand."

She left her sentence hanging and giggled again as Kyle laughed and kissed the top of her head.

"I just had too much time on my hands before Jack had the idea about the trucking company."

Teran frowned, confused.

"You mean J & B?"

Kyle grinned, realizing there was still much for him to explain about his life.

"Jackson & Benton Trucking. Jack's idea, with the initial financial investment coming out of my inheritance. Since Jack has his Master's Degree in Business, it was only logical that he be the one to run the business while I did the manual labor."

Teran said nothing for quite some time, simply staring up at the "stars" overhead for a long moment. So softly that Kyle had to strain to hear her, she finally spoke.

"Just when I thought I knew everything about you, I find out that all I've seen is the tip of the iceberg."

With a heavy sigh, Kyle told her about his colorful life, starting with the woman who gave him birth leaving both him and his father when the infant Kyle was only three months old. He told of his stepmother, who was the only mother he knew until the age of eleven, and of the ongoing battle with his birth mother, Darlene Godfried Benton LaCasce, over the will that left him the three trust funds that only Gram was able to touch until he turned 25.

When he started telling her things she already knew, she stopped him with a gentle kiss that soon deepened into something much more satisfying.

Chapter Ten

Early in the morning on Christmas Eve, Kyle awoke Teran with a kiss, prodding her out of bed and telling her only to dress warmly, his bright smile and sparkling eyes speaking of his excitement. As soon as they were both dressed, he hurried her down the stairs for a quick, light breakfast, then herded her out toward the garage, which sat a little to one side of the house on a slightly flatter portion of the hilltop. There, he picked up a lightweight chain saw and a large coil of rope, reached into his pocket and pulled out a key, then led the way to where a snowmobile sat off to one side and pulled off the dust cover. Its make, Arctic Cat, was written across the side in fancy letters, and it seemed to be just waiting for someone to come and play.

Teran had never seen such a thing up close, and her first thought was of her motorcycle. She studied the controls on the handle while Kyle watched her, grinning, then handed her the key. Without a word, he reached down and grabbed the handles at the ends of the skis and pulled the machine out into the snowy driveway.

"Start her up."

Teran's eyes lit up and she did as he suggested, smiling happily as the beast sprang to life with a roar. Almost before she knew it, she was on the seat with Kyle sliding on behind, his breath warm on her ear as he gave her instructions. The machine responded to her touch and they started off across the snow, Kyle lightly holding her waist with one hand while he balanced the chain saw across his knees with the other, the coil of rope slung over one shoulder.

Teran laughed as they roared across the hilly fields, her breath blowing back in smoky plumes. Kyle heard and smiled, glad that she enjoyed his little surprise. Making a mental note to buy her a snowmobile of her own, he got down to business, searching the woods they passed for the right tree to put in the entry hall. When he found it, he directed Teran toward it, pleased when she followed his every direction without question, realizing what they were doing as soon as she saw the massive fir at the edge of the woods.

Seated on the snowmobile, Teran watched while Kyle approached the tree, looked at it carefully from every angle, and then started the chain saw. In no time, the tree was down, and Kyle took the rope and started lashing down the branches to limit any damage that could occur while, at the same time, preparing the tree to go through the door back at the house. Teran helped as much as she could, but for the most part just stood and watched in awe.

When he was satisfied that the tree was as he wanted it, Kyle directed Teran to drive the snowmobile to where he could tie the ends of the rope to it. By the time all was ready for the return trip, Teran was starting to shiver and found that she welcomed Kyle's warm body against her back as they slowly made their way back to the house on the hill. Once there, she pulled up in front of the door just as Kyle instructed, then went to hold the door open while he untied the tree and dragged it in.

Next came a portion that Kyle had prepared the day before without Teran's knowledge. From his den, he brought out a large tarp, which he spread on the floor and rolled the tree onto to prevent the snow from melting all over the floor. Then he retrieved a box clearly marked "Christmas Tree" from a closet in the entry hall and set it in front of Teran's feet.

"Would you unpack this while I untie the rope?" he asked gently, and Teran happily nodded, thrilled to have Kyle include her in something that appeared to be a very personal part of his holiday. In quiet companionship, they worked side by side.

Teran watched in awe as Kyle revealed another of his little eccentric additions to his house, flipping open a hidden door in a part of the paneling to push two matching buttons on a four-button panel. There was a soft humming noise as two motors started lowering down two specially-made hooks attached to twin sets of pulleys, obviously installed for the task of standing up the large trees that Kyle liked to have in his magnificent entry hall every Christmas. At Kyle's request, Teran placed the star at the top of the tree and carefully attached unbreakable ornaments to the upper branches so that they wouldn't fall off during the lifting or lowering, but could be easily untied once the season was over and the tree was taken back down. He, meanwhile, tied two ropes in amongst the upper branches and attached the hooks to them.

With great ceremony, he escorted Teran to the panel of buttons and offered her the opportunity to raise the first Christmas tree that they would enjoy as a couple. She did so while Kyle did something he had always wanted to do but had never been able to: see that the tree got properly placed without having to keep running to the buttons to do adjustments. In no time, the tree was standing in the middle of the floor, its guide wires in plain sight, yet invisible to the girl who stood staring at it with starry eyes, thinking that, even with only a portion of it decorated, it was the most beautiful Christmas tree she had ever seen.

Chapter Eleven

Teran awoke on Christmas morning to find herself alone in the big bed. She listened carefully for a clue to Kyle's whereabouts, but no sound disturbed the perfect silence. Taking her robe off a chair by the bed, she set out to find Kyle, starting with the bathroom.

It was empty.

Thinking that maybe he had gone down to light a fire in the fireplace, she started for the bedroom door, but a glimpse of something on the balcony made her turn and go to the glass doors instead. What she saw made her stand and stare in wonder.

Kyle stood in the snow wearing nothing but sweatpants and a pair of sneakers, doing his morning mantra. His breath came out of his lips and nose as streams of smoke and his skin was covered with goose-bumps, but he seemed oblivious to the cold as his slow routine stretched every muscle in his body. She watched, entranced, until he finished and made his way back to the doors, moving as if it was a fine June day instead of a frosty December morning.

A lopsided grin told her when he saw her standing there, and as he slid the door open, he bent and gave her a quick kiss, his lips as cold as ice.

"Merry Christmas, Angel." He murmured, gliding off to the bathroom with an almost-silent tread.

Teran stared after him, wondering if such strange behavior should be taken as a warning for her to leave. Could a man who did such things as standing half-naked on a balcony in December be truly sane? Her doubts overcoming her love momentarily, she made a vow to get away from him the moment he showed any signs of becoming violent, then started for the door to get some clean clothes from her room and take a shower in the guest suite's bathroom. She had only gone a few steps when strong arms wrapped around her and warm breath touched her neck.

"Take a shower with me?" Kyle asked, his husky voice making her shiver with longing. With a half-smile, Teran finally admitted to herself that she could deny him nothing and gave her answer as a silent nod. Giggles trailed them as Kyle lifted her into his arms to carry her into the bathroom.

Cars started pulling into the driveway as soon as they finished dressing, the doorbell ringing as Kyle was tying his shoe and Teran was starting to put on makeup. With a wide grin, Kyle gave her a quick kiss and hurried to the front door, throwing it open and greeting Gram with a boisterous bellow that made Teran smile at herself in the mirror. Using just enough makeup to give herself a cheery glow, Teran soon joined them, opening the door when Jack and Kathleen's car was followed into the drive by Junior and Emma's. Bringing up the rear was an oddly-familiar, though freshly painted camper with a big red bow tied on the front.

Kyle looked as innocent as he could until the camper pulled to a stop, then Jack jumped out with a loud "Merry Christmas from the owners of Jack & Benny Trucking!"

"That means the transfer up here from down south and the new paint job come from all of us, dear." Gram commented as she passed Teran to help unload the cars.

Kyle grinned.

"Every adult here holds shares in the company, and the kids have some in trust for when they're old enough to help make decisions." Having explained the situation as much as he felt necessary, he went to help with the unloading of the presents, joking with Kathleen about how much they'd packed into the car's trunk.

In addition to the presents, they all carried in some form of food to contribute to their traditional Christmas potluck brunch, either oven ready or ready to serve. While the uncooked food baked and coffee brewed, presents were placed under the tree, all to the cacophony of many voices carrying on several independent conversations and the squeals of the children as they played with the toys Santa had left for them with their stockings. It was a big change from the quiet she had enjoyed for so long, but Teran found she felt right at home, especially when the master of the house brushed by and gave her a quick, gentle kiss or a light, loving touch.

For the second time, Teran was made aware of the reason why there was such a big table in the dining room. There was plenty of room for food, people, and even a few empty seats for future additions to the family. As if he could see her thoughts, Kyle squeezed her hand as she looked at the empty places, then leaned forward to whisper in her ear, having kept her close to his side for just such quiet exchanges.

"I'm always looking toward the future." His words seemed to bring everything into focus while bringing a warm glow to her heart. Without actually saying so, Kyle seemed to be telling her that he wanted her to be a part of that future, and she could think of nothing she wanted more. As she had sat watching the exchanges between the family members, she had come to realize that, despite his occasionally odd behavior, Kyle had always been very polite and easygoing, things that her stepfather had never been even on his best days. Why deny herself the man of her dreams because of fears of a man who could no longer hurt her, and who had, in fact, been put in the hands of the proper authorities due to the efforts of the man at her side?

Her dark eyes glowed with her happiness, and as Gram watched her grandson with his pretty little house guest, she felt happiness swell in her old heart. Here was the woman Kyle had always described when he spoke of the type of woman he wished to marry, easy on the eyes, yet sweet and gentle with no harsh words for anyone. Even when she had been going through the pain of the first few days of physical therapy, Teran had called on some inner source of strength rather than say anything that might offend the elderly woman who had held her hand. Gram couldn't imagine a better match for her grandson.

After brunch was finished, they followed the children out to the tree. All the other grown-ups found seats, but Teran found herself surrounded by the children and led to a blanket that had been spread on the floor for the younger members of the family, allowing Kyle to slip away from her side. So that she wouldn't notice he was missing, they clamored for her to sing Christmas Carols with them, and she went through every one she knew with them calling for another the minute she stopped. It wasn't until they heard the sound of jingling bells that the children quieted, and then only for a moment.

"It's Santa!" J.J. shouted, then helped Kitty to her feet while the twins scrambled to race for the door. It was yanked open by Chris, then all the children were hopping with excitement when a tall, broad-shouldered Santa Claus pushed through the door.

Teran giggled with delight as "Santa's" bright green eyes traveled around the room until they found her, then there was the suggestion of a grin beneath the fake white beard as her gave her a wink.

"Ho, ho, ho," the Santa with the oddly lumpy-looking stomach rumbled, and the children pretended not to recognize the deep bass voice.

"Hi Santa."

"Come in Santa."

"Can I get you something to drink, Uncle—I mean, Santa?"

The adults did their best to stifle giggles at the last remark from a rosy-cheeked Kitty, who earned herself a tickle from Santa as he rejected her offer, but thanked her for being thoughtful. She was the first to sit on Santa's lap to receive a special present, which she opened with great excitement.

It was a beautiful doll in a Mexican dress, and Kitty's obvious joy brought a smile to Teran's face. She looked up into dancing green eyes and returned his wink just before her attention was pulled away from "Santa" by Kitty, eager to share the beauty of her new doll with the newest member of the family.

Chris soon joined Teran on the blanket to show her a game involving Indian lore he'd been given, followed by Danny who showed her a book on bugs and a special container to catch and examine them in. J.J. brought up the rear with a logic puzzle that he showed off quickly before shushing the younger kids to allow them to hear what the adults said and see what they got.

Teran couldn't restrain her giggles as first Kathleen, then Jack, and on up through to Gram stepped up to the chair, each in their turn, and gamely sat on Santa's knee. Jokes a-plenty were tossed around throughout the proceedings, and Teran giggled uncontrollably, right up until Santa pinned his green gaze on her and called her to his knee, the last one in the house to be called. She smiled shyly as she found herself the brunt of the good-natured teasing, but had to bite her lip to control any outward display of trembling when the all-too-familiar hands guided her into place.

Despite his soft, padded stomach, his leg was still as hard as a rock, and she muttered a comment so softly only "Santa" heard it.

"Next year, you need to pad your thighs."

The green eyes definitely twinkled, but Teran couldn't see the smile behind the fake beard. His humor was evident in his voice, however, as he continued with the act.

"Teran, I understand you have been a very good girl this year."

Teran couldn't resist the wisecrack that came to her lips.

"Define good."

Deep chuckles erupted from the men in chorus with giggles from the women and children. "Santa" sighed as if his unending patience was wearing thin and slipped his fingers into the top of his suit. He pulled out an envelope with her name written across it in fine gold calligraphy and placed it into her waiting hands. With one final, searching look into the deep green pools, she opened the envelope and looked inside.

Several folded papers lay inside, and Teran pulled them out, noting as she did so that the number 1 had been written on the outside of one paper in pencil. The green eyes gave nothing away when she glanced into them while unfolding the marked paper. When her eyes returned to the page, they opened wide in surprise and her gasp was clearly audible in the waiting silence.

"My real birth certificate!"

The copy was too crisp to be anything but a new one, and the official seal of California made it legal beyond a shadow of a doubt. The next page in the stack was a new copy of her social security card, followed by a Georgia driver's license, issued to her with Bubba's street address and the picture from the license she'd carried as Tanya LaMonte, but with her given name on it. Hooked to this with a paper clip was a Maine license application with all the information typed in, ready for her to take to the nearest DMV office to get a Maine license with the office address for Jack & Benny Trucking, Inc listed as her residence. The registration to the camper she'd lived in had even been transferred to Teresanna Montesallo with all the paperwork for it typed up as well, so that she could register the camper in Maine the same day that she got her license changed.

Last, but by no means least, was a GED test date announcement telling her the date and time that she should arrive to find out what courses she would need to get her diploma. When she looked up into the shining green eyes that watched her, she was still in shock, but her eyes filled with tears when a familiar husky voice murmured "I give you back your name for Christmas as well as freedom from that monster you've been running from."

Without a word, she wrapped her arms around his neck and gave him a hug that thanked him more than any words ever could. When she could finally speak past the lump in her throat, she thanked him again and again, oblivious to the smiling faces that watched them—right up until the front door slammed open and a strange woman strode into the room as if she owned the place.

She seemed to be an older version of Kathleen except for her hair, which was a deep, auburn color similar to Kyle's. Her clothes under her open fur coat, though tastefully cut, were much too dressy for the casual group and in a bright, attention-grabbing shade of red that made Teran wish she was wearing sunglasses. With an oddly triumphant smile, she pulled off a pair of sunglasses that matched her outfit and revealed the same green eyes sported by Gram, Kathleen and Kyle. The only difference was the cynical look in the newcomer's eyes, so different from the warmth shown by the others.

"Hello Darlene." Kyle rumbled, and although she couldn't see his face behind the beard, Teran could tell that he was angry by the way his muscles tightened beneath her. The lady in red gave a dramatic sigh.

"Can't you call me Mother just once, Kyle, sweetie?" The lightness of her tone made it seem that her words were meant to be something of a joke, but no one seemed amused.

"What do you want this time, Darlene?" Gram asked, the sharpness of her tone surprising Teran. Whoever this woman was, it seemed no one in the room was particularly happy to see her. Darlene seemed oblivious to this fact, letting her coat drop off her shoulders as she came forward, obviously intending to stay awhile.

"I just wanted to come by and wish my family a Merry Christmas and introduce myself to the young lady I've been hearing about in town." Her cold gaze passed insultingly over Teran, seeming to rip her clear to the bones and find her lacking.

Beneath her buttocks, Kyle's leg stiffened even more as he fought to control his towering rage at the insult. When her inspection was done, Darlene gave a tight, chilly grin. "Doesn't look like much more than a baby, if you ask me."

"But I'm the baby, Gram Dee!" Kitty piped in, and for just a second, Darlene's annoyance at having been interrupted showed on her face. Then she remembered that she was supposed to actually care for her grandchildren and put on the sweetest voice she could manage.

"Of course you are, darling. I just meant that she looks *extremely* young."

Teran said nothing right away, but Kyle felt her stiffen, and something deep within him snapped. For the sake of Gram, who had given birth to Darlene, he had tolerated her interference in his life in the past rather than speak his mind and risk Gram's wrath, but when she burst into his house uninvited and insulted the woman he loved, it was too much!

He opened his mouth to speak, but Teran beat him to the punch, her voice soft, yet clear as a bell.

"Why, thank you."

Darlene frowned for a moment, wondering if the girl were too much of a dunce to realize she had been insulted…then the true meaning of the words struck home: The girl had understood the insult perfectly, but was proving herself more mature than the one who had insulted her by simply refusing to take the bait in front of the children.

When her eyes returned to Teran's, the brown orbs were steady, daring the older woman to try again. For some reason, Darlene suspected the girl would win a battle of wits and relinquished, deciding to attack from a different direction instead.

"What happened to the last girl. What was her name?"

Kyle's voice was as cold as a glacier.

"I don't think *my* love life needs to be discussed in front of *YOUR* grandchildren."

Darlene's eyes narrowed at the way the words were stressed, belittling her without presenting any obvious insult, and Teran could almost feel the hatred that ran between "mother" and "son". She began to wonder why the woman had come when it was all too obvious that she wasn't welcome here.

A cold smile crossed Darlene's face as yet another tactic occurred, but Gram had heard enough. Her own eyes dangerously narrowed, she stood and confronted her only offspring.

"If you can't be civil, you aren't welcome here, Darlene. Now either behave yourself or go somewhere else for the day!" As she turned and sauntered off to the kitchen, Gram muttered, "Probably only here because no one else will have you, anyway."

Darlene flinched slightly as her mother hit the nail directly on the head. Although no one in the room knew it, she was going through her fifth divorce, and had alienated all of her former friends when she married into money and took on airs. Now her rich husband was escorting a younger woman around to all the parties and she was home alone, with no money to even give herself the treat of a dinner out. But if she were to admit that she came here in another attempt to get some of Kyle's inheritance that she insisted should have been hers…

She shuddered slightly at the thought of what they might do, but was unable to turn herself away from her ultimate goal. Forcing herself to adopt a milder demeanor, she apologized, but something in her eyes made Teran wonder what she was up to.

"Santa" left soon after, and Teran waited for Kyle to rejoin the group, but one hour passed, and then two. She was starting to worry when she looked over at Jack, who was looking at the stairs, then at his watch with worry in his eyes. It made up her mind, and she excused herself to go up into the master bedroom and make sure he was all right.

She found him where she had that morning, out on the balcony facing the mountains. He was fully dressed, but wore no coat or hat. He brought his right hand up occasionally to drink from a bottle of Vodka and grimace as it burned its way to his stomach, but otherwise was motionless in the frigid December air. Biting her lip, she slid open the glass door and cleared her throat.

Kyle turned to look at her, but it wasn't the man she knew. Fury burned in the green eyes and he looked like he would cheerfully rip her apart if she displeased him. Unconsciously, she took a step back.

"Are you coming back down to join us?"

She tried to sound cheerful and even forced a smile, but her fear was evident in her eyes and voice. Kyle was just drunk enough to miss it.

"Is *SHE* still here?"

When he said "she", his lip curved up and he almost spat the word. Teran took another step back.

"Everyone is trying to be nice to her, but it's your house. If you want her to leave—"

"I should throw her out!" His snarl, followed by a derisive snort, frightened Teran more than anything ever had in her life. Kyle didn't notice that she took another step back.

"Right! Gram would rip into me for being rude and we'd have another Christmas with no one talking to each other!"

Surprise temporarily took the place of fear in Teran's heart as she realized that it wasn't the first time Darlene had disrupted her son's Christmas. She was wondering how any woman could find it in her to turn her back on her child when she looked up to find Kyle glaring at her, his good looks marred by his fury.

"Don't even think of feeling pity for me," he growled, then took another swig off his bottle, "because if that's all that you feel for me, the door is that way."

He pointed with the bottom of the bottle, unaware of how numb the cold had made his fingers. The bottle slipped out of his grasp, heading for Teran as if he purposefully threw it at her. Before it hit the floor and shattered, she was on the move, running for the door as if the devil were after her. The last time that a bottle of liquor broke during a confrontation, she had been in the hospital for a week for "making Big Daddy throw away his fun", and she wasn't waiting to find out how long Kyle could put her in the hospital for.

Kyle's eyes went from the broken bottle of Vodka to Teran's fleeing form, and his booze-fogged brain cleared just long enough for him to register the all-out fear on her face as she tossed a glance over her shoulder while pulling open the door leading to the main house. The sudden realization that her stepfather must have been drunk sometimes when he beat her struck Kyle like a physical blow, sobering him instantly, and he moaned softly as he went after her, unable to bear the thought of chasing away the one woman whom he ever thought worthy of making his wife.

"Angel, wait!" he yelled, but the door swung shut behind her with a bang. Kyle cursed as he started after her, hoping that Jack had pulled the keys out of the camper, suspecting that her past experience was telling her to get away while she had the chance. Those who were still in the entry heard the door slam and the sound of small feet racing down the stairs, turning to see Teran's white face just before Kyle stepped into view.

His bellow filled the great hall.

"Angel, please wait! It was an accident!"

Teran kept running, unaware of the anxious looks on the faces of those she went past. Her only thought was that she had made a disastrous mistake and had to get away while she could still salvage some of her pride. She heard the thundering footsteps as Kyle raced down the stairs in pursuit and ran a little faster, pulling the door open and racing out without stopping to grab her coat.

The fierceness of Maine's December winds hit her full blast and she hugged herself for a split second, looking for a place to run. Her camper beckoned, and she was just pulling the door open when the front door opened and Kyle stepped out. She pulled the door shut and locked it, but couldn't start the camper. The keys weren't in the ignition. Instead, she tucked herself behind the passenger seat where Kyle would have a hard time seeing her and tried to deaden the sound of the painful sobs that wracked her.

It wasn't long before she heard him approach, but instead of banging on the door and demanding to be let in, he dropped his head against the side of the camper with a sigh. His voice came out soft and gentle, ripping holes in her heart as she heard the sadness in his tone.

"I'm truly sorry, Angel. I didn't throw that bottle on purpose. It slipped."

"My name isn't Angel!" she yelled back, determined to stay angry. It was the sweet talk after the violence that had made her mother repeatedly drop the charges against Big Daddy Long—and resulted in both women spending more time in the hospital than out.

Kyle sighed.

"I know that." His apology came from the bottom of his heart. "I beg your pardon, Teresanna."

At the sound of her given name falling from his lips in that soft, slightly gruff bass voice, she thought she would burst with pleasure, but she forced the pleasure back and tried to whip up her anger. She was supposed to be trying to get away from him before he beat her! She was supposed to be scared!

"I love you more than I've ever loved anyone in my life." He continued, leaning against the side of the camper and turning so that all the woman inside had to do was look in the side mirror to see the sincerity in his face. "You're my dream woman come to life, the goddess I always waited for. I've already quit smoking for you. I can quit drinking, too, if you'll just come back inside with me."

The young woman who had been living in Maine under the name Teran Hodges peeked up over the top of the camper's passenger seat and saw the face of the man on the outside. The eyes that stared out at the side of the house were filled with pain and the mobile features were solemn, with no sign of the telltale brow. As she watched, he dropped his head in defeat, looking as if his best friend had died. It was that look that changed her mind. She opened the door a tiny crack and peeked out, ready to pull the door closed and lock it again if he showed any sign of rushing her. Kyle just stood and waited, almost holding his breath.

"If you have a problem with your mother, I think you should settle it now, regardless of what Gram thinks of you."

"But you don't understand what she wants." Kyle began, then thought about how much they needed to discuss.

Glancing back at the worried faces that watched from inside, he gave them a hopeful smile and suggested to the woman he loved that he step inside to explain, just so he didn't freeze to death standing outside without a coat for the amusement of those who watched.

When they were comfortably seated, Kyle explained the trust funds to her again, and the fact that he had been left a small fortune between his two grandfathers and his father. Darlene had long insisted that she was entitled to half of what he received from his father since she had been the one who gave Kyle birth, but Gram had stood firm that if she had been meant to have it, Andrew would have left it to her. Despite the bone of contention between them, Gram would allow no other to speak poorly about her daughter.

"So why don't you just give her half of what your father's trust fund was and get rid of her? Surely she wouldn't be able to keep using that as an excuse for ruining Christmas if you just give her the money."

"And especially if it's on the condition that she never darken my door again."

Kyle's smile suddenly returned, startling Teran/Teresanna with its intensity. His fingers were gentle on her cheek as he laughed softly.

"It's so simple, I should have thought of it years ago. Give her what she wants and send her packing and she has no more excuses to keep coming back."

His quick kiss preceded a warm, thankful hug, then he continued to grin as he took her hand to lead her back into the house.

Chapter Twelve

Standing in Kyle's office for the first time, alone while he gathered those he wanted at his impromptu "meeting", a girl who had been known briefly as Teran twisted her hands nervously, wondering again and again if she was doing the right thing. When the door opened and she saw the man who stood in the doorway, however, all her doubts fled. He ushered in Gram, Darlene and Jack, then carefully closed the door behind him while he urged them all to take seats, indicating that Jack should sit at the desk facing the ladies. Jack did as he was asked, then Kyle began to ask questions like a lawyer.

"Gram, how much did my father leave me in my trust fund when he died?"

Gram frowned at Kyle, but responded with the absolute truth.

"Twenty thousand dollars."

"And Darlene, you've always insisted that you should have received half?"

Darlene grimaced as she nodded. Ten thousand may not be enough to buy her a new house, but it would see to her bills for a few months. From where he stood behind them, Kyle's smile couldn't be seen.

"Jack, can you give me a ballpark figure of how much money I have right now to give me an idea if I can swing giving my Mother—" His voice dripped with sarcasm on that word. "— $10,000?" Jack suddenly saw where this small meeting was going and pulled up a pad of paper, writing down rough figures as he named off some of Kyle's holdings in a voice that may or may not have been called a mutter. "Let's see, there's J & B, then there's K.B. Enterprises, stocks, bonds, shares," after a brief time to total his rough figures, Jack looked up at Kyle with a grin.

"I figure you're worth about a million, give or take a thousand." His clear voice brought looks of shock to Teran, Kyle and Darlene, but Gram looked smug.

"How can that be?" Kyle finally managed to stutter, staring at Jack as if his friend had lost his mind. Jack grinned.

"You gave Gram, Dad and I power of attorney over your finances when you went into the service. Did you think we'd just stick your money into a savings account and let it sit there gathering dust?"

Kyle shook his head, trying to make sense of the amount Jack said he was worth. It couldn't be, could it?

Gram saw the look on Kyle's face and felt very proud of herself. From the time he went into the service, Kyle had sent home most of his pay to help Gram keep up with her bills, unaware that she had been left more than enough money between her husband and her son-in-law to take care of her for the rest of her life. Kyle's money, plus an extra amount that Gram thought of as Kyle's "allowance", was put first into Junior's, and then into Jack's able hands, and both had invested it wisely. By the time Kyle finished his six-year stint, he could have retired to the barn house and lived comfortably for several years without worrying about paying his bills, but his eccentric behavior worsened the longer he stayed alone in the secluded house, so Gram and Jack talked him into becoming a driver for J & B.

Darlene's face went a deathly white as she realized what she'd done. She'd agreed to ten thousand when she could have asked for the money with interest. She started to open her mouth to do so when she saw Gram's scowl and changed her mind. She closed her mouth and sulked.

Kyle still had some questions.

"How did you turn so little into so much?"

Jack grinned.

"Ever since you went into the service, Gram has been giving us money to invest in your name. Dad and I invested the money Gram gave us in small things at first—stocks and CDs, mostly—with guaranteed returns for your investment. The money we made from the initial investments went back in to make more guaranteed returns, and when we started to trust ourselves, we started to invest in bigger things. We suffered a couple of minor setbacks, but for the most part, we've doubled and occasionally even tripled your investment."

Kyle sat down in a nearby chair, astounded that this had been going on and he hadn't been aware. Then another thought struck him.

"My inheritance?"

Jack grinned.

"By the time you were able to touch it, Dad and I had already begun negotiations with a couple of companies to purchase some shares."

"What kinds of companies?" Now that he was hearing this, Kyle found he needed to hear it all. Jack's grin grew wider.

"The stable kind, of course! The kinds of companies that everyone needs at some point in their life or another, many of them fairly local at first. When you dropped the inheritance in our hands and basically gave us free rein, we already had your portfolio planned. We just kept using profits to invest in other stable companies, which would then grow and make you more money." Kyle was stunned. He had been made aware that he needn't worry about his bills, but he just thought it meant that the trucking company was doing well! It seemed the trucking company was just a single bauble out of a mountain of gems!

A small hand touched his cheek and he looked up into concerned brown eyes. He smiled, just a little, and welcomed the comforting touch of the woman he loved, pulling her close as he tried to believe that what Jack was telling him was true. It seemed somehow insane to think that he had taken so little money as an initial investment and turned it into so much in just 14 years! Taking a deep breath, Kyle tried to lighten the mood. "So I guess you won't be too upset that I went a little overboard this Christmas."

Jack grinned, then started to laugh, as did Gram and Teran. Darlene sat quietly in her corner, having achieved her goal, but feeling sick, nonetheless.

Chapter Thirteen

Much later that evening, Kyle again escorted his lady to the top of the former silo, laying down on the beanbag with her to stare up at the constellations that never moved. After the storm of their emotions had passed, peace again reigned between them, and Kyle couldn't help feeling thankful for whatever it was that had prompted his lady to trust him again despite his temporary lapse. His lips found a sensitive spot behind her ear and his warm breath stirred her curls, sending shivers racing down her spine.

"Are you still sure you want to stay? I'm not just a trucker with a nice body anymore. I'm a money-grubbing millionaire with an eccentric twist."

A wry smile touched the china-doll face and lit the dark, catlike eyes.

"Are you sure you want me to stay? I'm not just an exotic dancer anymore. I'm a runaway with a violent past who lied to you from the start."

Long, strong fingers brushed her cheek, drawing her gaze up to the two emerald pools that trapped her in their depths. There was no lifted eyebrow, no hint of a smile, and the woman who had been hiding from her past in a secluded hideaway under an assumed name saw her future in the steady green gaze. Instead of being afraid of the commitment she saw there, she was oddly comforted by it, wanting nothing more than to spend her life at the side of this man whom she adored with all her heart.

Kyle, too, was greatly pleased with the events of the day. Darlene had accepted Jack's assurance that she would see a ten thousand dollar deposit in her account on the next business day, and she even signed a paper, typed up swiftly by Jack and witnessed by Junior, who was a Notary of the Public, which stated that she would refrain from any further attempt to collect money from her son.

Gram had accepted the whole arrangement with less argument than Kyle expected, patting him lightly on the back and telling him that he'd done well on her way out to send Junior in. She had reassured him repeatedly over the long afternoon that the simple solution she had fought so long seemed to be the only way they would get Darlene out of their hair, and even apologized for not seeing its benefit sooner. Kyle's eyes had dropped to the woman at his side, who had first given the solution, then stood firmly by his side as her suggestion was carried out. He would, it seemed, never have a dull moment when a woman of such spirit stood at his side.

Sighing happily, he kissed her again, and they lay late into the night staring up at the perfect, never-changing sky above and talking about what they wished to find in the future. A future they fully intended to spend together.

Epilogue

Teresanna Returns

April 7, 1996

The prosecutor in the pretrial of Marcus Longley, alias Mark Long, which would come down to the decision of the judge whether or not to continue with the charges, was just winding up its questions to its key witness, one Kyle Andrew Benton. While he fought the urge to scratch the itches under the fake beard that was glued to his face to avoid letting Marcus know what he truly looked like, Kyle appeared to all those in the small audience to be calm, cool and collected. As the defense attorney stepped forward to begin the cross-examination, Kyle's cool green eyes observed him, but showed no real emotion. Trying to be just as cool, the attorney smiled and presented his first question.

"Mr. Benton, there has been a lot of press recently about truck drivers from Maine who falsify their logs in order to make a bit more money without paying fines. Are you one of those drivers, Mr. Benton?"

Kyle never even blinked.

"No sir, I am not."

"You do realize, Mr. Benton, that you are under oath, and that, since this is just the pretrial, we can subpoena your records and match them against the deliveries you've made."

"Yes sir, I realize that."

"Will you still swear that your records are clean?"

"Yes sir."

The defense attorney frowned slightly. According to his client, the trucker should have been at least beginning to sweat by now, as Marcus had insisted that the trucker was dirty. Ignoring his feeling that something wasn't quite right, he continued with his questions.

"What exactly did you do before gaining employment with Jack & Benny Trucking, Incorporated, Mr. Benton?"

A slight smile curved Kyle's lips beneath his beard, but didn't show in his eyes.

"I was in the Navy, sir."

The defense attorney's internal alarms all started screaming for attention. His information included no mention of a service record, but then again, he hadn't investigated the witnesses very thoroughly, believing his client, only the third suspect he'd ever handled, was telling him the truth. He could almost smell the trouble that was coming from this little faux pas! He plunged on nevertheless.

"What did you do in the Navy, Mr. Benton?"

Kyle felt the smile again touch his lips as the defense attorney wiped nervously at his brow.

"I was in the Seals, sir. To tell you anything more, I would need a direct order from the President." He turned to look directly at the judge before continuing. "With no offense to Your Honor."

The judge smiled at the trucker, liking the man's style.

"No offense taken, Mr. Benton."

The defense attorney rubbed at his temple, feeling the beginnings of a migraine. This wasn't turning out to be anything even vaguely resembling a good day, and he couldn't even bring himself to look over at his client. It had become too obvious already that the man who called himself Big Daddy had told his attorney only what he felt the attorney needed to hear to form some line of defense. He didn't like the line of questions he had prepared.

"You stated that you overheard my client threatening his stepdaughter, who was, at that time, your girlfriend."

Kyle didn't hesitate.

"Yes, sir, I did. He threatened to inject an air bubble into her IV tube, which would thereby cause her to suffer a heart attack."

The defense attorney turned his back and dropped his voice to a mutter.

"I'd bet you didn't hear a thing."

Kyle grinned, finding the adolescent techniques amusing.

"On the contrary, your client was speaking much more clearly than that, although his accent is much different."

The Judge covered his amused smile with one hand, frowning at the defense attorney slightly when he managed to control himself.

"There will be no more shenanigans in my courtroom, if you please." The Judge's voice was stern, and the defense attorney swallowed hard, feeling his chances of coming anywhere near winning this pretrial slip away. It appeared that, no matter what he came up with, Marcus Longley, otherwise known as Mark Long, would be spending a lot more time in jail while awaiting the full jury trial. He would have to do a *lot* of digging that he didn't really want to do.

In order to rattle the trucker, if only to prove him a less than worthy witness, the defense attorney tried another tact.

"I understand your girlfriend was an exotic dancer, is this true?"

"Yes sir, it is." Kyle's answer was crisp and clear, but his nostrils flared slightly, suspecting he knew where the lawyer was going with this line of questioning, but not liking it at all.

"Did you ever pay your girlfriend for sex?"

Kyle's nose wrinkled slightly for just a moment, then he responded in the same cool, collected tone.

"No sir, I did not."

The look of triumph that had briefly crossed Marcus' features was replaced by a fuming anger. Of course he must have paid for it! The twit sure didn't give it away!

The attorney pressed on.

"You expect us to believe that a woman who removed her clothes in public in front of total strangers wasn't getting money on the side as a prostitute?"

"Believe whatever you wish. She was a virgin the first night we slept together and I have never paid her for her services."

His words hit a chord and Marcus drew his lips back from long, rat-like teeth in a snarl. It was bad enough to have to think that Teresanna had been in bed with this man without the knowledge that she had given the big trucker the very fruit that Marcus had longed for the most! It nearly made him forget where he was!

The lawyer, scrambling for another question that might give the Judge a reason to find this witness less than believable, glanced over his shoulder in time to see the rodent-like snarl on his client's face. A shiver ran down his spine and he had cause to question his client's sanity before Marcus realized what he was doing and settled back in his seat, once again the picture of passivity.

"I have no further questions at this time, your honor."

The defense attorney's voice sounded strained, but he tried to ignore that as well as the glare that his client was giving him as he sat back down. Kyle was allowed to leave the bench and made his way back to the seat next to Gram, who patted him on the arm and nodded, feeling her grandson had done much to help the cause. Kyle placed his hand over hers and squeezed lightly, then turned his attention back to the front of the courtroom.

The Judge had just asked whether the prosecution had more witnesses, and the prosecutor stood with a broad smile.

"Just one, your honor. The People call Teresanna Montesallo to the stand."

There was a bray of laughter from the defendant and his words were clear despite his odd vernacular.

"Ya cain't call er to the stand, ya boob! She's dead an' buried. Watched em put her under the ground in Atlanta myself!"

The defense lawyer shushed the man as the Judge glared, then the back door of the courtroom opened and a guard accompanied a small, smartly dressed young lady to the front. Her chocolate-brown hair had been drawn back into a soft chignon, which looked perfectly at home with the soft gray business-styled skirt suit she wore. A soft pink blouse gave an interesting contrast to the somber gray and brought a flush of color to her cheeks beneath the almond shaped eyes. Marcus gagged when he saw her, jumping up from the defense table with a growl of anger.

"Ya cain't be here. I saw yer coffin goin' inta the ground!"

Teresanna's only response was a confident smile as she made her way to the bench, where she was properly sworn in even as Marcus continued to protest. Seeing the prosecutor step forward to begin the questioning, Marcus finally quieted, if only because he was interested in hearing what his traitorous stepchild had to say, determined even at this late date to see her buried rather than allow his violent behavior toward her to come to light. If he could just get the Judge to set some sort of bail so that he could get his chance before the actual jury trial.

The prosecutor smiled at Teresanna as she took her seat, having already assured her that she would only have to tell the truth. After the lies she had been forced to use in her past, she was only too ready to tell the whole truth to the world. His first question was more like a directive.

"Please state your name and spell it for the record."

"Teresanna Lee Montesallo." She stated in a smooth, clear voice, then spelled it slowly and precisely. Kyle felt a burst of pride, knowing how frightened she had been that morning when they separated so she could be kept safe. If her steady voice was any indication, she would do just fine!

To make her relax, the District Attorney asked a simple personal question first.

"Your name is quite unusual. How did you come by it?"

Teresanna's smile was slightly sad.

"My mother's grandmothers were Teresa and Anna. She combined the names to honor both women. My middle name is Lee because she said my father reminded her of Bruce Lee."

The prosecutor nodded, but Marcus's mutter was heard loud and clear.

"She were a whore who only knew yer Daddy cause o' yer Chinee eyes."

Kyle stiffened, but Teresanna pretended not to hear, her gaze flickering away from the DA for only a second to note the rat-faced man who glared at her, then she fixed her eyes on the DA again, ignoring her stepfather while he fumed. The Judge frowned at the defendant and warned him to remain silent throughout the testimony. When all was quiet again, the prosecutor continued.

Under his gentle yet persistent questions, Teresanna relived her life with the defendant, from the time when she first saw his rat-like smile until the night when she fled in fear after placing a 911 call. Tears welled up toward the end, but she held firm with a few gentle, ladylike dabs at the corners of her eyes.

As the prosecutor took his seat, the defense attorney stood, but it was Marcus who hurled the first question.

"Do ya know that Satan will feast on yer bones forever fer what ya jus' tolt ese folks?"

Teresanna didn't answer. In fact, she didn't even flinch. She sat staring out at a point on the wall the way Kyle had taught her and waited for the defense attorney to begin.

"Miss Montesallo," he began when he could control his voice, "I was led to believe that you were deceased. Would you care to explain how you have come to be here before us, alive and well?"

Teresanna smiled slightly.

"I have people who care for me greatly who spirited me away to a safe place. Others put together my 'funeral' to throw any who wanted to cause me harm—" She looked pointedly at her stepfather. "—off my trail."

The defense attorney shuffled, not liking at all that he had to find a way to make this young woman seem less intelligent than she was. Before he could speak, however, there was another mutter from beside him.

"You little bitch."

When the defense attorney looked at his client, he saw the vicious, slightly foaming grimace of a rabid rodent and inadvertently backed away a step. Marcus Longley, too enraged by the thought that he had been duped to worry about appearing docile in order to have bail set, was glaring at Teresanna and gnashing his teeth. Stuttering as he tried to avoid any possible fines the Judge might choose to levy for such conduct, the defense attorney gamely tried to keep the trial moving despite his client's odd behavior.

"Are these the same people who spirited you away from California on the night your mother was beaten?"

Once again, Teresanna ignored her stepfather to answer in her clear, precise voice.

"No sir. I didn't meet my boyfriend until last Labor Day weekend, and those who helped me escape this time were friends of his. When I ran away from California, I was totally on my own."

Once again, Marcus was too enraged by the thought that he had been fooled all those years ago by a teenaged girl to care where he was or who heard him muttering.

"You little Chinee bitch."

Teresanna gave Marcus a brief, cold glare, and no one in the room was prepared for what he did in return. With an animalistic roar, he leapt up, knocking his chair to the floor, and climbed over the top of the defense table like a monkey. He hit the floor on his feet and charged toward Teresanna, bellowing his rage.

"I tolt you to never look at me like that! I'll show you who's boss, that I will!"

Before the chair finished toppling backwards, Kyle was on his feet, leaping the gallery railing in a single bound. He launched himself at Marcus Longley and wrapped his arms around the man's waist in a flying tackle. Kyle was on top as they hit the floor, and Marcus was nearly knocked senseless, gasping for the breath that had been forcibly expelled from his lungs.

The bailiff ran to Kyle's aid as Kyle forced Marcus onto his face on the floor and pulled his arms behind him. When the cuffs were applied, Kyle let the bailiff and a pair of armed officers take over, brushing off his suit and looking sheepishly up at the Judge. Then his left eyebrow lifted to a jaunty angle.

"Sorry about the dent in the floor, Your Honor." Kyle murmured with all proper respect in his voice and manner, waiting until he saw the Judge smile at his joking remark, then glanced at Teresanna as he started to turn back toward his seat. The Judge's clear voice stopped him.

"Thank you for your quick action, Mr. Benton."

Kyle gave the Judge a half-wattage version of The Smile, and took another glance at Teresanna. She was pale, but a smile played about the edges of her lips. He gave her a smile and returned to his seat, unaware of the Judge's wise eyes watching him.

Hiding a knowing smile, the Judge came quickly to a decision about how to proceed. Clearing his throat, he looked sternly at the defense attorney.

"Was your client given psychiatric testing?"

It was the defense attorney's turn to clear his throat, nervously shuffling papers for a moment with a red face. Finding the one he wanted, he glanced at it and held it up to the Judge.

"According to this, he was given the basic exam and passed with flying colors."

The Judge nodded, knowing how crafty some of the more criminally insane could be. He looked for a moment at Teresanna, then sighed heavily.

"Although I know it will be harder on the victim to wait, I must rule that Mr. Longley shall have to undergo further psychiatric testing before he can be deemed fit to stand trial for his deeds." He covered his microphone and leaned toward Teresanna. "Just between you and me, I think you had every reason to fear that man. Thank you for coming here today."

Teresanna offered a watery-eyed smile and the Judge gave her a gentle one of his own in return. Turning back to the microphone, he completed the necessary ritual to postpone any further rulings until the psychiatrist's report was in and released those gathered, then offered his hand to Teresanna as he stood.

"Good luck, Miss Montesallo."

"Thank you," she whispered in return, making her way off the bench on shaky legs. Before her toes touched the floor, Kyle was at her side, his concern showing in his eyes.

"Are you okay, Angel?"

Teresanna nodded, unwilling to trust her voice when tears were so close. The Judge, pushing absently at a lock of gray hair, smiled as he saw that the gentle Kyle had returned, and carefully cleared his throat.

"Now that it's not going on record, do you have a passing knowledge of martial arts, son?"

Kyle looked surprised for a moment, then grinned.

"I have a Level 3 black belt in three forms, Your Honor."

The elder wanted to smile, but kept his face stern for one more question.

"Then I shouldn't have to worry that this young lady will be well taken care of?"

Kyle looked down at the lady at his side, his love shining in his eyes.

"Not at all, Your Honor. I plan to protect her with my life for as long as she'll allow me to do so."

Teresanna looked up at Kyle, her own eyes full of love.

The Judge saw this and gave in to the threatening smile before sending the young couple on their way. Later, he would sign the letter to inform them that Marcus Longley, who had called himself Mark Long in

California, on being ruled criminally insane and put into a penitentiary for those of his ilk, had been beaten to death by another inmate.

As they slipped down the courthouse stairs and into the waiting rental sports car, Kyle actually verged on being too attentive, only easing up when Teresanna gave him a fierce frown and snapped at him to behave.

"But Angel," he argued softly while his hand dropped to her tummy, which was still flat but wouldn't be for much longer, "It's my first baby in there."

Teresanna gave a snort that fully expressed her continuing disgust that the Pill had failed her before she and Kyle were married. After spending the better part of her life swearing she would never be like her mother, it seemed she was walking in the woman's footsteps, unwed pregnancy and all. The only difference was that Kyle was more than a one-night stand. So much more....

Seeing the wayward path of her thoughts in the thoughtful look on her face, Kyle leaned toward her slightly, his eyebrow flying high and his eyes twinkling merrily.

"You know…we could always fly to Vegas instead of going straight home."

Teresanna bit back a smile at his suggestion and tried to act upset.

"That's all I need, to have Gram take away my allowance because I let you talk me into eloping! Humph!"

Seeing past her angry facade, just like he always did, Kyle grinned as he helped her settle herself on the car seat, then pulled a mobile phone out of his pocket. By the time he pulled into traffic, they had reservations on a flight to Las Vegas, where Teresanna Montesallo would disappear forever, to be known from that point on as Teresanna Benton.

The End

Afterward

So, as I mentioned before, there were just a few minor changes, and hopefully it brought everything to a smoother conclusion.

I'd like to add a special "thank you" here to the people who inadvertently added some part of their personality to Kyle or Teresanna. There was Ernie from Florida for the muscles (though Ernie "batted for the other team"). There was Blair from BCC who smoked and liked Bloody Marys. There was Bob, a trucker who once helped me map out a trip from Maine to Florida and even had his times if his truck was running well on a clipboard, allowing me to plan my own trip with fair ease. Of course, the biggest contributors to the story were Dana, a trucker, and Luanne, a former dancer, who allowed me to interview them extensively and gave me far more material than I needed for the initial six-page story I wanted to write.

I think this turned into more than six pages.

The story continues in "The Tiger's Cub", with the little bambino that Teresanna is carrying, for those who want more, and I'm going to keep my mouth shut about what the third book is about. Suffice to say that other members of the clan are stepping forward to tell stories, so this series may be several books long…

And there are always other projects waiting in the wings that aren't related to this series…

For those who are worried that I'm going to suddenly stop writing, you can consider this: If I don't write, the characters all pile up in my head and start fights. I write for my own sanity, and am very honored that others are entertained as well.

Blessed be.

ABOUT THE AUTHOR

Debi lives in a small Maine town with her husband, Bill. Of herself, Ms. Emmons says, "I am tall and have brown eyes. The rest can change without notice."

www.ingramcontent.com/pod-product-compliance
Lightning Source LLC
Chambersburg PA
CBHW072307020726
47501CB00002B/422